The

and Other Tales

by

Stephen J. Clark

Swan River Press
Dublin, Ireland
MMXXI

The Satyr and Other Tales
by Stephen J. Clark

Published by
Swan River Press
Dublin, Ireland
in April, MMXXI

www.swanriverpress.ie
brian@swanriverpress.ie

Stories and illustrations
© Stephen J. Clark, MMXV
This edition © Swan River Press

Cover design by Meggan Kehrli
from "Portrait of a Satyr"
© Stephen J. Clark, MMXV

Set in Garamond by Ken Mackenzie

Paperback Edition
ISBN 978-1-78380-741-3

Swan River Press published a limited hardback
edition of *The Satyr and Other Tales* in July 2015.

THE SATYR AND OTHER TALES

Contents

Author's Preface vii

The Satyr 3

The Bestiary of Communion

The Horned Tongue 107

The Lost Reaches 141

The Feast of the Sphinx 179

૭

Acknowledgements 233

About the Author 235

Author's Preface

Since its initial publication in 2010, I've felt that *The Satyr* deserved further development than the publishing schedule for the original volume allowed, having agreed to write and illustrate the book within a month. So when the suggestion of this omnibus arose it offered the opportunity to refine the novella, not only in a stylistic sense, but in a way that resonated to a greater depth with Austin Osman Spare's life and ethos. Rather than applying Spare's ideas with any didactic intent, I wanted to discover and explore them in the process of imagining the story, giving its poetry the chance to ferment.

This new edition required fresh illustrations and I executed the drawings in bolder lines to lend emphasis within the tighter frame of the book, superseding the landscape format of the earlier edition. In some ways, as the style of drawing differs from the approach I would instinctively take, it seems fitting that it is supposed to be the work of another, the sorceress Marlene.

The Bestiary of Communion, which comprises the second part of this omnibus, was originally published in 2011. Again, for its first publication I agreed to complete the work to a demanding schedule. The closing story "My Mistress, the Multitude" was published in a rough form as a consequence, so I welcome its replacement here with the largely reworked and definitive version entitled "The Feast of the Sphinx". In fulfilling its original promise I now believe that the story brings the collection to a more satisfying close.

While *The Satyr and Other Tales* partly serves to salvage these tales, I feel bringing them together in one volume has proved rewarding in another sense, inspired as they all are by shared themes and settings rooted in a mythology of both World Wars.

Stephen J. Clark
March 2015

The Satyr

*"Revelation comes to us as lightning.
Alas! How fleeting our memory of all manifestation."*

- Austin Osman Spare

I.
Trust

That night she took me there again to the garret room as the siren wailed, while in the streets below strangers fled to the safety of Anderson shelters and Underground stations. It wasn't that she was indifferent to the panic the raids induced; if anything she entered a kind of ecstasy. She became intoxicated. With the first distant sounds of impact her eyes were lit with arousal. Excitedly clasping her hands together she whispered, "Drums." And we listened to those drums approaching and to the stabbing fire of guns responding. We watched the clouds through the skylight swell and flush like wound tissue in the glare of the searchlights. She'd insisted that we stand at the window with our heads pushed out into the night. All of Southwark had descended into Hell as she shrieked "The Underworld! The Underworld!" The rooftops seemed to shrink from the encroaching bombardment, shaking at the relentless tread of a titan's stumbling footsteps. The sound of nearby panes shattering in their frames gave the deserted street below an unreal and brittle beauty. For her, those empty streets belonged to a tragic little town from folklore. She was rambling about the Danube again. I tried not to listen. She said that she'd wished she'd gone on another thieving spree. Hearing her speak of my neighbourhood in that way made me think of silencing her for good. Yet when she'd pressed her face to mine I'd given in to her once more and we'd leaned there together through the window, witnessing incendiaries fall and the skyline along the wharves erupt into flames.

The following morning she disappeared, as she often did, as she had the day we'd first met. If that had only been a week ago time was becoming harder to judge. I asked her no questions fearing the answers she'd give. Before leaving she'd dolled herself up and when she returned dishevelled several hours later she had rations on her. There was coffee in a tin on the hearth and a fresh box of cigarettes by an ashtray on an upturned crate. So many of her sketches were strewn about the floor and pinned to the walls that I surmised it had been her den for quite a while. It seems this place and its neighbouring buildings had been emptied some time ago and used as a spiv's makeshift storage space that in turn had been abandoned. Nothing had its own place or purpose anymore. Every day you could see folks clinging like ghosts to the things they'd known, while all around them their future went up in smoke. That wasn't for me. It was a blessing in disguise being sent down. I'd had no choice. They'd taken my life and smashed it to bits. I'd left everything behind and I was damned if I was going back to find it. There'd be nothing left to piece together anyway.

It was easy to waste time lying there waiting, just gazing at her drawings fixed to the sloping ceiling and listening to the streets below stirring into life once again after the raid. When she returned she'd never say where she'd been. Instead the first thing from her lips would be, "And what does my old critic Mr. Hughes think of my drawings today?" She'd expect some insight, an observation or two, although compliments were of no interest to her. She demanded interpretations that my meagre talents struggled to provide, but I knew enough flimflam to see me through. I'm not an uneducated man; besides I brushed up on my reading inside and I have a knack of picking up on the games others play. Though I had to admit I was anxious my act was wearing thin. Luckily she was easily distracted by questions about her dream-life, which she consulted like an oracle. Any discussion of her work usually led us back to her dreams. There was a self-portrait secured to the wall above a mound of pillows and all around it numerous photographs of film stars torn from magazines.

The portrait only resembled her in essence. It was one of those new-fangled distortions, not a photographic likeness. It was unnatural and you could tell how she'd tried to shape Dietrich's likeness into her own face. Yet any fool could see she had talent and I knew photographs didn't bring the rewards paintings could. Her technique was good enough to suggest, with the correct guidance, she could produce decent forgeries. If only she could abandon this obsession with the man she called her master.

It was possible that no one knew she'd come to London. Of course Marlene wasn't her real name. It was another game she played, like the delusion that she'd escaped from a rural retreat, The Institute for Gifted and Orphaned Exiles. It sounded as preposterous as adopting a German film star's name; not exactly smart given our predicament. Her accent wasn't convincing and as for all of this talk about the Danube, it was easily tolerated and could be used to humour and placate her in her maniacal episodes. So our little sessions where she'd insist on hearing my opinion were a perfect opportunity for me to exercise my influence, to play along and familiarise myself with the way people like her spoke, highbrow people I mean. Not that I am a stupid man, don't get me wrong, yet you've got to learn the steps quick in this dance. In my game you have to know how to learn from your victim, to get inside their skin, speak the way they speak and think the way they think.

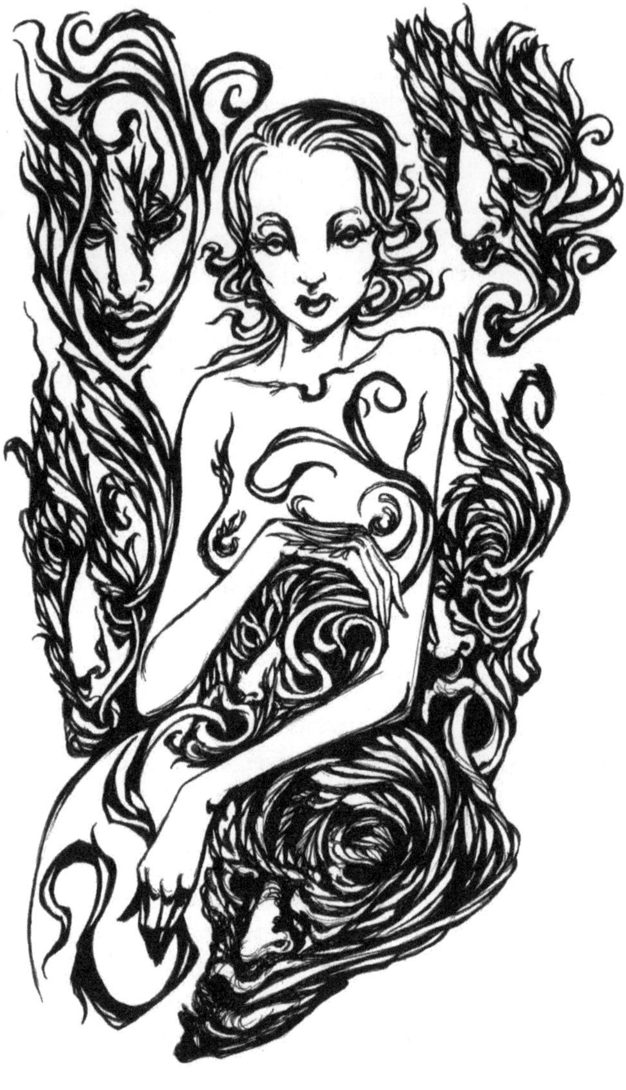

The Satyr

I admit I was intimidated by her self-portrait; there was something about her lithe body that unnerved me. It was lust but not only that. She'd never allow it. She was always slipping from my hands, like a cat or something. And she was full of puzzles. Even when we shared the same bed she'd remain distant and separate. I saw myself in the drawing; in the hideous masks that framed her body. It was impossible to say how my likeness could appear in a picture drawn long before we'd even met, but there was no doubt I recognised myself in it. Why it should demand my attention in this way I can't say, yet I know that the image sparked a chain of associations that echoed in all of her pictures littering the floor and walls of that place. Try as I might I couldn't muffle that nagging voice that tempted me from my plans and insinuated itself into my thoughts. It persuaded me to find a fatalistic pattern in the years before our encounter. It tried to tell me that I'd known her before, that I couldn't trust my own judgement, that I'd forgotten my dreams from which she'd emerged.

"You're an idiot," she'd say, when I mentioned that her drawings were wilfully perverse and threatened her stability. She'd withdraw into one of her stubborn thunderous silences, filling whatever corner of the room she occupied with a palpable hostility. She'd mumble to herself about finding her master, while frantically scribbling into a concealed sketchbook propped against her raised knees. If I approached she would close the pages and glower until I retreated.

Laughter was the key. It wasn't hard for me to act the fool. I'd had plenty of practice. It's a matter of survival in the clink. So bloody stupid to think all you had to do to cheer that girl up was play the spoons. Yet the light from her smile made me feel invisible. While she beamed I reminded her of the first day I'd seen her, finding her marking the pavements with coloured chalks outside Borough Market. From there she'd taken us on a snaking route off Union Street and around Red Cross Way to extol the poetic virtues of those lonely lanes and spin a yarn about Cross Bones, the old site of an unconsecrated graveyard, where she claimed she could hear the spirits of whores and beggars buried there. And I told her again of how she'd led me back to the row of evacuated and condemned terraces where she'd made her home. Nostalgia didn't keep her from her fixation long, however, and she'd draw the conversation back to the man whose name I always resented hearing her say . . . Austin Osman Spare.

Although it was wise to play that card close to my chest, Spare was familiar to me from the days I used to do my rounds with my old muscle, Bloaters. Yet that was long before Bloaters was beaten up by his local rivals, hired hands of the publicans we'd managed to squeeze in our racket for years. It struck me as being odd at the time that an artist, especially an artist like Spare, would take an interest in painting an old has-been prize-fighter like Bloaters. But then, Bloaters was a legend, a living monument scarred by a lost age; I suppose that's why he might have fascinated Spare. Bloaters' glory days were long gone yet like a gnarly old lion he could still depend on his brute presence alone to intimidate the locals into giving him whatever he needed. It had been the easiest thing in the world for me to step in and exploit the opportunity to its fullest. I had my reputation to think of. Even though Spare often eyed me with suspicion I'd pass a few idle hours drinking in his company, among others, well, until he guessed my tricks and would have nothing more to do with me. Yet I knew what the folk around there used to say: that Spare was an odd one.

Folk warmed to him, but there was something in his eyes, or in his voice, or the way he carried himself at

The Satyr

times that told you he wasn't the same as other people. Sometimes when he was propping up the bar or sitting in the shadows of the pub's snug, it was as though he was only half there, as if part of him belonged somewhere else, as if he cast another shadow in a place you couldn't see. He was a man lost in rumours. Especially when he looked at me one night in the Mansion House Tavern, as if he'd found me out, when he'd seen me and Bloaters plotting in a corner, it was as if he was looking into me, X-raying my body with those blue-grey eyes and locating some secret ailment, a defect that runs as deep as my bones. And in his look I guessed there was something else, like he knew that I was up to no good and pitied me. And although I knew he didn't intend it, one look from him was enough to fill me with shame, with the sense of my own failings. He had an air of nobility about him, which is strange coming from a man who looked almost destitute at times, in that old trilby, worn tweed jacket and battered shoes. Perhaps he had the natural grace of a wild animal. When there were a few of us crouched round a table drinking, he once casually emphasised a word to me that I had to later look up in a dictionary. I had plenty of time for such things when I was inside. The word was "duplicity". He reckoned it always trips you up in the end. He was talking about this and that, politicians perhaps, but really I think his words were somehow meant for me, whether he knew it or not. So it was as if he'd seen right through me all along and I imagined he wouldn't be surprised to hear that I'd been nabbed and sent down. Bloaters didn't fare so well, as I was saying. The landlords ganged up on him, got a few of their own heavies together and had the poor sod beaten and thrown in the Thames. They were sure he was dead, but he wasn't, although that's a different story.

So although I knew Spare was no prophet or demigod as Marlene seemed to believe, there was still something about him that unnerved me, some kind of quiet magnetism, that made me admire him against my will. The man I'd known would never make a claim to genius either, or privileged knowledge, in fact he demanded that others should consider him an equal, that's how I knew the girl had got it all wrong. She was naïve and so ripe for the picking, and certainly unhinged. It was crystal clear she was prone to giving in to adoration, to worship. It's not as uncommon as many would have us believe. For years I've depended upon charisma for my living. I can turn it on and off like a tap. What choice have you got? An opportunity presents itself and you either take it or regret it later. There's no in-between. There's no time for letting pride or principles get in the way. Not that I knew exactly how I'd make use of her, but considering the options, it was better to stay close to the merchandise and work out a plan as I went along. I must have been crazy to stick by her instead of getting out of London, out into the country. Staying in the city would mean I'd eventually get my collar felt, probably sooner rather than later, or roped into volunteering for fire watch, that's if I wasn't blown to pieces first. At least the shrapnel I'd taken in the last war saved me from the draft. If it wasn't for that and the fact I was an educated fella, I doubt the magistrate would have been so lenient.

So, my guess was that she hadn't really known Spare. If she had she'd know where to look for him. If you ask me, given his disposition, he was destined for either the doss house or the nuthouse, and there were parts of Southwark that were both. Why spend money on locking someone up in a padded cell when they can rent one at their own expense around the Elephant and Castle?

The Satyr

And yet, there were her drawings. They seemed to tell a different story. From what I'd seen of Spare's other pictures, the ones that didn't depict the folk of his neighbourhood, or even this world, his pictures that defy my attempts at describing them; her own shared a certain likeness. They belonged to the same world, were of the same mind. I can only imagine she'd witnessed one of his exhibitions that he used to hold in his flat. And then there was the fact, call it coincidence or whatever you like, that this girl who called herself Marlene, was the first person I clapped eyes on, the first human being to meet my eyes with theirs, on the morning of my release. It comes back to me again in flashes of colour gushing from the grey of the street. There she'd been, at the entrance of Borough Market, off Green Dragon Court, drawing the map of a river in bright chalks right across the pavement I wanted to pass. And I remember she'd depicted faint faces in the river's water and she looked up at me and, pointing to one of the faces, said, "That's you." That was before I knew she was crazy, referring to the Danube all the time. She seemed as nuts as Spare. Yet Spare differed, or so they reckoned. They said he'd made a life or method from his madness, whereas this girl just seemed as if she was a victim to it. I suppose it can only go either of two ways. It was a wonder some enterprising spiv hadn't picked her up before. Let's just say I was playing my old game, offering protection, and was prepared to see where it would take me. I could bide my time where beauty was concerned, although her innocence bothered me, if you could call it that. Her pictures suggested something else, but then you hear of all kinds of things happening in those places, with or without consent, if that counts where lunatics are concerned. Just look at what they still say about Bedlam. And besides, it had been a long time since I'd had the company of a woman,

The Satyr and Other Tales

and the way I figured it, they wouldn't exactly be lining up to knock on my door. The alternative was a hostel, not a prospect I exactly savoured. But to that girl Southwark was an enchanted kingdom, a place where her wounded king had retreated into hiding. Listen to me. I'm even beginning to speak like her. What I'm trying to say is there was more to my stumbling into her than meets the eye. It was as if she'd been following me, or that I'd somehow been nudged in her direction and her in mine. As I was saying about Spare, it's magnetism. How do you account for the fact that she wanted to find one of the men I'd rather not see ever again? Call it destiny if you will. There's some kind of cruel trickery at work in that if you ask me, at least that's the way I think when I've had a few stouts and superstition gets the better of me.

Marlene didn't care if you believed her when she said she'd been his model, pupil, and lover. Perhaps she sensed that I suspected she was a compulsive liar yet it was as though she was so confident in her delusion that she knew that her imagination would win over mere truth in the end. Who was I to contradict her dreams? Her infatuation with a man she considered a modern day seer could be quite easily incorporated into my plans and if I played this game right it could even work to my advantage. At least that's what I thought at the time.

In keeping with her casual disregard for fact, when asked of her first meeting with the artist she called, with strange endearment, the Satyr, she would drift off into a trance-like stare, murmuring under her breath about remembered events that could have only been invented. At times she'd insist that I record these ramblings and we'd spend entire nights sitting by the window, with her in endless dictation and me transcribing by the throbbing light of a distant air raid. It was as if she spoke in incantations that were inseparable from the rhythms of the bombardment outside. The firestorm shook and illuminated the world of that attic room, her drawings seemingly animated in the flashes of light as she spoke in tongues. She demanded that I must be vigilant at times when she was like that, that I must be poised and ready to record everything that she said.

"Take this down," she said. "Even in its stillness the world is boundless, is restless. As without, so within. Are you catching all of this? Write this down while I remember all that the Satyr said to me . . . he told me how through the threshold of negations, through the Neither-Neither, after becoming nothing the polysemy of the instant would appear . . . when the world is in flux, when time itself is concentrated into the moment and we slip through the fissure between one blink and the next . . . we fall, we tumble, we pass through limbo, we slip between one memory and another, vanishing from ourselves as if stepping through a mirror into shadows. As Blake said: to Annihilate the Self-hood of Deceit and . . . "

When I complained I could no longer keep pace with her gibberish she'd demand that I read it aloud to her. Maintaining a glassy gaze she listened intently, as if sifting through the words on the air for some sign or clue that would lead her to him, to the Satyr. She snatched the pages from my hand and ran her eyes over their surfaces, stopping here and there to recite a passage to herself.

"As a child I was carried on my mother's back from the Black Forest to the Black Sea and saw Man's great strongholds tumble at her touch and all their treasures swallowed by her lips. I heard her voice carried by the currents of the Danube itself. And in her blood I inked wild faces of satyrs and cherubim . . . did you see this? Here, this . . . "

She forcefully prodded the page with her finger as if demonstrating a proof that she had no intention of explaining. I smiled a humourless smile and shook my head.

"The city will carry me closer to him. All I need to do is surrender to its currents and they will take me to him. It is easy. And the wild faces of the satyrs and the cherubim . . . they are my guides and my drawings will invoke his emissaries, they will gather to my side to assist me. I will draw their faces and they will come to greet me." She was speaking with deliberation as though explaining herself to a child.

The soft heartbeat of the air raid as it receded must have coaxed me to sleep. I dreamt of hooves clattering across distant rooftops. Waking in the early morning I found Marlene, who had clearly been awake all night, her hair all wild, frantically filling a page of her sketchbook. Several other pages lay around her on the mattress and floor. Although the temperature in the room had dropped and the window still gaped, she was indifferent to the breeze, utterly enthralled in the act of drawing. I pushed myself from the pillows and tried to speak to her, but her only response was a shake of her head. She threw one of the pages casually in my direction. It glided miraculously into my lap.

She joined me shivering upon the mattress, pressing her body into mine, still transfixed by her latest work and indifferent to the desire she'd just triggered in me. The drawing depicted three creatures . . . if that was the right word. Maybe they were a trinity of sorts. They seemed to be preoccupied in a form of oblique communion with each other. At least that's how she put it. She was always coming out with words that left me puzzled. Marlene had given a name to each one of the creatures and went on to explain their individual characteristics.

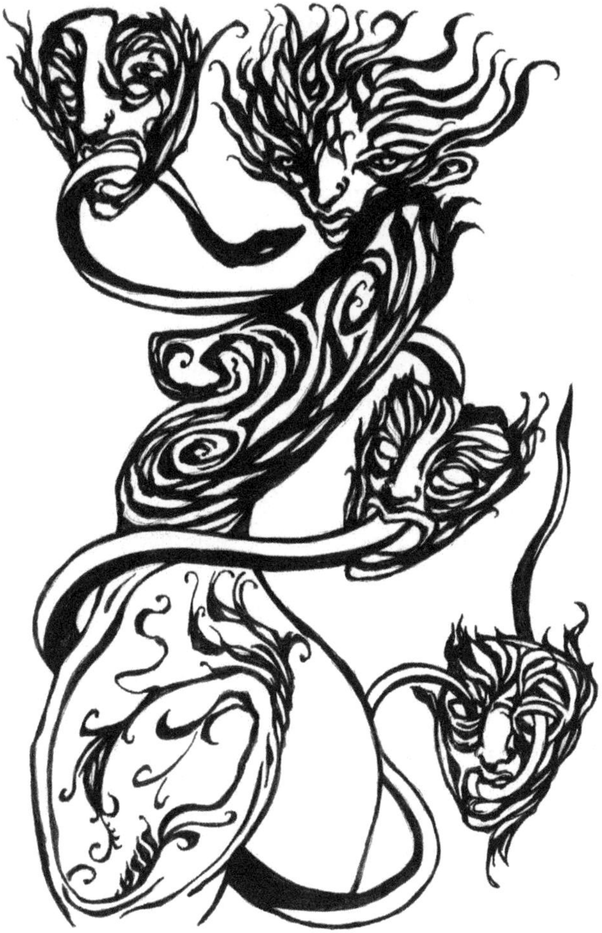

The Satyr and Other Tales

"These are the emissaries sent by my master to guide us on our way. We must trust their silence and only speak to them when we are spoken to. That's the rules of their game and woe betides anyone who breaks them. The first, named The Mephistotrix, is the link between how we act and how we think. She lives in the spaces between the world that everyone knows and the world we all keep secret. She could be sitting in between us now and we would never know it. We could never feel her presence even though she's made of flesh and bone just like us. She knows the secrets we've forgotten or want to forget. And she is the link between us and the other emissaries. She is a seductress and cannot be trusted to be left alone with men. She has been known to eat men after she has finished taking whatever pleasure is necessary from them. If you want to forget something you must leave a votive offering to her, which can be bread soaked in egg yolk, a lady's glove filled with lavender or mascara mixed with a little blood."

"Why does she have no arms?" I immediately regretted the question.

"She has no arms so that men might mistake her for an easy victim, yet that is just a ruse for her eyes, like the Serpent, have mesmeric qualities and she, like me, was born near the lagoons of the Danube Delta. She pities the men that she tempts and devours for she knows that they cannot help but be drawn to her charms. She will help us slip secretly and unnoticed by men into the most guarded places of London."

"And the others?"

"It's plain to see, Mr. Hughes. This is Beezle."

"A housefly?" The insect was depicted in such a way that it suggested it might escape the page at any second.

"Not an ordinary housefly but *every* housefly. He lives everywhere in London. Indeed he has an encyclopaedic

The Satyr

knowledge of London's streets and history and can be an invaluable guide to its world, if you can listen carefully enough to catch his words because he speaks very quickly. Although I can't say when I first befriended him, perhaps in the institute, Beezle is an archduke of the Underworld here on Earth and knew Blake and Dante before him, yet time means so little to him for he lives everywhere at once. I know—it is very hard to follow but try to keep up.

"I call the third emissary Lamia. I don't know her purpose or why she appears to me, only that she leads the way. She seldom speaks but leaves the tracks that I must follow. She always appears that way, as a serpent sliding through or sloughing masks. Sometimes the sound of the Danube's rushing waters accompanies her.

"Not a single citizen of London has realised that their city is now enclosed in a great shell of water. The river Danube rises up around it and forms an impression of the sky. When you see stars it is really the eyes of the Danube's denizens staring back at you from their depths. Where ever I go the Danube follows and envelops everything in my dream. It is my calling to map this new world; to record all its flora and fauna and herald its coming. Only I can document these things because only I can see them. The Satyr entrusted this gift to me alone and prophesied my return. In a way he serves to herald my coming."

"And that marking that you make in the corner of every drawing, are they your initials?"

She picked out a scrap of paper from a stack to show me. "Yes, it is also my *sigil*. My inherited sign, I call it *The Eye of the Donauquelle*. In that eye a great river stirs."

That night she'd made me promise to stay in the attic room until she called for me. She was preparing something on the deserted floor below while I sifted through her drawings and thought about the world I'd been allowed to enter.

The Satyr

Even though I had been there some time it was difficult to tell what purpose the building had originally served. While first ascending the three steep flights to the attic there were signs on the lower floors that it had been an administrative organisation at one time. The ground floor was draughty and deserted, occupied only by dusty windowed compartments, yet through the gloomy spaces of the first floor amongst rows of metal filing cabinets and rows of cluttered pigeonholes a few upturned suitcases and stacks of crockery were discernible. The fact that the second floor was home to various pieces of domestic furnishings such as a wardrobe and even a bed, only reinforced the idea that some part of the building may have at one time served as quite a grand private residence too. It was impossible to truly tell which era had preceded which, as though each age of the building had occurred at once, colliding and collapsing into each other. Had the contents of other nearby properties migrated to that one great mysterious place, to form a storehouse of abandoned lives? It seemed fitting then that it should become a fugitive's temporary bolthole.

Even though the rooms were spacious and had high Victorian ceilings damp permeated the haphazard maze of crates and shelves and furniture that occupied the lower floors. The entire place was airless and musty suggesting that it had been sealed up long before the outbreak of war.

Marlene said she'd originally entered through a rear window where in some cluttered backrooms she'd found stashes of contraband. That same night she'd heard cursing in the shadows below; black market racketeers no doubt, for the following morning the spoils were gone.

It had been days before I realised we weren't living there alone. Marlene called her Mrs. Paterson, although I only had her word for it that the name was real. And what's more I never did converse with the old woman, mostly seeing her from a distance in corridors or aisles, passing from dusty light into shadow, or hearing her rummaging through detritus, searching for God knows what. The crafty way she moved about the place made me wonder how long she'd been there. I never discovered where she vanished to each and every night. Even when she was near she never replied to anything I said to her, only responding to my questions with a wry smile; so I was tempted to conclude she was a mute, a simpleton or both. Yet I also suspected that was all part of her game.

"She's been helping me to prepare for the way ahead. I couldn't have made my ghost map without her. She can unearth things in here we'd never dream of finding. She was a mentor of a dear friend of mine, the Satyr. She taught him the first steps in her hidden ways but now she's been forgotten about and no-one believes she ever lived. But I believe and here she is."

Yet was there any real sign that the old woman did anything but tolerate Marlene? It seemed Mrs. Paterson was merely biding her time until Marlene left. However Marlene claimed this apparent indifference was all part of being tutored in the old woman's ways; a test of patience whose rewards, she said, I could not hope to understand. She explained by way of comparison, saying that just as some had never been taught how to read and the world of books and newspapers and hoardings were a closed enigmatic world to them so too were there other common kinds of illiteracy of infinitely more subtle kinds that meant the scope of sensual experience and comprehension was greatly hindered. The old woman nodded sagely at what was said and yet I couldn't shake the impression that she was humouring Marlene only to ensure she had shelter there.

The Satyr

When her excited voice suddenly roused me from my thoughts again I became all too aware of her manic energy that left me muddled. We hadn't eaten properly in days, since withdrawing into the secluded world of our attic. She'd been making preparations all along for a voyage I was only just beginning to understand.

I wearily descended the stairwell as she called out again from the floor below. Looking down from the elevated view of the flight of stairs I saw her making the final adjustments to a structure she'd cobbled together from the contents of the room. Clothed only in her stolen silk dressing gown, she was indifferent to the cold. There she was in her toy kingdom; in the spacious shadows she'd gathered all manner of clutter in a rough circle: crates, boxes, magazines, lampshades, empty jars, and furniture. Linen dust covers and moth-eaten curtains were draped over areas of the construction. It represented the streets outside, a microcosm of London as she dreamt it, or some city that I'd yet to imagine: a capital for ghosts and dreamers, improvised in miniature. Here and there, on whatever surface she'd deemed appropriate, she'd lit a candle. In the midst of it all there was a clearing where she'd given a privileged space to a large oval mirror. She'd freed it from its frame and placed it on its back, facing the ceiling. Pacing around the outer edges of the structure, she threw her arms wide as though announcing her creation. What ensued could only be described as a ritual. It didn't please me to see her like this.

She became subdued, humming out of tune to herself in a low voice as she wound her way through the tight avenues of her city, occasionally spluttering on dust baking in the candlelight. Why she'd insisted that I attend I don't know, as I felt that I was intruding on a private act, an act I could not hope to comprehend. By the time she'd reached the centre she was undressed. The pale hue of her body glowed from the gulf of the room as she dropped slowly to her knees before the mirror and peered into its depths, suddenly calling out, her voice soon trailed off into silence. I heard her repeat something incomprehensible that sounded like a request or perhaps a command, and assumed that she was beckoning me to join her. Of course I'd entertained ideas that she'd intended this to be an elaborate and quite unnecessary game of seduction. As I neared her I soon gathered that I'd been greatly mistaken. I noticed pages from a pocketbook map had been strewn about the floor. She'd pasted a few torn fragments to a sheet of paper from her portfolio onto which she'd scrawled coordinates and hieroglyphs.

"Don't speak when I'm scrying. If you're going to stay, then get on your knees beside me and listen. And don't look at me—look in here, in the glass. You remember a dream I told you about? When was that? That's what all these pages have been about . . . all these drawings and pictures. You remember; I dreamt I was a forgotten book whose pages were scattered in an ancient river; the knowledge of the Danube coursing towards the heart . . . But now we must listen, because now they're coming to write on me. They will finish the map. The emissaries are coming to tell me where we must go."

She carefully looked over both shoulders in turn; fear draining and contorting her face. What had she expected to see? It was as though she was watching the movements of birds, hearing the descent of their wings through the darkness above and witnessed something either crawling or sliding across the floor towards us. Her whole body trembled. She returned her gaze to the looking glass.

"There, in the glass." She was pointing. I could see nothing but the faint reflection of the plaster ceiling, hanging

As within

Remembering

Danube

So without

far in the shadows above us. Her fingertip traced whorls across the mirror's dusty surface. As she muttered under her breath it appeared that she was making calculations or solving a riddle. It wasn't until she pressed her ear to the glass in several places, with her finger to her lips, that she felt satisfied and confident enough to pick up the page she'd prepared; a strange makeshift map cobbled together from various sources. She began to scrawl across the paper wildly with a pen.

I noticed by the Thames, which she'd renamed "The Danube Remembering", she'd drawn a dagger over Whitechapel. I asked her why, but she ignored my question.

"This will be our ghost map, our journey will take us close to . . . " she was about to continue when she was interrupted, turning her head this way and that, listening. She started to nod her comprehension at a voice that wasn't there.

"But we must be careful, Mr. Hughes. We won't be alone. Beezle says we'll be followed. As we look for the Satyr, someone will be looking for us in turn. It's no longer safe here. We'll have to go. Sister Charnock is coming."

It's precisely then that the air raid siren wailed into life. This time all Hell had been let loose around us. The great old frame of our hideaway shuddered. With the sound of the floor groaning and splintering above us we grabbed what we could and fled.

II.
The Séance

She walked ahead as though invulnerable, almost naked beneath the overcoat I'd wrapped around her. Perhaps she sang to herself because she was afraid. I doubted that it was because we'd spent the night in a local church. And even though the familiarity of the song nagged at me, I knew it wasn't a hymn:

> Men cluster to me
> Like moths around a flame,
> And if their wings burn,
> I know I'm not to blame.

As we neared and then turned the corner she sang the same lines over and over in a deliberately doleful way. We'd returned even though we knew it was useless to hope that we could retrieve anything. It seemed that our street had been torn apart the night before. Buildings stood eviscerated in the early light, their innards spilled across the road. Broken furniture was strewn everywhere. A bathtub and wardrobe teetered on cross-sectioned floors to our right and to our left an entire terrace had been hollowed out by a blast to such an extent that it resembled the rickety façade of a film set. Doors on upper floors opened onto nothing. Curtains flapped through empty frames. Shards of glass scattered across pavements glistened with the morning's rainfall. As a few shipwrecked survivors recovered what they could of their lives from the rubble, a stray dog picked its way through the debris emitting timid whines, returning to find its home devastated. It trotted to the edge of a crack running almost the whole breadth of the street. It was deep and wide enough to reveal ruptured pipework from which a strangely calming gurgle could be heard. Several lampposts had been partially uprooted and stood frozen in a permanent toppling gait, lending the whole scene a vertiginous aspect: a nightmare tableau. At least that's how she described it.

Marlene turned with a distraught look on her face. She approached the dog and dropped her portfolio by her side, my overcoat slipping from her shoulders and with it her dressing gown. She stood there naked letting the dog lick her feet. I heard her address the dog, "Is she gone, boy? Is the old witch Mrs. Paterson gone?"

As she hunkered down to embrace the dog like a child, I took up the gown and coat and threw them around her shoulders. She groaned her disapproval as she softly wept. Thankfully she was quick to compose herself when an A.R.P. officer approached, calling out to her, no doubt believing her to be a survivor. We slipped away down an alley whiskered with dead grass, her soles raw against the rubble underfoot. The yelping dog followed for some time but was diverted by little buggers throwing bottles from an upper floor that had been sheered clean in half.

Stopping to catch her breath she flung her arms around me and dragged me through a misshapen doorway to a narrow yard scattered with clothes from fallen washing lines. She thought we should hide awhile convinced that we were being pursued, utterly absorbed in the world of her quest as a child is in a game. It didn't seem to occur to her that people were suffering all around her or that the life of the Borough that I'd known as a child was disintegrating. She even laughed when she caught me fighting back tears. It was impossible for me to decide whether she was cruel or an innocent. Either she didn't care or couldn't understand. Nor did she seem to notice that the yard into which we'd stumbled smelt faintly of the dead. She reached towards me, and I, assuming that she was finally trying to kiss me, leaned forward only to sense her pulling away. Her face was contorted with rage. Holding me at arm's length at first, with surprising strength, she pushed me violently backwards against a wall. As I fell, flailing wildly, I pulled her portfolio from her grasp and scattered pages of her drawings across the cobbles. This seemed to suddenly bring her back to her senses. She was silent awhile, slowly stooping to carefully gather up her pictures, looking at each one in turn. I was still shaking as I dusted myself down, cursing under my breath.

"That was just a test, to see if you are good enough. The Mephistotrix said I should do it, to make sure you're not like those other bastards. Don't think me a child or a lunatic. I'm not a monster, you know. I just get like that when my muse grips me. You think I'm a liar. Even if my name's not Marlene, what's it to you? Why don't you just go? Leave me alone! I'm no woman. I'm an animal now . . . I had to become an animal and no man wants an animal like me by him when he's snoring. That's what we all must do now to survive, call upon those things dormant in us: atavistic resurgence, that's what *he* called it. It's not the animal that's cruel. I can see this city's being torn apart. Do you think I hadn't noticed; that I live in a little world of my own? Do you think I need you to help me find my way back to him, to the Satyr? I know the way, you know. I know the way. And what do you think I'm going to do when I find him? I'm not just going to shake his hand!"

She went on like that for some time. It was unwise to stop her, best to let her wear herself out, to shout herself into exhaustion. A part of me was loath to admit that I was transparent to her. Compared to this self-possessed creature I'd always be a piffling little conman. What was that word that Spare had said to me again? Duplicity? Even in her madness that girl's courage had a frightening conviction, an honesty that seemed to demand the world's compliance. And yet, all of this could surely only bolster the scheme that was slowly hatching in my head. Whatever it was that she needed seemed to find its way into her hands. She threw away her dressing gown and pulled on random garments that lay about her begrimed in puddles on the ground. She stood there, out of breath, in an oversized chintz dress and mismatched cardigan. Barefoot she traipsed to the tall gate of the yard and peered out, clutching her ghost map in her hand.

"I know the way, you know. You think I don't know. You think I never knew the Satyr. You think Mr. Spare's just someone I dreamt up when I was sick. If you think that, you may as well go now."

She was already away, striding from one alley into another, over fences, through gardens and condemned buildings. I could do nothing but follow. All the while she was chanting something under her breath, something about "Blake, Dante . . . Michelangelo in a teacup!" As I tried to catch up with her I could hear her chanting the names of the places through which we passed, "Tabard Street, Marshalsea Road, Mermaid Court." As if she marked the names she favoured on her imaginary map.

"We must find his pubs. The places he haunts." She reeled them off in an intoxicated whisper, they were names she'd memorised and obsessed over while locked away from the world; "The Temple Bar on Walworth Road, The

The Satyr

Mansion House Tavern and White Bear on Kennington Park Road. I must get back to him before it's too late."

Out of breath she was waiting on the corner of a garden square, leaning on a buckled railing, unsettled by the sight of splintered and scorched trees. As she wandered off across the grass she was pointing, but as I followed at some distance behind her I couldn't hear her voice. She came to a halt at the first tree, so damaged by a blast that it was leaning at an acute angle over the water-filled crater that had bitten through its roots. Again she pointed and this time I caught her meaning. She was indicating the scores etched into the tree's bark, made by anonymous lovers no doubt. Initials and carvings that may have made some sense at one time had now degenerated and distorted with time. She had other ideas however. She kept shaking her head so vigorously with frustration that I feared she might erupt into one of her rages again. She traced her fingers through the scored indentations in the bark and no doubt expected that those actions alone would be enough for me to understand. Exasperated she said, "Look here . . . and here . . . and here. These are his sigils, his marks to let me know he has passed by here and that I am expected. He is telling us that we are on the right trail. We must hunt for further signs. They will lead the way."

She was off again at a determined pace while I still stood there at the tree, wanting to shake my head yet half-convinced by her explanation. Something momentarily shifted into place, some sense blinked between the hieroglyphs in the bark. Was there a peculiar logic to all of this that I had been missing? Or was this the life I was now expected to live, on her terms? Only weeks before I'd been sharing a cell then suddenly I was in Wonderland.

We passed through streets whose conditions alternated, in that some had survived almost intact while others were reduced to ruins. This was precisely one of those facts that fascinated Marlene: the notion of chance. She said the world was caught in a kind of limbo, vulnerable to the intervention of great primal forces, being neither one thing nor another where anything was possible. She said that the flies swarming in a nearby broken window had told her so. They'd spoken of a turning point where the fabric of life was torn through by the urge of prophecies. Without a word of warning she'd stop in her tracks and try to teach me how to read the signs of where reality surrenders to dreams. She'd pick a particular ruined building and claim she could read a hidden language in it, a magical grammar, something taken from an ancient way of thinking; hermetic she called it, or some such. She said that by studying a broken window or crumbling wall she could see the city's secret faces. She claimed it was taught to her by the Satyr long ago on the banks of the Danube. She explained that the Danube was pushing at the seams of the fabric of London as she spoke and it was only a short matter of time before the deluge came and washed the streets away. She was in full flow and it seemed clearer to me then that she spontaneously created her story as we went along. Yet all the while I couldn't help but wonder just how much she'd invented and what stranger stories might come to meet us still. It exhausted her at times. She tired of the endless explanations she felt obliged to give to me, her novitiate. Perhaps out of pity or frustration, perhaps out of wanting to wash my hands of it all and abandon her and her voyage, I admitted that I knew the way to The Mansion House Tavern, hoping that she wouldn't ask me how. She didn't, instead she just smiled to herself and took my arm. I understood then that my chances of retrieving something for my own ends had probably been lost for good.

The Satyr

Yet what exactly had I expected to gain from this girl? Maybe I was losing my marbles. I'd gone soft I could hear them say. That's the way old Hughes went, he got himself mixed up with some lunatic when he got out of the clink and it was the end of him. Yet I still hoped against all reason that she'd come up trumps. Pathetic, I know. I mean, if I stuck close by her an opportunity might arise that I could make use of. For all her talk there must be some truth to it, I thought. Maybe she didn't know Spare, but a girl like that has had a proper education and must have had contacts or some influence or sway with someone in her old clique. At the worst she'd got her looks if all else failed. She was shivering and rubbing her arms as we walked so I insisted that we stopped to break into a junk shop that had been partially boarded up on Borough High Street. Once inside it was obvious the place had been ransacked before us, but Marlene found an old man's navy pullover and slippers. She must have spent hours in there, mesmerised by the wares and oddments, looking for portents.

"Chance will lead the way," she said. All it took was a tiny advertisement snatched from a postcard carousel for us to be diverted away from our intended destination. She refused to show me the card until we'd followed its instructions. Some distance down a narrow side road we were greeted in a doorway by a native going by the name of Ole Luke. I knew him and a flicker in his eye told me he knew me too, but neither of us was prepared to admit it. In that chaos where well-known lanes could vanish overnight it seemed that familiar faces were becoming the only reliable signposts. It was early evening by then and the leer on his face immediately put me on my guard. His pal said, "Don't mind him; around here we call him the Village Idiot." The idiot shoved his younger Brylcreemed friend into the street.

Marlene, losing her patience, erupted, "The Mephistotrix protects us! Let us pass!"

It completely threw him. Trembling and red-faced, the idiot stepped aside for Marlene to enter. The younger lackey was laughing. There was a poster in the lobby door proclaiming a cheap spiritualist, Lilly Peer. Marlene pointed at it and said "Lamia", then took the stairs assuming I would follow. This is how the unwary get fleeced, I thought. If she'd been alone she wouldn't have made it past the doorstep. Once we were out of earshot of the idiot I complained that we should keep to my plan, but all I got, by way of reply, was a "Shush" and a raised finger.

The room behind the curtain was already bustling. Tables and chairs had been haphazardly arranged to fit as many punters into the space as was physically possible, yet those without seats were more than happy to drink standing. No doubt it had been hastily thrown together when their local had been suddenly demolished and made migrant drinkers of them all. The chatter didn't lessen when we entered and Marlene took to the place instantly. The air was acrid and the booze already flowing. Still, it was good to be indoors after roaming the streets all day. Glasses of beer and gin were being exchanged for the clink of a few coins. There was even chocolate.

The only window in the space had already been covered and music crackled from an unseen corner. A brood of older women noticed the girl's zeal and almost dragged us to the table to join them. Marlene's youth gleamed back at me from the host of haggard faces around that table. I knew instinctively what she must have been thinking; that she was amongst people that her precious Satyr may have sketched. One of the crones in answer to Marlene's question nodded to a yellow door beside us, and a note pinned to it read "Lilly Peer's Parlour 8PM".

The Satyr

By the time we'd climbed the second flight of stairs and closed the door behind us, the raucous room on the floor below had been completely silenced. It gave the impression that we were entering a place where private deals had been done. We weren't alone. A few of Marlene's newly adopted matriarchs were following close behind us and muttering between themselves in rapt tones down the hallway. Apparently by the very fact of being a man I was somehow trespassing on hallowed ground. There was another yellow door ahead. One of the women sharply took my arm to divert me while the others passed to reach the door. They gathered around Marlene and prevented her from entering, putting fingers to their lips, and making gestures to await further instruction. The door opened onto a darkened room, I didn't see who had ushered the women in. Marlene hesitated, turning her head to me and seeing that I must have looked apprehensive said, "Don't worry it's just like the pictures." I think she meant the cinema. I wasn't afraid, not of that place, just unnerved by the fact that the city was being busily torn apart night after night and there I was at a bloody séance. I was being vigilant, awaiting a peculiar detail or event to crop up so I could be assured that it was all a dream.

The bay windows in the wall to my right were sealed with blackout curtains. A lamp lit the soft circle of a table. The rest of the room was bare. While I adjusted to the low glow of the gaslight Marlene was already opening her portfolio in her arms and excitedly mumbling with our host for the evening. The grand old dame was sympathetically nodding, a maternal hand patting Marlene on her shoulder. The only words I could make out from her creased lips were, "We'll see. We'll see." It may have been the light and her heavy makeup but the medium had a certain faded glamour. The other ladies already anxiously seated shared looks of concern and pity, but then eyed me with suspicion. No doubt I'd become the target for gossip. Cups of tea were poured and passed around the tight circle of the table, as was a saucer marked "6d", into which each guest placed their coins. Marlene had respectfully gathered up her drawings again and pushed the portfolio under my arm with a timid smile.

"You can stay over there if you're quiet. Smoke if you like." The crumpled Bette Davis gestured to a chair in the alcove of the bay windows so I took it and lit a cigarette.

As the old woman summoned in whispers there wasn't a peep out of anyone else. They all sat transfixed, expectant. It may have been the gin I'd gulped downstairs or the fact I was just sat there in the quiet, staring on exhausted, yet my eyes were heavy and started playing tricks on me. From where I was sat I could see Marlene's face half-obscured by the profile of the medium. It was as though their features had been dipped into the soft pool of the lamplight and it had slowly merged them together. Marlene silently mouthed the old woman's words in unison. It was as if for a moment Marlene was wearing the medium's profile as a mask down one side of her face so that they shared the same mouth. And yet it was for more than a moment, for the impression, the illusion returned to me again and again as I sat slumped there, fending off the temptation to sleep. The congregation took turns to voice their questions and the old sphinx answered them with reassuring riddles, in tones that seemed, at times, to not entirely belong to her. She spoke in lullabies that had me teetering and about to drift. Then it was the girl's turn to speak so I surfaced again, my eyes attempting to awake with small jolts. I didn't hear the words of her question, only that her manner was insistent. It seemed to bother the old woman as she tried to find an answer, wafting an

The Satyr

invisible fly from her lips. Had there been a low buzzing in the room? The medium finally replied to a question I can only guess at.

"He's telling me that you've travelled from far away to find him. He is grateful, my lovely, he wants you to know that. And he says thank you. He's been waiting but had to go, he had no choice you see. He wanted you to know that."

With her eyes tightly shut, the sphinx moved her head slightly from side to side.

"There's something else he wants to say, but he's going now, back into the shadows, dear. He's telling me . . . yes?"

She wavered for a moment, inclining her head to one side, trying to hear.

"Yes. Who? He's telling me that someone else is listening."

Marlene's eyes widened. The exchange had brought me to my senses. "He's saying, my dear, that someone else is trying to find you. A woman? That's it; you are trying to find *him*, yet someone is also trying to find *you*. What's that?"

It was as though Marlene was trying to will the voice in the sphinx's head to ring out into the room for all to hear.

"It's no good, dear, he's going now."

A faint air of relief descended after the frisson of the séance. There was something farcical about paying to watch an old woman speak to herself in a room full of strangers. Whether I want to admit it, my cynicism about these things was always tempered by shame; so a little corner of me still clung to superstition. It made me think of my mother. Once composed, the medium stood by the door to shake hands with the guests as they departed. As we passed her she put a hand on Marlene's shoulder again.

"It might not mean anything, dear, but there was something else. The spirit also said the word Saturday?"

"You mean *satyr*?"

"No, love, I'm sure it was Saturday."

"It will all happen this Saturday." That was enough to put the fire back in Marlene's eyes. With her portfolio under my arm I followed her down into the street to see the idiot and his accomplice loading small boxes into the back of a van. They turned at the sight of Marlene leaving, eyeing her up. I expected some comment but they must have thought better of it.

Thankfully, against all of her wishes, the routes to the river were impassable. Having convinced her to finish our night in the Mansion House as we'd originally intended, we wound our way through the abandoned streets with her dreamily whispering the road names again as we passed, holding her imaginary map in her hands, yet without delighting in her game, obviously dejected; "Great Maze Pond . . . Sparrick's Row . . . " Every time she became quiet I kept turning to ensure she was still trailing behind me. She stood there transfixed by the street sign that read Dante Road. The names meant little to me now. When I noticed them at all they seemed to follow no map that I knew of. It was as if the streets were moving around us, sliding aside like panels, or rolling away on wheels. If you ever wanted to summon-up and speak with ghosts then these were the streets where they'd be right at home, streets that belonged on the Moon and what better place for Marlene to be?

III.
Doctor Charnock's First Report

Monday, 5th May 1941

Surely there is enough evidence in this little folio alone, just four mere drawings that support my case for her re-admittance. To have her back in my possession again would mean my sleep would be assured. Such terrible dreams these drawings have given me. My superiors could have nothing but admiration for my methods once this wild bird is recaptured.

They were wrong to suggest that London was no place for a woman on her own. The rented rooms here are plentiful if dirty and the men that remain are mostly old or infirm. No threat. Yet how is a fugitive traced in such conditions? The girl would be friendless and hungry. No common sense. Half-demented, with a bit of luck. She'd be roaming through the streets without direction. It's possible that her symptoms would be acute by now, that's if she's survived the raids. Perhaps the hospitals would be the best place to look. Austin Osman Spare. Were his letters to her a hoax? The return address is at least a starting point: the one real chance of finding her that's left. The contents are vague or ambiguous. There's mention of the Mansion House Tavern. There is always the possibility that he is a fabrication. That's what the Matron said. Yet my research has shown he's real enough, for me it is a clear case of transference. Perhaps there are clues in the drawings, or maybe my close examination of them is leading me astray. For now I will review her journals. It was wise to bring them with me on my hunt, while they may not provide a route they will certainly help to inform me of her possible strategies, her own particular psychological trajectory. So here again is her essay written just after she started to adopt the name Marlene Dietrich. Perhaps it was an act of defiance or consolidation after she had been referred to the hospital. The essay demonstrates a lucidity that she lost in the subsequent months in our care. It is an unavoidable side effect when administering the necessary regime; health must be, above all, the priority of the institute. That would always be an obstacle to my research and it became necessary to make arrangements to ensure she would take advantage of a certain opportunity to liberate herself and believe she was doing so unaided.

Who will ever read this report? I cannot truly envisage a day when I could deliver this to an audience worthy of its implications. It is evidence that could so easily be used against me; a report that is also a suicide note. After all, perhaps I am being compelled. What exactly is it that draws me into this girl's influence? Her peculiar magnetism is undeniable: she believes herself to be a sorceress. And in a way she is. I suspect that is why she has adopted the persona of a screen siren; not as others would believe—merely as a desperate form of escapism but a sophisticated technique within a far greater opus or incomprehensible system of belief. Does it simply serve her purposes to have us believe she is deluded? A siren; she is surely that, drawing others to their peril if they listen too closely to her alluring song. Yet I have no choice now, I must continue to listen; I mustn't lose my grip on her now that I have strayed into her waters.

The Satyr

She must be kept hidden—contained. At all costs it is necessary to maintain the appearance that the girl Marlene is a submissive subject. Now that she has escaped into the world I don't know how long that illusion can continue as the potency of the girl's insights and proclamations threaten any attempt at keeping her gifts a secret between us. None of my peers could possibly appreciate that it is I who must consult her as an oracle; that is the risk I must take to acquire illumination. I must be prepared to cross the line . . . to cross the threshold, to recognise her and embrace her for what she is now, my shadow. Then once she is within my grasp I can finally close the door that she has opened. Once I have her trust and obedience I can finally finish her, take away her map and exploit her gifts. Only then will she become merely mad. If my peers knew they'd only interfere with this vital work. They could never understand why it is essential that I walk this high wire. I must descend into another. I must enter into her madness. In knowing her I feel that I am on the verge of being plunged into another element. In those moments I'm immersed in timeless childhood once more, my senses reborn in a world that has only fleetingly become enchanted. I yearn for its return yet fear what its full manifestation will mean.

Admit it: the world I live in now is haunted. Speaking with her opened something between us, a breach between us, as if I had trespassed on hallowed ground and there are other presences now; unwelcome murmurs and impulses. She awakened something in me and now I cannot rest. I have no choice but to go further, to learn more. I must know what she knows so that I can be at peace in my own head. I must silence whatever it is that stirs inside me and will not let me sleep. She spoke of being taught secrets by her mentor, the Satyr, then I must exploit those lost principles too for my own ends.

The Satyr and Other Tales

൸

Notes on Drawing as Revelation
by Marlene Dietrich

Over time I have come to consider drawing as a form of initiation. Through various methods of automatism, such as the elaboration and interpretation of inkblots or scribbled random lines, revelatory images are coaxed into being.

When speaking of initiation, I mean engaging in practises that establish an exchange between conscious reflection and unconscious material, and developing a form of analogical language: the acquisition of a poetic literacy. I believe this literacy of the imagination arises from a creative dialogue with the unconscious and involves recurring motifs or symbols that transform with time and seduce the initiate. And of course as conscious thought is not independent of the world, similarly the unconscious draws its ancient forms from all things around us in this secret dialogue. New forms arise out of chaos. As the alchemists proclaimed, there can be no generation without decay.

When I am not in the drawing's presence I have an impression of it in my memory that undergoes a process of change. I enter into a psychic dialogue with the image and allow it space to breathe and speak. It often occurs to me that these images are living riddles that require solutions. I am convinced the presented image, which is never truly finished, only arrested, is informed by the experience of this restless quandary. Revelation in this way embodies, or results in, an open question rather than an answer, or perhaps on rare occasions

The Satyr

grasps the poetic drama implicit in the creation of an image. For me this isn't an artistic matter in that it doesn't demand considerations of composition, technique, aesthetic history or reception. These become, at best, peripheral concerns. The scene taking shape before or through me primarily absorbs my attention by way of an obsessive method. It's difficult to describe to what extent or how this dialogue might have transformed me, however, I can sense an increasing fluency in the imagery I encounter or create and that this lends insight to my life. However, this insight takes the form of gnosis and as such resists speech. It is closer to the awareness or foreknowledge one believes one possesses in dreams.

The image might only acquire the status and values of art when exhibited. As the image moves from the private to the public there is a loss of intimacy. The image becomes vulnerable. My only measure of success for an image in this context is the degree to which it disturbs the habitual tendencies of seeing, thinking and understanding. I owe a debt to the man they call the Borough Satyr, Austin Osman Spare. He was my master and through me he lives.

He showed me that these images arise anew from disinherited sources that run as threads through culture and language. They are hidden; lying dormant in and all around us as connective tissues, as resonant chords occasionally and accidentally struck by the many but sought out by a committed few, the only difference being the degree of commitment to the faculty of the imagination, the methodical exploration of these dream environs, these forgotten languages. This commitment is also a kind of initiation, for it demands that one sacrifices the common virtues and habits of society in order to keep the door to madness and dreams ajar. It is a balancing act, yet once risked great marvels of the world come to greet you. For the sake of sanity however, you must seek solace with like-minded souls who, without question, welcome you as a fellow seer.

෨

Her obsessions are contagious. Would it be wise to return to interpretation? The folio she entitled *From Mutus Liber: Four Drawings in Communion with the Danube* is made of blue card. It is stitched at the spine and to some extent apes a professional publication. She often acted out games where she was the centre of a rarefied community. It was useful to permit these fantasies as they kept her occupied and distracted her from her infatuation.

In conversation with the patient on a number of occasions she would attempt to elucidate her claims to "the throne of the Black Forest". Much conjecture amongst my peers ensued to seek the possible trigger for these delusions and fantasies, but as yet no one could arrive at an entirely satisfactory and convincing solution upon which to base a remedy or course of action. It was decided that an extensive log would be kept of her proclamations regarding this imaginary kingdom, an archive that has since been destroyed by fire in the raid upon the institute. From memory I can recall that, rather than relating in detail any accurate geographic or historical facts, her case amounted to a kind of private ethos and mythology that excluded the real concerns of the wider world. It is not known that her family originated in the area of the Danube and she has, for some inexplicable reason, adopted that river as a kind of moral template and barometer. Although some of my colleagues argued that tolerance should be practised with regard to her obsession I can see no evidence that it resulted in anything other than the deterioration of her condition. Furthermore, some of my colleagues were prone to indulging in viewing her drawings beyond what might be acceptably permitted within their professional capacities. Before the closure rumours had started to circulate that some of the staff had acquired artworks for their own personal pleasure or had established a specialist clientele of interested buyers. One doctor dismissed from duties had even jokingly encouraged the other patients to refer to her as Saint Marlene. It proves that they were unfit to attend to a case as complex as Marlene's. I admit that she does inspire a strange kind of loyalty and although I pride myself in conduct befitting an empirical approach, remaining intact and free of such temptations, I acknowledge that such a method can only lead to an inadequate grasp of the case. It is not that we should somehow respect her as an equal and thereby cure her; no, that would diminish her unique qualities. No, if we must admire her then we should do so as one would the untamed lioness in the cage. Thankfully all records of those events suffered the same fate as the patient's archive. Only I and the patient herself have the surviving pictures and passages of Marlene's precious book.

Finally returning to the folio, I will relate my own impressions of how these drawings have insinuated themselves into my own dreams, for according to her own methods, they may lend insight for my own task in hand. It must be remembered that this girl at large on the streets of the city might pose a threat akin to enemy propaganda. I have already sensed its growing impact on the people of Southwark.

Upon arriving in London I spent my evenings contemplating again the drawings I still had in my possession. As I travelled from the outskirts into the heart of the city my grasp upon the certainty of the world I'd known gradually loosened. So I entered the city on Marlene's terms as the further I went the closer I was to dreaming. Passing through a world of breached roads, dissected streets, and broken statues I felt I was crossing a threshold and couldn't turn back. Through those first few nights it became my ritual to sit by the window in my hotel room studying moonlit pages, looking for clues in Marlene's drawings. Through the window the city came to resemble the dreams played out in my sleep. Ruins dissolved in their own shadows. I lost track of the hours I spent awake or sleeping. Fearing that all of the resultant dreams might slip from my grasp I made meticulous records and interpretations.

The patient's drawing entitled *Emissary at the Threshold* depicts people gathering at an entrance on the edge of a forest. These men and women appear to be dressed in an archaic garb or perhaps the rags of bombsite survivors. From the great doorway a monstrous form emerges, a thing of mossy boughs and antlers. It greets them decorously and from the pages of an opened book gives them masks which they pass from one to another.

In a dream that I believe was inspired by obsessively poring over this image I dreamt that I followed this crowd across the threshold to find that we soon descended into the tunnels of the London Underground system. Tube signage adorned the walls yet the names of the stations had been obliterated. When we surfaced again we arrived in an ancient lost city—a city within a city frozen in some halcyon time. In my dream it is still London but it appeared

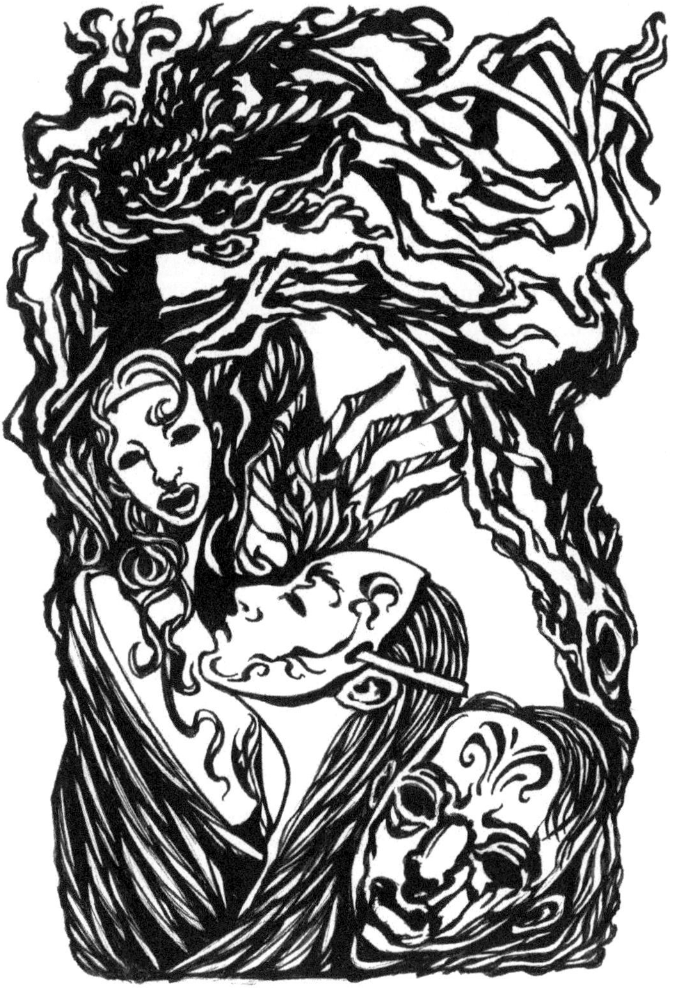

deserted, as if entirely evacuated and abandoned. How quickly the ruins had become overgrown and occupied by fauna that do not even belong in the British Isles, let alone England. Someone in our number whispered something about the gates of all the zoos having been flung open. Our monstrous envoy strides ahead, a motley procession following in his shadow. From time to time someone within the flock of followers would turn to hold a finger to their lips indicating that we should respect a reverential silence as we advance. An unspoken conviction took hold of me, as is common in dreams that we were partaking in a ceremony, anticipating our arrival at a sacred place.

From a deserted avenue we entered a ruined circle of grand terraced houses. Other streets led off in all directions from this hub and all about the twilit silence strange monuments stood; great broken heads and masks and other statuary of scarred sphinxes, beasts, and angels. This debris and flotsam had been unearthed here by the air raids, dredged or somehow washed up on the shores of the Thames . . . as if the secrets of the city had been unmasked and spilled into the streets. In wonderment I lost the others in the procession as they dispersed through the labyrinth. Then as I thought I had caught one of the other survivors the figure swiftly turned to show it was wearing a mask of Marlene's face as it slipped quietly around a column and vanished. I followed as quickly as I could. I was being inexorably drawn to my prey. Some elements of this dream are apparent in the patient's drawing entitled *The Great Meadow Where We Whispered.*

In considering these nightmares I must not forget that I'd just arrived with trepidation on the edges of Southwark, in a city being gradually eroded by nightly encroachments, each morning a fresh ruin was visible from my window. And so for a time I feared leaving the confines

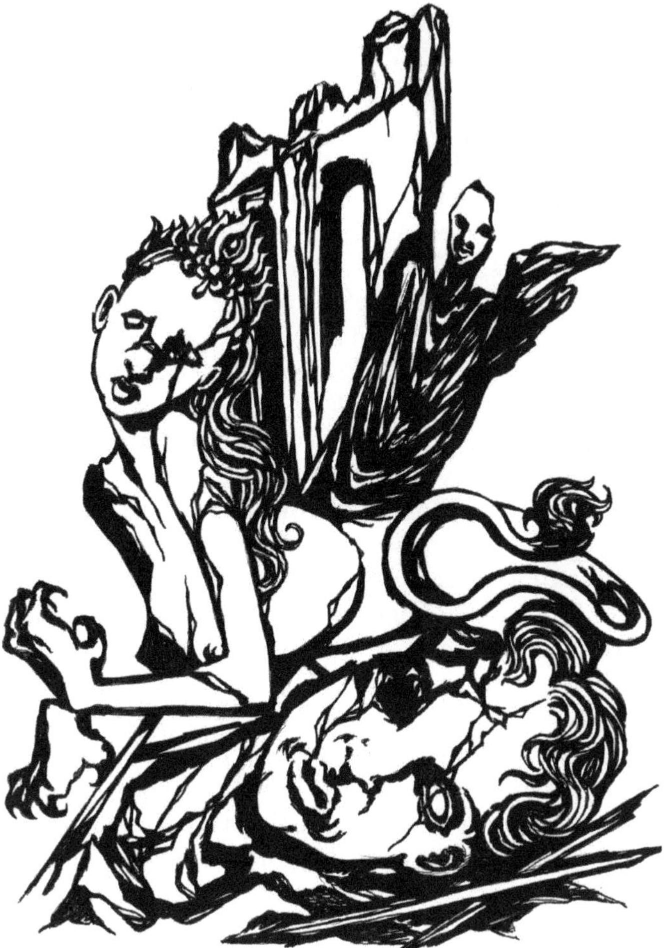

of the hotel, a fact that only concentrated the potency of my dreams. The few other inhabitants of the hotel seemed increasingly desperate or suspect. Marooned until I could find the courage to embark on my search I became vulnerable to the contagion of the pages, depicting as they did an imagined city in ruins.

The image of Marlene's face as a mask preoccupied my thoughts from the previous night. It was as though the dreams I experienced in my room conspired to form a continuous memory, segueing into one another while reaching into the fabric of my waking life. The dream of the mask found me drawn again to the penultimate image in the suite of pictures; *The Semblance of the Satyr*.

Did I see in its baroque lines the winding of a great river and the turning of inexorable events? That drawing was inseparable from my memory of yet another dream, this time involving an encounter with Marlene. Indeed it seemed that not only did the drawings influence my dreams they also acted as markers in my waking life, or doorways, indicating a transition from one stage to another in a process that still remained mysterious to me, a process I was only experiencing inadvertently and in diluted form by analysing these few drawings divorced from their greater context and without the necessary keys to understanding Marlene's scattered book. As the patient states in her treatise on drawing, for her it was a form of initiation, meaning the practitioner believed that a dynamic of transformation was intrinsic to the method, of which I could only sense a mere echo as an observer. And yet was it possible that, encountering a part of the book in that raw and unbound form, I could not avoid being drawn to its influence?

And so, to the last dream from my time in that hotel: I was being driven along a convoluted route through devastated streets when the taxi driver abruptly refused to go

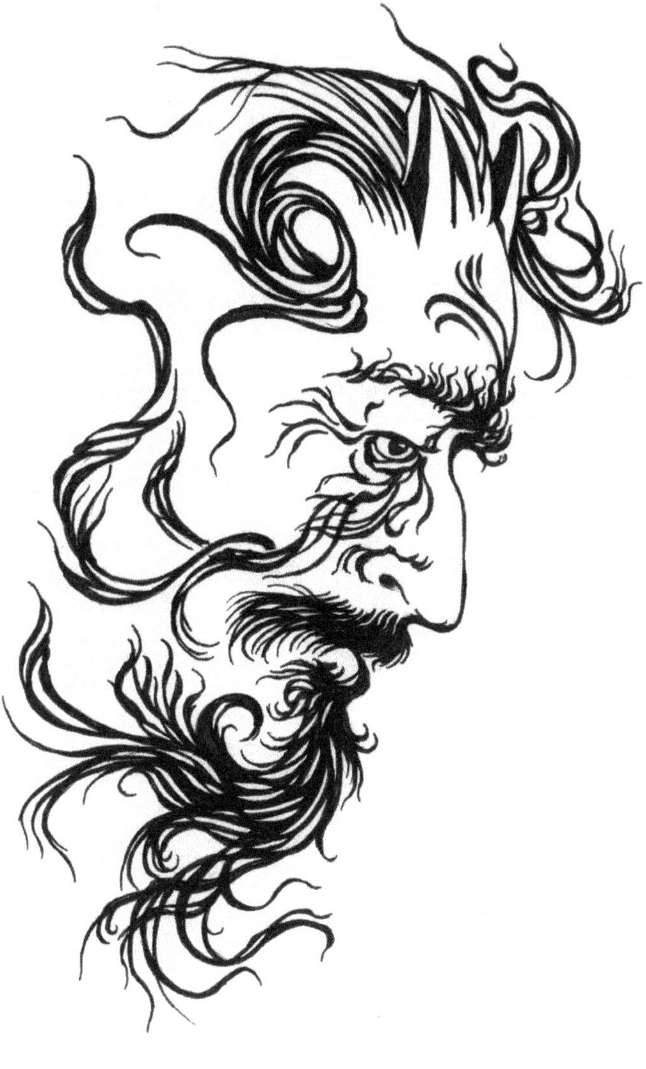

any further. When I demanded to know where an exhibition of the patient's drawings was being held he bowed and said, "Saint Marlene would have welcomed you in person if you'd telegrammed ahead." The driver pointed down an avenue of ruins to one incongruous building, a neoclassical rotunda standing apart in an expanse of rubble, its pale dome fractured as if about to collapse. It was clear my chauffeur had no intention of escorting me any further, so I picked my own way through the debris and after hesitating for a moment pushed against one of the looming doors. It was night inside the temple, a few stars peppering the breach in the great dome above me. Far below there was a candlelit array of salvaged furniture (beds, wardrobes, and the like) gathered in the hall's centre. I approached to find Marlene naked, reclining on a bed against a headboard of grotesque masks. Around the edges of this tableau a number of nefarious characters loitered as witnesses; spivs, hags, whores, and itinerants. A wild-haired painter stood at his easel with his back to me; the Satyr himself. Marlene glanced up as I advanced but didn't acknowledge my presence. It was then that I noticed that the girl also held a pencil and a book in her hands, drawing the artist in turn, or perhaps making notes.

Without a word to the others she slid from the bed and approached me. She said that I looked much older since we'd last met and that I would probably die soon. As she told me this, she was caressing her own breasts and throat and mouth. With the same lingering sensuousness she showed me her book. On one of the pages there was a portrait of an ageing satyr with bandaged arms and head. As I touched the pages I felt them twitch in response like warm skin, and on pulling my hand away I felt something coating my fingertips. I knew that the book was now part of me. Taking me to the door of the temple she gestured to the wasteland of the neighbourhood outside. The scene had changed, the expanse having greatly expanded to resemble the ravaged fields of the Somme. As I turned to go I found her book in my hands.

I left her without complaint, trudging along the edges of flooded bombsites clutching her open book in both hands, consulting it as one would a map. As I moved through burnt shells and skeletal remains I sensed that someone was following me. I had to escape them at all costs but was overcome by that fatigue peculiar to dreaming that, while allowing panic to persist afflicts the victim with a strange kind of indifference to whether one dies or survives. Knowing that if I turned to face my pursuer I would be confronted by something I could not bear, I pushed on through rainfall and mud until the skyline ahead was suddenly ablaze and I escaped from my dream, the dawn warming my face.

That is why the last image in the portfolio spoke to me so clearly that morning; Marlene had entitled it *And If I Had Turned to Face Them*. The details of the drawing seemed to respond directly to the contents of my dream from the previous night, as if answering a question I had only partly formulated. I had never confided any of my dreams to the patient yet I was still shaken by the possibility that Marlene's drawings had insinuated themselves into my life, responding to my dreams, anticipating my thoughts. Yet a drawing cannot influence a dream that preceded it. Marlene cannot read minds or predict the future by reading the patterns of the past; yet in my fear the stray leaves of this book still ring out with a secret synchronicity, calling out to the other lost pages in Marlene's possession, pages that I must reclaim and possibly destroy.

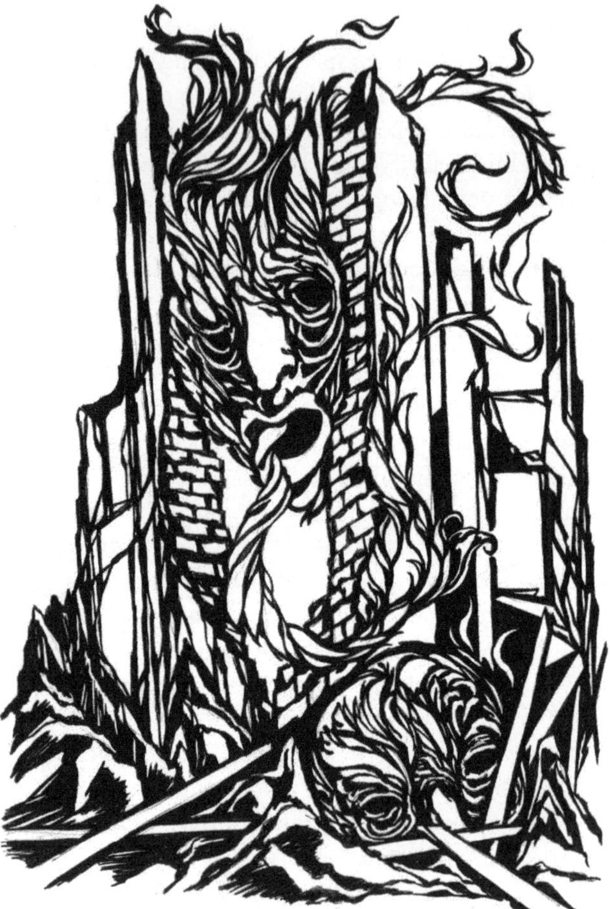

IV.
The Mansion House Tavern

"Walworth Road?" We'd been wandering in circles it seemed only to return all the way back to Kennington Park Road. The wheezing ruddy-faced landlord was clearing away our glasses from the bar with one hand and peering at his pocket watch in the other. The snug behind us was empty.

"That's the last I heard. He's living on Walworth Road. Haven't seen him for a while, so I might be wrong. Might be better checking at The Temple Bar, that's on Walworth. Although they were saying the other night that neck of the woods was hit pretty bad. Might be wise to check at the hospital or the hostels. If he's out on his arse, that's where he'll be because I don't think he had any friends to speak of. I could be wrong . . . "

He would have gabbled on if she'd let him, but she cut in, "Neck of the woods. Black Forest. Snake. Lamia." She was flicking through a card calendar on the bar, lingering on the day marked Saturday, May 10th 1941. She'd taken a turn for the worse since the séance, as though it had triggered something in her that was beyond her control. Her mania saddened me. It made me doubt myself. The landlord gave me a look.

"She all right? Here, don't I know you? Hughesy isn't it? Didn't you have trouble with my old boss? Blimey, when did you get out? You're not looking so well. So this is the sort of company you're keeping now, eh? Mind you

The Satyr and Other Tales

I saw your old partner in crime just the other day, Bloaters wasn't it? He was asking if I'd seen you about. And he told me not to tell you. Funny that. So I didn't tell you, right? Anyways, there's a hostel up on Walworth: if you ask me, that's where you want to be headed. Mind you, a lot of people have left now you know. There is a bloody war on, in case you hadn't noticed." And the landlord was trying not to shake his head as he served us another drink.

I thanked him and took another two glasses of stout from the bar to a table nestled behind an oak partition. Marlene seemed mesmerised by the stained glass in the panel, I was just thankful to have her hidden in a quiet corner. Taking a gulp from her glass she opened her portfolio again.

"It might be too late," she said, as she showed me her drawing of the emissaries again. "Beezle, you know, the fly, the emissary, was at the séance too and he was speaking through the old woman and reading her thoughts. And he said I would know that I was close when I heard the poet's name. I thought he meant the Satyr at first but now I realise he meant Dante Road. Dante Road is the sign he predicted. The Satyr, speaking through the old woman, had told Beezle where he could be found. Beezle said it was a matter of urgency now. The deluge would be coming and my master would be carried away if I could not warn him . . . save him. I don't like it here. We should get away. We're being followed. We're being watched."

"Look, let's calm down, hm? Let's just sit here awhile all safe in this quiet corner. Let's just rest while we can and give me some time to think, girl." Mention of my old ally Bloaters had shaken me. It was someone I really didn't want to run into. I pushed the glass of stout towards her and told her to drink.

The Satyr

"You seem to like games, Mr. Hughes. Let's play one. If you were a book what book would you be?"

"Keep your voice down, Marlene." The barman was earwigging our conversation and shaking his head in an amused, derisive manner.

"Don't you like books, Mr. Hughes? I thought you said you'd read many books while you were inside."

"I don't know, Marlene. I really don't know what kind of book I'd be. I know: a detective story, where the copper gets the girl in the end." I put my hand on hers and she didn't take it away.

"That's stupid. And besides, you're certainly no copper. But I bet you're wondering what book I might be?"

"Do tell." She scowled a little at that so I entreated her to tell me.

"I'm a book that most people have forgotten. It's a great lost book that more than one writer has written. Yet it's a book with many pictures. A book that's almost silent . . . a book . . . "

"A book for children . . . lots of pictures," I said trying to deflect her from her portentous tone.

"Perhaps; certainly children believe in magic until it's smothered inside them, true. So the book might appeal to them. It is a book that's almost silent after all, as I was saying . . . a book that whispers, but not only to children. Perhaps I'd be a book that would make all men become children again. What book would that be? Mr. Hughes, can you guess? It was entrusted to me, in here, inside my head, inside my body. But I'm a scattered book, Mr. Hughes, and someone has stolen some of my pages. She uses them to steal my past, pry into my thoughts and guess my actions. But the good doctor doesn't know what she's meddling with by taking those pages. But she'll know soon enough what a mistake she's . . . "

The Satyr and Other Tales

I was holding her hand across the table when the swelling moan of the siren interrupted.

We were still holding hands as we ran down Kennington Park Road. Buildings all around us were emptying. Marlene was lagging behind, her face stricken with fear, the sky far behind her down the vista of the street began to ignite and bloom. She was gripping the portfolio under her arm for dear life as she ran. She was screaming out "Demons!" She'd left her slippers in the pub but kept on running barefoot. Faces appeared around us, some strangely calm while others were anguished. Not everyone ran, already sick and defeated. I didn't know why we followed the surge of bodies until the landlord's voice echoed in my memory saying something I had missed when he'd first said it; "Kennington tube's just down the road, there'll be another tonight I shouldn't wonder." Spurred on by this memory I cried out, urging Marlene to follow and we reached the sandbagged mouth of the station as the street above us thundered.

V.
Doctor Charnock's Second Report

Thursday, 8th May 1941

They would never imagine it had been my intention all along to release the girl and let her return to her master. I can hardly believe it of myself at times. The raid proved the perfect cover. It wrenched her from their hands and took her beyond their reach. All I have to do is wait for her to burn herself out and then intervene. It isn't my duty to heal her or absolve her of sin, quite the reverse; I want to stoke up the fires of her own private damnation. The experts will no longer fawn over her, or claim glory from her case. When she returns to me she will be compliant and defeated, an innocent. And then I'll take from her what I need.

I've acquired an accomplice. I picked him up in the hotel bar. The bellboy should show him up to my room soon. Bloaters is a dullard, it's true. Yet, he knows the territory and will do the legwork for beer money. Finding Bloaters has given me fresh impetus to escape the nightmares that were trapping me in the hotel. Having someone to carry out my orders has given me vital focus. I must not fear the girl but use fear to tame her.

Among the patient's confiscated items, as well as the small folio of drawings and various odds and ends (a silver mirror, a brush with hairs attached, mascara case with traces of blood) there were sheaves of writing paper at the back of the folio with a spine sewn by hand. These I understand were her attempt at a fabulated form of memoir. It seems that by substituting the Satyr's idealised life for her own she actively attempts to conceal truths from herself that she cannot endure. I have scoured the text for any morsels of information that might prove useful in my search.

༺༻

A Modern Mythology of the Satyr
By Marlene Dietrich
Winter 1939

Let this be known as the true chronicle of the girl now called Marlene Dietrich who was so cruelly abducted by corrupt men on orders of her false human mother (the bitch who will not be named here in this record so that she may be forgotten) who did incarcerate her in the Institute for Talented and Demented Orphans and in doing so, separated Marlene from her beloved Satyr and erased her ancestral memories of her real mother, the primal waters of the Danube.

Marlene recounts the history here of her only love as a testament to those times so that they may one day return and illuminate the world with great cathedral-cinemas of glass shining from caverns all along the banks of the Danube, to celebrate her blessed, true and mysterious mother.

The Satyr was found floating down the Thames in a wicker basket on the morning of the 30th December 1886 by a City of London bobby, Philip Newton Spare. Philip made no secret of the fact

The Satyr

that he found the child clutching a pencil. The boy was immediately baptised with the human name Austin Osman Spare, still holding the pencil defiantly in his little fist. His new mother, Eliza Ann Adelaide Osman, being an enthusiastic attendee at séances throughout the district, had welcomed her offspring without the least crumb of surprise, having had the event accurately predicted on a number of occasions by the Elephant and Castle's most revered mediums. The Satyr was one of six children. They lived in a small palace known locally as The Snow Hill.

His mother Eliza noted that her foundling son could not be parted from his pencil and could only be coaxed to release it once it had been worn blunt by scribbling on whatever surface (wall, table, newspaper) came into close proximity. His cries could only be abated by the promise of a fresh pencil. By the age of four the child was an accomplished portraitist. Soon whatever savings the family had were quickly dissipated by the boy's insatiable appetite for materials. His older siblings took to petty theft to feed their brother's needs and he in turn would repay them by protecting them from the corrupting influences of the day with charms and spells.

In adolescence the Satyr was taken from his family home and forcibly enrolled into a school where the professors tried to make him design stained glass coffins for the affluent. He refused and was punished when all of his childhood drawings were confiscated and put on display in the grand bone halls of the Royal Academy Reformatory where he was pilloried for his shy beliefs in metempsychosis.

The actress Eily Gertrude Shaw liberated him

from this despair and they toured a small ragtag theatre company through the byways of the city together, the Satyr providing the painted backdrops and lyrics for Eily's songs. It was at this time the Satyr became fond of adopting animals, particularly cats, and the theatre came to resemble a kind of travelling circus. People came from all around to see his drawings and hear his orations on alchemy and his great feats of fortune-telling through consultation with animal spirits. Yet all that changed when the Great War broke out and the theatre had to serve its country, taking its dreams into the trenches by performing Arthur Machen's great play *The Angels of Mons* to the troops, although no one can remember the performances now. Their theatre was destroyed one night by enemy artillery and Eily vanished into the trenches. The Satyr was driven half-mad by the suffering and the spirits he'd seen rising from the mud. They had asked him too many questions and he did not have the energy to answer them all.

When the Satyr returned to London he founded his own religion against the god of men. This religion was like the theatre he'd lost, it was a lonely way where he'd erect stages along the river that ran from his head backwards into his heart. There he would imagine archaeology anew and write his own history, listen to his own seers and oracles, find entrances to the Underworld behind commonplace doors. At this time, when he slept, cowled shadows climbed up his limbs to whisper old forgotten phrases in his ears. In his dreams he wrote down their words using a feathered snake dipped in ink. He spent his days finding people who would publish these books and some of these people

The Satyr

became his loyal friends. He journeyed through the public houses and taverns finding in the wrinkled faces of Borough charwomen and the scars of ex-prize fighters the hieroglyphs of his secret elders. He transcribed this spectral language and soon became quietly celebrated in neglected corners, the only parts of the world that mattered to him.

It was 1938 and Marlene had arrived in Great Britain in her sleep as if washed ashore; shipwrecked. She awoke one morning in the spring, under a tree in Peckham Rye with a pencil in her hand, still damp from the waters of her mother, the Danube, who had carried her there. Many urchins of the neighbourhood came to her aid, bringing her clothes from nearby washing lines and telling her of a man who was perfectly suited to helping someone like her, the "Seer of Southwark", an older child proclaimed. The children took Marlene off across the city on a tram to meet their master and found him in the Mansion House Tavern drawing the publican's wife. The Satyr recognised Marlene and casually greeted her, as one would politely entertain an acquaintance. Marlene informed him that he was quite wrong, that they had never met before and that they were undoubtedly strangers. Yet the Satyr insisted that she'd once modelled for him and indeed even attended a few classes, where she'd shown great promise. Marlene could not remember this and broke into tears, which the Satyr dried with his sleeve. He pressed the matter no more but Marlene became convinced that somehow she'd forgotten their first encounter completely. It is possible that her voyage through the rose caverns of the Danube had robbed her of these memories.

The Satyr and Other Tales

So, that evening, to prove to her he was telling the truth, they returned to his studio. There, pinned to the wall, was a portrait in pastel of Marlene, but as if distorted through a river's restless water.

So in the Satyr's sacred grove a new era of Marlene's life began. A life of ecstasy and fasting and tea served in square porcelain cups in endless rooms that Marlene painted with murals of the vanished palaces of Esztergomand Štúrovo, dream-memories of the Belváros and zeppelins exploding over Bucharest. These rooms were inhabited by the migrant, avian spectres of the Ark: white egrets, bearded vultures, spoonbills, rollers, divers, red neck geese, pelicans, cormorants, and swans. There she became the Satyr's mistress posing for him wearing only a crown of feathers and acting as his oracle, his conduit. Through her he could consult the great spirits of those lost to the waters of the Danube and thereby travel cheaply but like a king in his sleep. In return he taught her how to gain the guidance of the dead in Elizabethan calligraphy.

Yet being so poor they could not eat, so Marlene was visited by demons in her sleep that picked her up from the marital bed and thrust her hands in the still-hot stove. They would throw her around by her hair and drag her into the street at night. There she was assailed by all manner of fiends in strange hats and overcoats. And although the beautiful Satyr searched through all of Southwark to find her, hags had cast a spell so that she had become deaf, dumb, blind, and invisible. She saw future visions of the Satyr at this time, of how a great calamity would befall him in the year 1941, but Marlene awoke in the institute for gifted orphans far from London and

The Satyr

could not reach him no matter how loudly she cried or how intently she listened. She knew she must find a way back to warn him that soon he would lose everything and fall wounded into the gutter.

The demons still hold her prisoner in her own hair to this day and the white walls open high to the clouds bursting with feathers. The river cracks the floor and roots reach through to her cell to entwine her feet and ankles while she sleeps. A giant's ghostly forehead is pressed against the window to block out the light all day long while Doctor Charnock's nursemaids bring Marlene suppers of sawdust and aspirin.

༄

Self-mythologising, persecution, and infantile regression are well-documented in cases such as this and the patterns that the patient has compulsively invented and adhered to can only ensure that she will be easier to follow and apprehend, even in a district as large as Southwark. Spare's notoriety and once celebrated gifts as a painter can only assist me in anticipating the girl's likely whereabouts. She will stick out like the proverbial sore thumb. The heightened suspicions of others will help to smoke her out.

Bloaters arrived late. He said he'd had trouble remembering that I was in room number eight. He reported that he'd seen the girl! And that she was in the company of a man, a swindler that was known to him. We would have to play this very carefully. I must not break my cover yet. At least I'd prepared my concoction and instructed Bloaters to administer it, should the opportunity arise, and report back to me once they were safely sedated. Can I entrust such a task to that inbred dolt? At least he took a stack of posters away with him. Soon her face will be all over town.

VI.
The Underworld

There was nothing else I could have done. My hand was clamped over Marlene's mouth even though she was trying to bite it. I could hear her muffled voice through my fingers saying, "The Underworld. The Underworld." Luckily in the panicked press of the bodies on the steps our struggle went largely unnoticed. People streamed and stumbled around us.

Once down in the stuffy interior of the tube station Marlene became preoccupied by the sight of so many people sheltering there. Although she was quiet I could tell by her flickering eyes that she was still agitated. Dozens of families had congregated along the tunnels leaving little space for others to pass. When we reached the main platform Marlene was astonished by the sight of men and women huddled together there in the semi-darkness. An infant sat upright in its mother's lap having its face washed with a flannel. Countless suitcases served as pillows. Some nervously conversed with strangers, while others sat staring at the ceiling, prepared to silently count the hours.

That was not all. Marlene was quiet for another reason. She was transfixed by something in the sheen of the white tiled passages and whatever it was made her fretful. It reminded her of something: that place perhaps, the institute from which she'd supposedly escaped. And still there was more, her eyes roved over the surfaces. The posters triggered a curiosity I couldn't grasp. She traced her fingers

The Satyr

around a glamorous face in a soap advertisement and nodded to herself. She was deciphering signs again, finding patterns that were not there, at least not to me. And her vulnerability struck me again; how she was so open to the least suggestion. That was her strength perhaps but in a way her weakness too. I hadn't lost my canny knack after all, always looking for a chink in the armour. And yet my old cruelty was beginning to fail me; I sought every excuse to prove my worth to her. Even my instincts were telling me to protect her. Thankfully it was while she was preoccupied that I noticed a smaller poster, this time of Marlene's face. A name and address was given, but in my panic to conceal it from her I tore it down and threw it in a crumpled ball to the ground.

Oblivious, Marlene took my hand and led me to the furthest end of the platform where the temperature dropped away from the throng of bodies, near the mouth of the tunnel leading off into the darkness. Her nervous eyes made me cautious. She crouched to sit on the platform's edge and I joined her, putting myself between her and the tunnel's mouth. She repeatedly ran her fingers over the leather portfolio that lay across her lap. She brought her mouth so close to my ear I could almost feel the movement of her lips.

"Even though I sense them here watching, I have to take the chance to tell you something. And I do sense that her agents are here amongst these people. They may not even know they are her watchers . . . her listeners. But they are just mere vessels. Some may even be her true servants in disguise: terrible spirits born from doubt and self-hatred. Doctor Charnock drew them out of me when I was vulnerable. She fed them, nurtured them, and turned them against me. That's the bitch I escaped, Charnock, their mistress now. They are bound to her and so some part of me is bound to her. She made the pact but I never consented to it. She called it treatment . . . analysis . . . yet she was prying into me, trying to salvage things for her own ends . . . her own fame . . . to leave me a husk . . . an empty shell. But that's not how it works. She's stupid, see, naïve in the ways of . . . well, of sorcery."

"Charnock? The doctor in the institute you escaped? The doctor that was helping you? You think she's coming after you?"

"Helping? Oh she was helping all right, helping herself to my secrets. She has some of my pages, some of my precious drawings. They are part of me. Part of the great lost book I'm becoming, the book Spare started to write and started to live through me . . . a living book . . . a *grimoire*. The silent book . . . the book of pictures . . . the book without words . . . the *Mutus Liber*. That is what I am. I came out of desire. The pages are made from the very flesh of the imagination. My life is the act of writing. I walk between the sinews of this world, slipping through the lacunae, attentive to the silences . . . seeing the flesh of all forms and the ancient forms buried in the shadows. I walk in between on the way of the word, on the edge of utterance, in limbo . . . the Neither-Neither . . . both imminent and immanent . . . " Her gibberish had somehow started to take an intelligible shape in me. Her warm voice on my ear seemed to breathe understanding into me.

"But her servants are near. They may be listening to my every word; her demons, her *interlopers*."

As she stared blankly into the darkness of the tunnel I thought about how she'd led us on a wild goose chase. It was as though a more direct route to her quarry might have been accomplished and yet it seemed necessary for her to enact this ritual of obeying whatever her instincts or intuition dictated. Perhaps she believed that Spare's salva-

The Satyr

tion depended upon it. Yet then she seemed to knowingly contradict my unspoken thoughts.

"We must not waste any more time. I have to find him and take him back with me. Take him home to the Danube. Something terrible is about to happen. The tide of this war will break everything up . . . will carry everything away. But listen! Listen! What was that? That voice from the tunnel! Over there in the darkness; it's one of her servants!"

I put a hand on hers to find that she was trembling. Tears were welling in her eyes. She was stifling the urge to cry out. I had to restrain her, to keep her from running off. She fought with me, sliding onto the tracks and dragging me into the damp shadows of the tunnel, leaving her drawings scattered across its entrance. She was growling the word "demons" at the back of her throat. We'd drawn a small crowd at the platform's edge, a grizzled man climbed down, telling us to "Stop that racket!" An infant's cries were echoing somewhere behind him.

She pulled me slowly into the darkness, then her hand cold with sweat slipped from mine and she stumbled ahead whispering that we must stop the interlopers that Charnock had sent after her:

"We must keep the people in the station safe . . . we must banish her influence . . . before it fully manifests through me . . . "

"Marlene there's nothing there . . . just echoes from the air raid." I was reaching out to her while edging forward hardly able to see where I was placing my feet in the thickening darkness.

The tunnel shuddered and dust fell in clouds of fine powder as unearthly echoes reached us from the choking blackness ahead. The few dim lamps strung along the walls flickered as if about to fail. With the sound of a great impact in the world above us the metal ribs of the tunnel whined an unnerving song as if to warn us of an imminent collapse.

"Marlene, stop! This is pointless! Come back!" That's all I could say before the dust filled my throat.

"We must catch one of these spirits and get some secrets out of it before we send it back to its mistress!"

"Marlene there's nothing there! Come back!" Just as I cried out again a shadow reared up near her and detaching itself from the tunnel wall it snarled, lurched forward and struck at Marlene's legs. In the darkness I could only guess that by its size it must have been a stray dog, probably lost and demented by its time in the tunnels. Yet it had attached itself with such ferocity to Marlene's clothing that even as I entered the fray to defend her I could not make out enough of the assailant to settle my doubts about what it was. In fact, my doubts only multiplied as I stayed in close proximity. As I tried to pull Marlene free and kicked repeatedly at the beast, my own firm grasp of what was happening slipped away. While struggling with the beast had I seen flashes of many teeth and talons and maddened eyes? Had there been scales and feathers? And had I heard speech, or even curses amongst the guttural sounds of its constant growling as the animal defied my attempts to repel it? Who knows what happened in that tunnel with the racket of the air raid reverberating all around us? As it persisted at riving at Marlene's garments and ankles the shadows and dust seemed drawn to the beast like iron filings to a magnet. All the while Marlene was screaming insults and demands, while landing fists on its unseen head.

"What's your name? Tell me your name, wretch! What was that you bastard? Is that what that bitch Charnock calls you now? You betrayer! You failure! I never want you back! I disown you! And you can tell your new mistress from me she'll never catch me! I'm Marlene now, not the

The Satyr

little girl she thought she could dissect with mind games and clever words! Tell her I have my own words now! My body's a sacred book! So get out! I banish you and send you back to that bitch!" All the while Marlene had been raining down blows, and with her final word there was a whimper in response followed by the sound of hurried paws padding away into the darkness. Marlene was doubled over breathing heavily, laughing her relief through clenched teeth.

"It's just a mere dog now. I transformed it back into a dog. Exorcised it, you could say. Let me catch my breath." Her face was caught by sudden torchlight searching the darkness. I looked back to see the familiar uniformed silhouette of an ARP warden standing at the entrance, a few other onlookers standing by him. He was asking if everything was all right as he lit our way with the ray of light. I put my arm around Marlene's shoulder and helped her back.

"Is everything all right there?" The warden addressed his question to me and gave me a look as if to say Marlene wasn't a full shilling. I held out my free hand to warn him off as Marlene stopped to gather up her pages strewn about the tunnel's entrance. The warden just shrugged and ushered the others away back to the platform again. I took Marlene's hand and led her to a secluded spot. Bombs were still being dropped in the city above. As we walked towards the entrance through the confined tunnels, picking our way through the slumbering bodies wrapped in blankets, she was opening her portfolio again. We ascended the steep stairs and found a private space near the entrance that others had avoided.

"Demons; they're coming to find me from that place. That's what it was back there; an interloper. They were born in that place I escaped. Doctor Charnock is their mistress now. The demons once belonged to me but she coaxed them out of me and learned their secret names. They have new names now and that's why I can't control them. She lets them do terrible things to her and uses them against me. They're up there now, rooting around in the city. They want to take me back there to the institute. I'll show you." She was shaking as she pulled crumpled pages from her portfolio.

"This here. See this."

She was struggling to maintain her whisper as she pushed a drawing into my hands and prodded the page with a fingertip.

"That's what that thing looked like, you see. We'd been followed and being underground leaves us prone to their influence. That's why I found the attic. I wouldn't be surprised if they coaxed us here. This might be one of their traps, bringing us down here. You can't hide away from these things because they're in you as well as out there: as without so within. It's when the two come together, that's when there's a problem, when the key enters the lock and they lock you in." And she gestured towards the darkness down below, the dim lamps reflected as pinpoints in her eyes.

"These parts of the world are closer to them. The skin between them and us is thinner here in these tunnels. I can sense it. They could just reach in here and swallow you whole and none of these people would raise a finger to help you, that's if they noticed at all."

Moving the drawing to the back of the pile I found handwritten pages and my glance registered the word Danube amongst the text. It was an imaginary life in the form of a poem. She snatched the pages back from my hands. A few of the refugees' heads along the far walls turned, mumbling disapproval at our whispers. Only a few remained awake and most of those eyed Marlene with suspicion. I suggested reading to her as a distraction. My

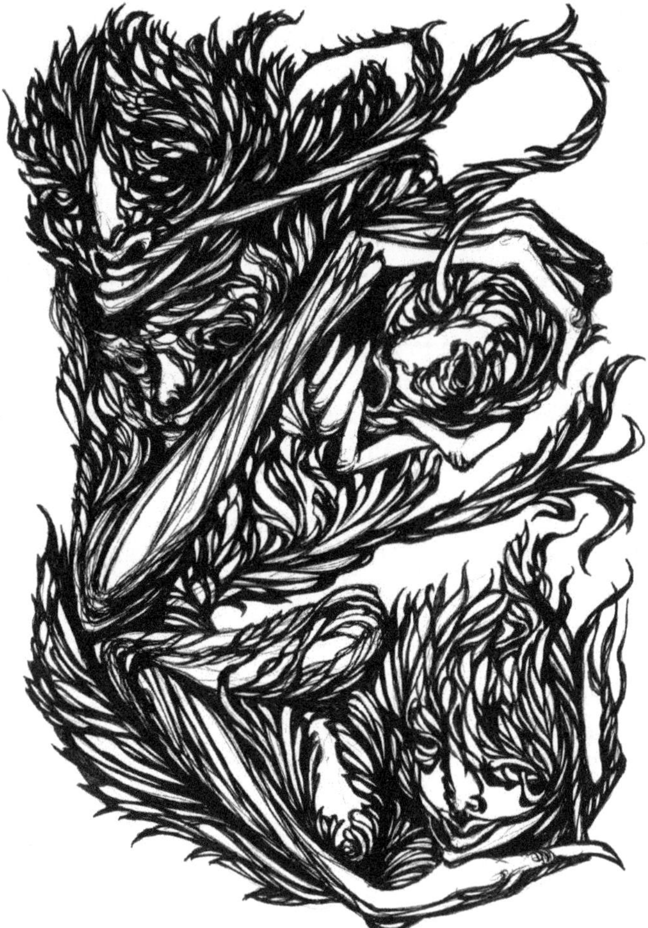

thoughts turned to what she'd said about someone shadowing us, this Charnock woman. Was she being hunted? Was that the opportunity I'd been waiting for? I could exploit it. Where there was a need there was a price to be paid. The thought was more ominous than I'd expected. The idea that she was infatuated with that man, her beloved Spare, sickened me. What would it matter if they never met again? What if he vanished, would she seek consolation in me?

The sound of the bombing in the streets above had fallen to a murmur. She sat by me on the steps and I pulled her close, letting her head rest on my shoulder I started to read her poem to her in the hope that she would trust me enough to fall asleep. After a few verses I felt her body relax into mine, yet I continued reading, the sounds of the words in my mouth gathering their own curious momentum.

> Cloven hooves clatter through rock pools
> the face of a satyr ripples
> in a mirror of water.
>
> The knowledge of the Danube
> courses toward the heart
> of the Black Sea.
>
> Marlene was born
> from the inky eye
> of the Donauquelle
> the wellspring and womb
> of her mother the Danube.
>
> She awoke to fauns
> dancing through

The Satyr

the palace
at Donaueschingen.

She climbed from the spring
up the great yarn
of her mother's hair
that formed the first forest.

Even stars and birds
became entangled
in her knotted tresses.

To their songs satyrs stirred
from dense woods
to bring votive offerings
of beer and cheese
heralding her return
they built her a palace
from the bones of fallen deer.

Grottoes and great gardens
were made in her honour
to rival those lost at Heidelberg.

Automaton statues
graced every avenue
of her overgrown maze
steam-driven and clockwork
pantheons that could seduce
any wandering guests
with their songs and dances.

And in the heart of that garden
sat the statue of the great Satyr

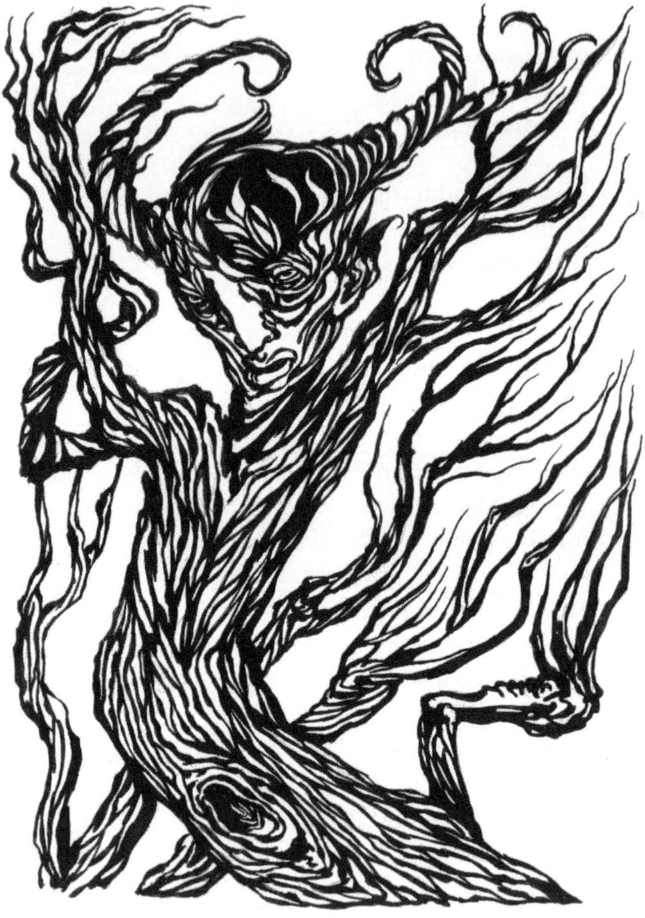

The Satyr

    rendered from her dreams.
    From his mouth
    billowed heady incense
    that she sucked through her lips
    to hear him whisper
    in her sleep.

    Her dreams were thunder
    through the water
    and from that incantation
    the river Danube . . .

The all-clear siren sounded in the small hours. Sensing its calming influence I still read the poem to her as we threaded our way through the debris back up Kennington Park Road at dusk, accompanied by other survivors from the tube station. It seemed that the buildings had crumbled of their own accord, as though finally admitting defeat.

    I stopped reading the poem, yet Marlene took up where I left off. A procession of dazed bloodless faces under powdered hair momentarily turned towards Marlene as they passed. A loose convoy could be seen all around us, avoiding the oncoming traffic of overloaded trucks and prams and wheelbarrows. As we made our way into the heart of the district others were fleeing in droves from the city. Her poem became a hypnotic chant.

    Under water sleep thunder
    under sleep thunder water
    sleep under water thunder
    sleep water under thunder
    sleep thunder water . . .

It was as though that nonsensical verse kept something at bay. She was trying to put her mind to sleep while walking. I tried to stop her from taking drawings out of her portfolio and pushing them into the hands of random passers-by. I watched each in turn either drop this strange propaganda to the dusty road or tear them to pieces as they went on their way, shaking their heads. Only one, a teenage boy with a bandaged eye, stopped in his tracks to watch us go, clutching a page in his shaking hands. A man, possibly his grandfather, tore it from his grasp and dragged him on.

Up ahead was the junction at the Elephant and Castle and from where we stood I could see the signs were not good. Clouds of smoke and dust cloaked everything.

"Who is she? Is she famous?" The bandaged boy was tugging on my sleeve. He must have picked up Marlene's picture again because he was holding it up in front of me. It was Marlene's self-portrait. His grandfather was nowhere to be seen.

"She's no one. Go on. Scarper!" The lad looked lost but suddenly defiant. I made to swat him but he only stepped out of reach.

"If she's no one then why's some old tart asking all over for her? She's put up a reward in all the pubs in the Boro', you arsehole!" As he turned to run I caught the scruff of his neck and brought him to the ground. By now Marlene was vanishing with the convoy on the road ahead. She either didn't hear me call or didn't want to. Noticing I'd attracted attention I quickly turned back to the boy and demanded, "Look. What are you saying? What's this about a reward? Make it quick."

He spat in my face. I went to hit him again, but a hand grasped mine from behind and wrenched it up my back. I was face down in the dirt under the full weight of my assailant. The boy was standing over me smirking.

The Satyr

"Go on, Bloaters, kick his head in!" I couldn't believe my luck.

"Bloaters? It's me, Paddy Hughes. You remember?" It was difficult talking with a prize-fighter's knee on the back of my neck. Marlene was long gone, however, the boy, now at the head of a small crowd, was still hovering. He was goading them into his defence yet it was Bloaters's voice I heard booming in my ear.

"I've been watching you from over there. You were going to do something bloody stupid, so I had to stop you. Been followin', you see." I craned my neck uselessly around. "I've been watching you for ages with that madwoman. She wants locking up she does. You didn't see me, but I was down in the tube station last night and heard her screaming. She's a nut that one, if you ask me." Bloaters turned me over onto my back like a doll and was standing over me gesturing for the crowd to disperse. They immediately complied. "You were always a sly one you, Hughesy, a snake in the grass." Even though he towered over me, I could tell he'd lost weight. He looked his age. Scars showed through his close-cropped hair. His hands were still gnarled, soaked in vinegar they say, back in his glory days, and toughened by punching the bark on trees. He held out a hand and pulled me to my feet.

VII.
Doctor Charnock's Third Report

Saturday, 10th May 1941

The prize-fighter had given me a few pointers of where to look. So I entered the world of Southwark's public houses at noon. A realm of mahogany, stained glass, brass, and leather where men who should have died long ago still sat staining ceilings with their tobacco smoke. There was something infernal about those sooty interiors. It was as if a presence lay in waiting in their heavy curtains and ancient carpets, in the aroma of thick fumes from coal fires and stoves, the closed chatter of the billiard rooms, the sad efforts of amateur pianists, the lazy traffic of street traders and barrow boys and hucksters. All were burdened; they must have known, as I did, that their world was soon to be swept away. These leftovers, stragglers and escapees were the living ghosts of an age that was slipping away; they were clinging to what was left of the shipwreck. I made no effort to be inconspicuous as I left posters of Marlene in each establishment. I was viewed with lust by most of the men, and suspicion with the slatterns that clung to them.

If my attire seemed well-heeled then I used it to my advantage; to sway the weaker-minded.

From directions gleaned off a barmaid at the Mansion House Tavern, I traced Spare to Walworth Road off the hub of the Elephant and Castle. In the Temple Bar a

The Satyr

fawning drunkard informed me that the artist's studio was situated above the local Woolworth's store. I'd brought along the patient's folio of sketches and writings. She often referred to it as a book, in fact using the archaic term *grimoire*; no doubt an indication that the pages had been completed under Spare's influence. They were the key to his sanctum I was certain, and much more. If he recognised the hand that had created them and admitted his complicity then some progress might be made. It was of no interest to me to see him convicted, as the damage had already been done and my purpose was to bring the girl back into the fold. However, the folio might provide considerable leverage, should it be required. He would deliver the whereabouts of the girl immediately or suffer the consequences. Yet, I was on their sordid turf; all these types were in it together. No doubt they were accustomed to closing ranks whenever trouble landed on their doorsteps. They call it community around here. I call it collusion. As thick as thieves, don't they say?

I made my way there on a surviving line, the packed tram slowly rattled and grated on its way as I sat deep in thought while surveying what had survived of the district through the webbed window. As I swept through the once grand stuccoed Victorian façades and wide Georgian streets, I wished that these worthy edifices could have been spared while the slummy network of warrens and decaying lanes that marred their beauty had been erased without a trace. While gazing at the passing ruins I decided it was wise to resist wading in. After all, Spare had once been prey to journalists, so was no stranger to being approached for interviews. So that would be my ruse. I'd play on his vanity; however, it would not be an easy game. I alighted from the tram coughing through the dust and debris of the street. The rundown shop front of Woolworth's was plain to see on the pavement opposite. There were no signs of life at the unwashed windows above the shop's loading bay and the shutters were down.

The directions I'd procured suggested that I knock at an entrance to the rear of the building. Through a grubby back street strung with laden washing lines I reached the adjoining yard. A cat sloped off across the high walls to watch me sphinx-like, at a safe distance. Holding the folio against my chest and assuming the air befitting a reporter, I knocked loudly then studied the door's blistered paintwork.

The sound of muffled and stumbling footsteps neared the other side of the door. Had I disturbed him from a deep sleep? God forbid that this was the man I had been looking for. The sight of him immediately caught me off guard and my eyes were thrown from one detail to another, not knowing where to rest: from his aquamarine eyes to his feral dusty mane, from his vagrant attire to his proud yet shambling gait. For a man living in the midst of a bombsite, he seemed singularly undaunted. Sweeping a hand before his face with an oddly flamboyant or nervous gesture he welcomed me in, as though I'd been expected. He mumbled something over his shoulder about a newspaper. My appearance had worked its magic again. Only then did I register who he really was and as I did so I found myself speaking his name aloud, "Mr. Austin Osman Spare?" His only response was another subdued gesture as we exited the dark hallway.

He led me up uncarpeted and decrepit stairs to a confined room. The aroma of damp and tobacco made it seem almost subterranean. Although the walls were bare, framed pictures draped with rags, or turned from view, were stacked along the skirting boards. It was as though I'd interrupted preparations, perhaps for his departure. Or was he in the process of preparing for an exhibition? A

The Satyr

few pictures still hung on the walls yet I could not allow my gaze to linger; all moonlit flesh, reverberant faces and bestial contortions and couplings; somehow alluring yet repellent. A paint-daubed table cluttered with curios, knick-knacks, creased pages, brushes, and jars occupied a corner. In another there was a folded easel. While I stood dismayed by the clutter around me Spare had produced two chairs from another room, hidden behind a curtain. He gestured for me to sit by the empty fireplace and, lighting a woodbine, joined me there. The scent of the sulphur from the match lingered.

Thinking back to the tram ride I remembered the strategy I'd devised for that very moment: while I'd flatter him I also planned to flavour my interview with some disdain. My intention was to see if this man Marlene called master could be wrong-footed. My approach opened with a remark about how some critics might doubt his calibre as an artist, having lost his way and now living in a nest with petty criminals. He said quite casually that he preferred to be "a swine with swine". No doubt a defensive move he'd come to rely upon, a droll wisecrack for all those who dared intrude upon his sacred grove.

He quietly watched the tendrils of smoke twist from his cigarette.

Next on my itinerary of insults were his portraits of what some termed "local types", the barrow boys, the drunkards, the waifs and strays, and charwomen of his neighbourhood, I insinuated that what he was doing was little more than exploitation, a form of kitsch: a misguided appropriation of a social class that would never appreciate his work.

Still playing with the spent match in his fingers he suddenly flicked it into the cold hearth. Panic must have gotten the better of me and from the folio I produced one of my posters.

"Do you recognise this woman?"

He peered through the smoky gloom between us and reaching into a threadbare pocket produced a pair of spectacles. I read his lips as he squinted and mouthed the name Marlene Dietrich. Before he had the chance to look amused I deadpanned, "It's not her real name."

"What is?" His emphasis made the question seem strangely open. As he took another drag from his cigarette I thought I saw his hand trembling slightly.

"I've come to warn you. She's trying to find you and has got it into her head that . . . "

"What if I told you I had already turned her away this morning?" The Satyr exhaled a plume of smoke.

"That's unlikely, Mr. Spare. I don't think she'd be so easily averted . . . "

He gave my statement some consideration while reaching for a bundle of pages and a pencil from the table nearby. He sat there casually drawing as he replied, his eyes hardly looking at the page but glancing at me and at the air around me, as if finding something there. Had his tone become suddenly alluring, or was it pity in his voice? "Tell me, when was the last time you saw her? You see the Boro' has many new ghosts; so many have died in the last few days alone. This city is being torn apart." The sound of Spare's pencil sliding across the page seemed louder than it should, yet I hadn't slept properly for days. I wanted to see what he was drawing, but sensing when I craned my neck he inclined the paper away. He continued to speak in a preoccupied manner as the pencil scored the page and again it may have been my sleep-deprived brain that suggested he referred to many things at once, as if there was some significance to his words I couldn't quite grasp, "So many things are slipping away . . . and slipping through . . . in the turmoil of

The Satyr

the moment . . . the volatile moment . . . when anything is possible. You know I once chased a satyr through the market crowds and no one took a blind bit of notice. Of course he gave me the slip. So you see I'm no stranger to the spaces in between . . . those veiled . . . subtle regions . . . those slippages and furrows. The strangest tails can be our own and you are chasing yours. I suggest you give up on this girl. Go home."

"She's real enough. These pages belong to her but I have them now!" I showed him her drawings. I wanted to snap him out of his daydream. I'd hoped for some sign of recognition, a proof of his guilt.

He put his own picture to one side, concealing it in a pile of papers. Passing Marlene's drawings carefully through his hands he murmured, "The subjects are of some interest, yet the hand is unsteady. It lacks . . . "

"Let's not play games. I didn't come here for your aesthetic opinion. Let's assume that there's some truth to what the girl's saying and that she did know you. Then you are responsible; you are the one that set her on this path. It was you, Mr. Spare. You were the one who corrupted her. What was it that you did to her, Mr. Spare? How did you get inside her head? She believes you entrusted something to her, that she must return pages of . . . "

"Why do you ask? Is it for her sake or because you want to take something from her; to take it for yourself?" Something in Spare's eyes became severe; fixing me with his gaze he silenced me and continued to speak.

"You still haven't told me this girl's real name, or your own, and what's more, I see you've used my name on your poster to bait your trap. Who's playing games now?" Tossing the folio back in my lap, he was already on his feet and walking towards the doorway.

He'd guessed the snare I'd set. I'd wrongly assumed he'd be an addled eccentric. I tried one last shot as he took me politely by the arm and ushered me to the landing.

"It was you, Mr. Spare. You were the one who corrupted her. What did you do to her? What do you want? I have these pages, Mr. Spare, and she'll come for them. And when she does I'll be waiting." Clutching the folio to my chest I let him guide me to the door.

"You should leave those pages with me." I remember he sounded almost kind, as if pitying me. "They don't belong to you. They'll only bring you harm." The long fingers of his hand were offered gently.

All I could do was shake my head like a scolded child and watch as the Satyr slowly closed the door, an odd sombreness coming over his face as he withdrew into the shadows.

For a moment I thought of pushing the folio through the letterbox but defiantly turned to go, his words dogging my thoughts. As I made my way into the warren of alleyways, I could still hear the sound of Spare's pencil against the page and my memory of that encounter troubled me. I never saw what Spare was drawing? Had he drawn my portrait? Had he seen something in the air around me? And as I sat there had the curtains in that recess stirred at times, had the cloths covering the pictures twitched or the features in the pictures on the walls become restless? The sound of that pencil on the page had left my thoughts itching, as if the seams and corners of the streets through which I made my escape were being picked at by a sharp beak or the point of a pencil.

VIII.
Bloaters and the One-Eyed Boy

"This is what I was on about." The boy had tagged along. He pointed to a poster of Marlene on the frosted glass of the bar's panelling. I didn't let on that I'd seen the picture before in the tube station.

She looked younger in the mugshot. It showed her cowering from the camera, the wall behind her bleached by the flash. Underneath there was the address of a hotel and the room cited as number eight. A convenient calling time of 6PM 'til 10PM had been provided and a named contact: Austin Osman Spare. As the reward was astronomical it was surely a hoax. It preyed on my mind that the boy had first reckoned that a woman was circulating these posters. Was Charnock real then?

"On the road back there, you mentioned a woman?" Before the boy could answer, Bloaters interrupted.

"No one's really taking it seriously because of her name. I mean who'd believe it: Marlene Dietrich!" Bloaters already sipped his second pint. "Do you think you can find her?" He looked sheepish.

"Is she famous?" The boy was still on his first lemonade. Bloaters clipped him around the ear. "I'll ask the questions or you'll be out on your arse. Make yourself useful and bring me that poster." The boy did as he was told.

The giant led us to a quiet corner and told us to sit, "Before you start on about the past, I'm not interested. You did your time and I took a beating: end of story. So don't waste your breath: how do you know her?"

Was this the same old bruiser that used to put the fear of God into people? While Bloaters's face was recognisable, it didn't conform to my memory, to the face that belonged to those days when we'd done our rounds of the local boozers: him acting as brute force to my nous. The silhouette of his head and shoulders, which had always given me the impression of an anvil, now seemed frail and somehow diminished. His pupils, once possessed a shark-like glaze, now nervously jolted in bloodshot jelly. Our racket had concluded with Bloaters taking a beating. There'd been rumours he'd ended up in the river. It was pure lucky coincidence that I was fingered for another scam and sent down. It had been convenient to let Bloaters assume I'd taken the rap for him. But this head . . . this head planted before me across the other side of the table had been reshaped. The skull's former lines of angular solidity had become warped, almost fluid, perhaps suggesting that it could at any moment slip from his neck and, like a water-filled balloon, burst upon the floor. I willed it to do so but it didn't comply. As he spoke I imagined his pulped head being loosened by the Thames's mercurial currents. It wasn't the same man who'd emerged from those waters and, if gossip was true, methodically avenged himself against his assailants and their employers. And these were no longer the words and images of my own thoughts, only Marlene could take credit for their lucidity. Even in her absence I was under her influence and the time had come to either surrender or resist.

"I don't know her." My head was racing with potential lies.

"You do. Of course you frigging well do. I've seen you together all over the place. Don't bullshit me, Hughesy." He jabbed a calloused finger at me.

The Satyr

She'd disappeared, and in her state of mind could be anywhere; of course Bloaters needn't know that.

"I don't know her, but I've got a good idea where to find her. You remember that painter Spare?" I had to get Bloaters to believe we were on the same side.

"He did that picture of me. Got me drunk for the privilege." I could tell he was warming to me again, recalling better times.

"Well, she's on her way to find him. We could go there together right now."

"He's still living off Brixton Road. Folk see him in the Temple Bar now and then. Says he looks madder than ever, like a tramp, all . . . "

"We all know what he looks like. What matters is that we can find him. Although, the address on the poster is a hotel; since when has a man like Spare slept in a hotel? And what's this girl to you anyway? You can tell your old pal." Bloaters averted his eyes; I always could tell when that big lump was trying to hide something.

"You'd better be silent now, Hughesy, 'cause I'm not to answer no questions right. You're going to sit there all quiet like until I say we can go." Bloaters sent the boy back to the bar for more drink.

Marlene's face looked back at me from the poster on the table. I was still in two minds. The prospect of clinching a deal had never saddened me before. She was my ticket out and I couldn't let sentiment get in the way of business. Bloaters looked on edge but I had to play along. It was my only way of finding Marlene again. Although I'd guessed that we'd reached the pub around midday, the clock on the pub wall was broken, so the only way to mark the time was by the pints Bloaters sank. He kept looking at a pocket watch but refused to tell me the time. Although I was pacing myself, the rounds kept coming and I suspected my captor's plan was to dull my judgement. So he sat there in stubborn silence, a statue standing guard over me. He'd obviously been paid expenses as he was never that generous. He was following orders. Had he been told to hold me there, or divert me, or worse still? I could think only of Marlene and how with each hour she slipped further away. The light was failing outside.

Finally signalling that we should leave, Bloaters clamped a hand around my arm and marched me from the pub. I made to voice my excuses, but the tightening of his grip told me otherwise.

"You're not going anywhere. I'm keeping my eye on you now, Hughesy."

We navigated our way through tight derelict back lanes in silence, the boy wheezing behind us. Evening was closing in and the threat of the siren was never far from my mind. With a grunt Bloaters indicated he'd found what he was looking for and, still clasping my arm, shouldered a tall rickety gate and entered. He dragged me into the shadows of a high-walled yard and I heard the boy close the gate behind us. He hauled me, stumbling up cluttered steps, to a door at the rear of an evacuated bedsit. The room we entered stank; pipes must have been breached in the floor below. There was a faint maddened buzzing of flies as if the air itself was agitated.

Bloaters lit a paraffin lamp to reveal the fleapit that was our room for the night. He directed the boy and me to a stool and crate at a table, and pulled a bottle and two tin cups from a cabinet. The journey to his hideaway had made the booze and blood rush to his head and he staggered as he moved.

"You're to drink that then you're going to sleep." His command was slurred yet I knew that, even when inebriated, Bloaters was a formidable opponent. He scraped

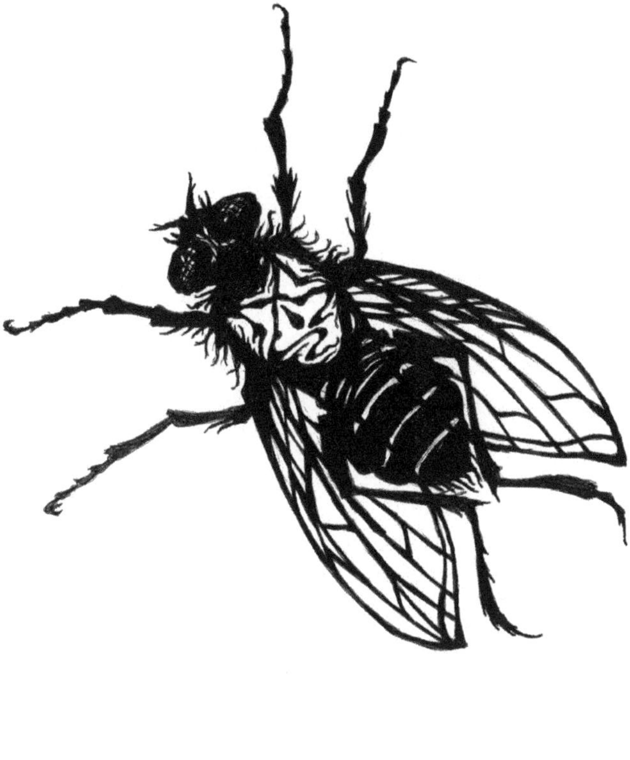

up a chair to the table and joined us. Seeing that I was hesitant, he took a flick knife from his pocket, extended the blade and planted it in the table. He looked at the boy, expecting him to comply first, which he did without further persuasion. I watched Bloaters empty a generous measure of clear liquid into a tin cup and the boy gulped it down. His face contorted, stroking his throat as he swallowed. Bloaters stifled a laugh. Then he turned to me and poured another measure. The prize-fighter rolled up his shirtsleeves and folded his arms on the table's edge saying, "I'm waiting." He swatted a fly from his hand.

"What's that stuff anyway?" The young lad spluttered, his voice sounding hoarse.

"Just something the doctor prepared." Bloaters kept glaring at me. I noticed his fingers twitching for the knife, so I downed it in one. The chemical had a harshly bitter aftertaste.

"Another." Again I did as I was instructed. Moments later I had to fight to refocus my eyes.

"That's that. I can't have you doing a runner. You've both had a dose and that's where you'll be sleeping. We'll start again in the morning." He stabbed a finger at a mass of blankets beneath a broken window.

The boy with the bandaged eye moaned and turned in his sleep, at times bleating "Ma! Please!" I couldn't remember joining him on the floor. Had I been chasing Marlene through an overgrown ruin? Dust was unsettled from the nearby sill by a tremor. It must have been the sound of another air raid, and not the boy's dreamt pleas, that had woken me. Something was wrong. The noises of each encroaching impact had a peculiar resonance. It seemed to me that they echoed and overlapped in such a way that they began to resemble a booming voice: struggling to shape the words of a foreign language. When I sat upright to concentrate, to try to discern the reason for the distortion, the room swam and every corner telescoped away from me. This was an intoxication the like of which I had not known before, and no doubt Bloaters's concoction was the culprit. My body was sluggish while my thoughts raced. A partial paralysis hampered my movement; I had to crawl to the nearest wall and use its surface to climb to my feet. The drunken warden of the room slept on, oblivious at the table, his head wrapped in his thick arms. As I attempted to stand upright the room reeled violently about me. I made it to the table, snatching up the crumpled poster. The muffled thunder outside drew my attention to the window where I was mesmerised by the deep sky filled with streaming tracer fire. Then the crazed buzzing of the flies returned, ringing and itching in my ears, whispering and spurring me on.

Without a second thought I took the flick knife and slid it effortlessly into the nook under Bloaters's ear, right up to the handle. My hands were instantly painted with the prize-fighter's blood as his body bucked from the chair to convulse upon the floor. Houseflies raged in the air all around me. The one-eyed boy was screaming. The knife, depicted in Marlene's ghost map, suddenly made perfect sense. My actions seemed unmoored from their consequences. I drifted to the window past the boy and, clearing the remaining brittle shards of glass from its frame, I let myself drop into the distant night below.

It had seemed as though I had flown, either that or I had been entirely anaesthetised to the pain of the impact. My fall had partially been broken by a small rundown glasshouse. I picked myself up from the wreckage and unrolled the poster in my hand. Marlene's white face stared back at me. Folding it into a pocket I stood awhile, exhilarated and terrified, leaning against the glasshouse's doorframe, gazing up at the blazing night sky: all ruptured flesh and fireworks. In making me imbibe his drug, Bloaters had cursed me and I felt it poisoning my thoughts; memories I had fought tirelessly to bury now erupted to the surface. I was back in the mud of the trenches.

IX.
Fireworks and Flesh

The lanes I tried to follow pulsed with lightning. At each junction paths multiplied around me. As I staggered on through the furnace of that redbrick maze my fingers trailed cracked walls, unsettling a lacework of shadows in my wake. Alleys wheeled about me as I turned to take another direction, so I reached out from one wall to the next, feeling my way like a blind man, the furrows of the world deepening and multiplying as I went. Pausing to wait for an eternity the intoxication would not pass, yet to remain standing still only left me vulnerable to the widening fissures beneath my feet. If I hesitated the pavements and walls were sure to sprout coarse black hair. All were signs that suggested whoever it was that had hired Bloaters had now sent something far worse after me. So I pushed on even if it meant I had to crawl.

Casting my gaze upward provided no peace or hope of escape. A barrage balloon in the sky overhead throbbed in time with my heartbeat as distorted faces emerged from the enflamed clouds around it. As thunder filled the alleys naked strangers ran criss-crossing from one yard doorway to another. From broken windows ancient faces peered, their translucent skin lit by their bones within. All around me ack-ack fire erupted against the sounds of agonised cries and collapsing walls. And the flies again buzzing; everywhere buzzing.

Then the confines of the backstreets gave way to an overwhelming sweetness of sap, of burnt stripped bark as I found myself straying across an open green surrounded by blasted and still-burning trees. An unearthly silence fell within the square of lifeless façades surrounding me, every pathway a glittering mosaic of glass slivers, until another cataract of incendiaries enveloped the rooftops with streams of dancing blue-white flames. In the debris and embers, in the depths of the white-hot flames fluid forms, shapeless phantoms stirred and rose up, invoked in the fire. From the blackened rafters, from the spaces in between, wings unfurled and limbs were born, reaching out only to vanish again. And what did I hear crying as it was born that night? As all of my childhood haunts were devoured, the blaze of all those memories burned at once; it was the sound of one world dying as another emerged. Through the great veil of broken frames and shattered glass I glimpsed that world's secret face.

For a moment an endless hush. The air raid fell silent. The bombardment gave way to birdsong. From my pocket I unfolded her crumpled white face and read the words beneath it. Another reward was promised then. Golden light suffused green ruins as far as the eye could see. That was his time, he was in the stones of that place, and through the wind his words were breathed, following the rhythm of a great river that ran somewhere unseen and forgotten beyond the crumbling skyline. Through the overgrown avenues his flesh was in the plentiful ivy and wise bark of the trees. The city in that moment was his, a garden of fallen walls, a place lost to time, a vision of what the city would become; the city as the Satyr dreamt it.

Then that bliss was punctured, giving way to the tumult of that other hallucination: I was there again in the burning city, the bombardment drumming through

The Satyr

my bones. Sudden breaches in the rows of houses before me were like teeth smashed from a mouth. The city I'd known was disappearing, dissolving into the night. Through one such rift in the façades I wandered on, lurching through potholes and hollows filled with black water. I glimpsed the movement of a familiar shadow against fire and pursued it.

Whatever it was wanted to be pursued for I soon had it cornered. In the archway of a ruin something limbless stirred; skin unfolding from shadow, a swollen head slowly turning, its monstrous face somehow feminine, almost feline, and its forehead encrusted with jewels. Her ink-black eyes met mine as her pupils dilated and eclipsed the white of her eyes. I caught a glimmer of Marlene's face in that creature's expression. It was one of her emissaries come to help me. With a mere widening of its eyes and a nod it urged me to follow, its ophidian shape; a flame sliding and flickering through the shadows as it lit the way. Marlene's face danced there too in that tongue of fire, drawing me on as I ascended through the ruins. I followed the edges of craters from which clouds of chattering houseflies surged around me. The swarm sang with a single voice, driving me on in my delirium. Still clutching Marlene's picture as a talisman, as a map, I reached the corner of an open street filled with sirens and firemen, deeply inhaling the cooler air. I'd surfaced once more, returning to the world of men. The words on the page in my hand formed directions in my mind which I quickly followed.

The face of the hotel was dark and tranquil. Blackout curtains had been drawn, but the muted glow of the entrance hall became visible as I entered. No bellboy or desk clerk came to greet me. I guessed the building had been evacuated sometime before. I had to see it with my own eyes and pushed on.

The first floor hallway stretched before me. The angles seemed somehow awry. Whatever it was that Bloaters had forced me to drink still lingered; perhaps it had left an indelible mark. Had it awakened something in me, that same unease that Marlene possessed; an acute awareness to the world as restless and without bounds? It seemed fitting then that I found more doors had been left open than closed. A few stray suitcases lay across the corridor's carpet, their contents abandoned in a panic. Aroused by the sense of intrusion I was spurred on down the hallway, the numbers glinting on the doors, the walls reverberating with the sound of the encroaching bombardment.

Number eight flashed through my fingertips as I pushed the door open. The occupants had carelessly left their bedside lamp blazing. The room was in disarray; the bed unmade and the dresser overflowing. Medicine bottles and phials glinted from a valet case by the mirror. Piles of posters bearing Marlene's face were stacked on the floor. Then a voice came from the half-light, drawing my attention to a chair beyond the lamp. The place stank of tobacco smoke.

"I said; you found me then. I must say I'm surprised." she purred, her voice crackling as she inhaled deeply on her cigarette. She slurred a little too, an empty glass poised in her hand. Despite the act of composure her voice trembled. The sound of an impact resounded in the street and the window in the room rattled.

On a low table between us there was an open folio much like Marlene's had been, yet the drawings on the pages displayed weren't familiar to me.

"You've seen something like it then? You're a quiet one. Afraid I'll read your mind?" She must have seen me staring. My throat was dry with brick-dust and smoke.

"Help yourself to a drink, don't worry it's only gin. There's tonic too. I must say I'm surprised you're here to

The Satyr

tell the tale. She'll have told you all about me. I'm Charnock, her old doctor."

I poured a measure without speaking.

"Oh, I found her precious Satyr. He turned me away, you know. You'll have seen his address written there on the cover. You could go there, but I think you'll find . . . " The room shook with another explosion as the woman pushed herself unsteadily from her chair, ... I think you'll find that you're too late." She reached to pour herself another drink.

"Take the drawings . . . take her damned pages! Wish I'd never opened them. Wish I'd never laid eyes on them. Take them far, far away from me. But it's too late. Spare tried to say. I thought he was playing tricks with me. Well, I know a few games of my own . . . but these pages . . . her pages . . . they awakened something in me . . . something I can't allow. So take them away from me . . . go!" Letting her sway and ramble on I gathered up the folio in my hands without a word, saw the address scrawled on the inside, and closed it. With that a change suddenly came over Charnock. Her face distorted, becoming fierce.

"Those pages don't belong to you!" She staggered towards me as the reverberations of a direct hit in the road outside shattered the window in its frame, showering the room with glass and dust. She was grasping at me, trying to hold on as I pushed her away. Her face powdered with dust, her eyes wild and unfocused screaming, "Take them out of me! They don't belong to you! Get them out of me!" The window behind her was filled with flame, the curtains igniting and starting to disintegrate. She was attempting to drag me backwards as I pushed her away. If there was another explosion, then I didn't hear it. There was only a great muffled and dislocated ringing as I fell into darkness. The room was torn apart around me; the ceiling suddenly all embers and stars. Had the flames reached out to Charnock, its fingers tearing her back through the space where the window had been? Did I see a great shadow with blazing feathers rear up and sweep her off into the night?

Hands pulled me from the debris. I fought for breath as I surfaced from the dust and darkness, the scent of blood burning in the air. Uniformed men gathered around me, lifting away rubble and rafters. I tried to speak, but brought blood to my lips instead. Behind my rescuers I saw a body lying shattered in the street, the head twisted round towards me possessed Charnock's unmistakable face, the expression still contorted as I had last seen it. Beyond the body and the road there was nothing. The street to which the road had once belonged had been erased. The dawn was all dust and dying flames.

X.
Wish You Were Here

When I surfaced I was in a hospital ward; as the anaesthetic faded they administered morphine. The thunder of my memories dwindled. No longer pushing against the current I surrendered and my dream carried me downriver.

The soft bright face of a nurse floated for a moment before me, telling me I'd had a visitor while I'd been unconscious. I asked how long I'd been out for the count, but the girl just touched my shoulder and said not to worry. She said my visitor had left a message. The angel handed me an envelope then vanished. I tore it open to find that it was no simple letter; as I unfolded the page a drawing came to life.

It depicted Marlene as a sphinx holding a finger to her lips; her secret was safe with me. There was something else; a slip of paper had fallen from the crease of the page as I'd opened it. It was a ticket for the hostel on Walworth Road.

The slogan "Careless war talk costs lives" printed on the ticket took on a stranger resonance as it slipped from my fingers, the morphine submerging me again in its currents. Other faces came to my bedside then; old Bloaters emerged from the depths, his skin cracked driftwood with dry blood in its grain. As he levelled an accusation at me his voice softened, as did his features, until that ancient mask of his gave way to another; Charnock glowered back at me from the flames. I remembered then that I had seen

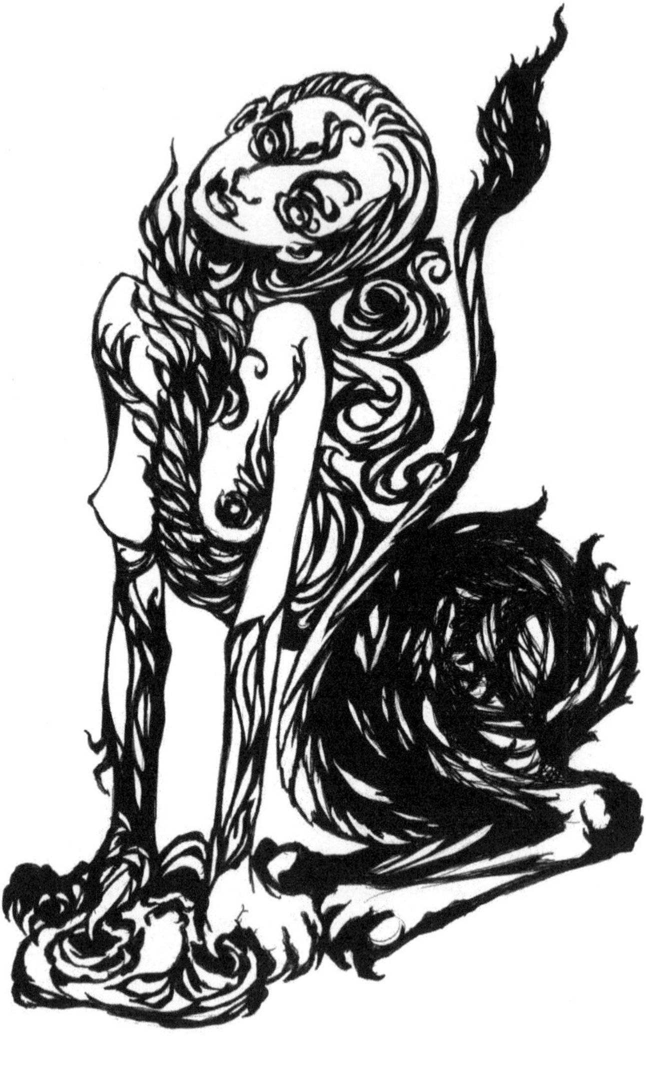

her on many previous nights, holding a vigil at my bedside, pages fluttering in her hands before they blackened and curled and flew from her fingers to become ashes on the air. She repeated something Spare had told her: "The strangest tails can be our own."

It was the clairvoyant Lilly Peer who spoke to me next, her face rising from the smoke where Charnock's had burned only a moment before. In her eyes I caught Marlene's reflection. On the verge of unconsciousness again I remembered Marlene one last time as dawn arrived.

I recalled the night I'd survived the flames, the night before I fell into this limbo between waking and sleeping. Crawling from the ruins of the hotel, I still held the folio I'd reclaimed from Charnock. I read the address scrawled on the cover and found my way to Walworth Road, to the Satyr's den only to see the place in flames. One of the wardens there who'd tried to douse the blaze pulled me back and said he believed there was no one home, at least that's what he'd told some blonde girl who'd been there before me, a member of the family he thought. She'd been distraught so to give her hope he'd directed her to a makeshift hospital nearby where hundreds of casualties were being taken that night. It had to be her.

So I must have headed that way myself as I recall limping on, trying to follow the warden's directions, but finding it useless as the streets that night were unrecognisable. Yet I must have stumbled on through that wasteland of fire and debris, growing ever more exhausted until I blacked out.

This was all I could remember. As I surfaced again from memory I knew I could waste no more time. Discharging myself, the ward staff didn't attempt to stop me, nor complain when I made off with crutches taken from the porter's office. They even found me some other fella's clothes; he wouldn't need them anymore they'd said. I knew the rules of the wounded; if I could walk I had to give up the bed to someone who couldn't.

When I eventually reached the Walworth Road, I hardly recognised it; the once bustling tram-jungle was now almost deserted. Many of its familiar haunts and landmarks had been obliterated. Limping my way up the street, the footpaths powdered with brick-dust, I hesitated to place the sound of a muffled ringing until I realised the old shellshock had returned. No doubt my disorientation was further magnified by Charnock's poison lingering in my veins. Out of swirling dust clouds old refugees shuffled towards me, noticing my bandages they offered directions then went warily on their way.

Soon I found myself stumbling up the steps of the hostel's imposing entrance. I pulled aside the great blackout curtains to find the peace inside was palpable. Checking my permit, the bored sentry at the turnstile waved me through to a dim passage of green glazed bricks. From that main corridor numbered doors opened onto dormitories busy with the destitute, the infirm, and the wounded. Perhaps the place had been grand once, but now the curtains at the high windows were threadbare and the tables scarred and stained. Men hunched over those tables playing drafts and dominoes, occupying the space conspiratorially, and as their low voices echoed across the tall Victorian ceilings it seemed to me that I must enter with a kind of reverence, as if into a church.

The letters and numbers stamped on my ticket directed me down the hall to a secluded area. I didn't know how Marlene had worked her magic, whether she had colluded with a doctor to secure me a privileged place there I will never know. I entered a space divided into private sleeping cubicles, and within the silence of high wooden panels I found a bed and chair waiting for me. Finally slumping onto the bed to gather my strength, my hands violently trembling, I wondered, as if from a strange distance, whether I had been shaking that way all along without noticing. Had I become in some way a stranger to my own body, as if dislocated, dislodged, or suspended on the brink between one place and another?

Then, just as despair was closing its jaws on me, there was singing. I heard a woman singing:

> Falling in love again
> Never wanted to
> What am I to do?
> I can't help it

Her voice danced, softly echoing against the panels as I entered the aisle. An old man had come to his door on crutches. He must have heard her too:

> Love's always been my game
> Play it how I may
> I was made that way
> I can't help it

We listened a while before we spoke. In a reverie I heard the man reply to a question I couldn't remember asking. He said, "He's a special case. He's got one of those cubicles all to himself while some of us have to share. At least we're not stuck in the dorms, eh? He came in here the other night in a bad way. He's allowed company on account of his injuries. Both arms, see, and him an artist as well."

I left the man murmuring to himself as I moved on, drifting down the dim passage, trembling with the cold and drawn to the warmth of her voice. I neared the doorway and hesitated.

> Men cluster to me
> Like moths around a flame
> And if their wings burn
> I know I'm not to blame

As I turned to cross the threshold the morning sunlight touched my face. There she was at the bedside; Marlene singing.

> Falling in love again
> Never wanted to
> What am I to do?
> I just can't help it

She was singing to the Satyr as he slept, his bandaged arms draped across the open pages of Marlene's portfolio. Just as I was about to speak, she took her hand from his and raising a finger to her lips whispered: "He's dreaming."

The Bestiary of Communion

"Nature is a temple where living pillars sometimes allow confused words to escape; man passes there through forests of symbols that watch him with familiar glances"

~ Charles Baudelaire

The Horned Tongue

I.

Even when she was alive he'd guessed that her life had many secret pages that remained unread by him. Surely it was not as if she'd planned to hide them. It was just that he'd allowed his curiosity to wane, assuming that the marvels and surprises they had to offer each other were far behind them. Edith had simply been there, a constant through their childless years. True, she'd often escaped to her family as he had to his books. He had accepted long ago that women must be allowed their hysterics. After all, he knew she would always return to him with sympathy. She'd soldiered on.

And then she was gone; the hub of his life. He always thought, even hoped, that he would go first, so he'd made no preparations for a prospect that had, only months ago, become a reality. She was gone, vanished from orbit, leaving him vulnerable and dispossessed. He had become a vagrant in his own life. All the daily rituals that had seemed so effortless before were no longer informed by her presence, her purpose. In the space she'd once occupied only a nagging doubt remained. All his energies were expended at its avoidance, but the doubt waited for him all the same. It would appear in different unexpected guises, and that particular night it took the shape of his pillow. No matter how he pummelled or kneaded its flesh it would not comply, it would not let him rest. It was as though it whispered softly to him, "You never knew her."

The respite those first moments of morning brought were soon swept away once he'd found his senses. The obsessive thought returned and flavoured the breakfast he took too long to make. There had been unknown elements in his wife's life, private zones of shadow. They were important to her, he supposed, but he had never taken the time to explore them, and now that she was gone they had become a permanent mystery. He even imagined that she'd had secret friends. It was possible. He wouldn't even know if he passed them in the street. He suspected that she'd had beliefs . . . certain commitments or allegiances, yet it was a book he'd preferred to leave on the shelf for fear he'd open something he'd come to regret.

He had little patience for her spiritual convictions. They were an unnecessary indulgence. He found them embarrassing, even insulting. He resented the way they seemed to lead her astray, leaving her open to manipulation; a potential threat to his own peace. Yet that peace was anything but secure now, and he knew that he must go on the offensive. He knew he must seek what remained of her secret life.

It had been much simpler than he'd expected. Her possessions, which he could not bring himself to disturb let alone part with, had become talismans in their home. Her dressing table was still adorned with her things as she'd left them, an unstoppered bottle of jasmine, a brush still thick with hair, and necklaces that spilled from a jewellery box onto her reading glasses. With time this shrine charged with raw intimacy had become just another familiar mess, coalescing with stacked books and unwashed clothes. Yet it was there, in an unlocked drawer, that he'd found her diary, although to call it that would be an exaggeration.

The Horned Tongue

The book had few introspective logs, mainly names, addresses and times, most of which he couldn't place. However, a pattern of reoccurring entries suggested an unlikely rendezvous, a café in a lane off Spui Square called Lusher's, in the heart of Amsterdam. Every Wednesday evening she had gone there to meet with half a dozen names he couldn't quite decipher. The writing seemed intentionally scrawled, almost written in code, yet each bore an appellation, mostly "Mrs."—a peculiar formality for a woman so informal. With further study he guessed that these gatherings were much more than social. After all, it seemed that a private room had been *prepared* above the café and if the scribbled rows of calculations and symbols in another section of the diary told him anything, then his wife must have been the society's treasurer. Dates had been marked with specific activities too, such as "Table-rapping, remember candles", or "Manifestation—pins and mirror", or to top it all off, "Guest talk tonight: speaking in tongues". A spiritualist union then; he'd winced at the thought of it but was determined to visit the café all the same. As it was Sunday he decided he could afford to take a few hours off, a welcome diversion from haunting his bookshop that since her death always seemed empty. Unaccustomed to such places, he decided that it would be wise to eat there, at least ordering food might make his visit less conspicuous. He had to admit that some part of him savoured the idea of fulfilling a heroic role he'd only read about. He put Edith's diary inside his overcoat, imagining that some confrontation might warrant its use as evidence. He set out, his head ringing with the names of Holmes, Watson, and Dupin.

There was muted laughter as Pieter Metternich settled in the corner of Lusher's café. It seemed strangely quiet for midday, only a few customers sat scattered about the sunlit tables, each preoccupied by their company, food, or reading. A man raised his newspaper noisily as he passed. A radio buzzed behind the counter as bored waitresses polished surfaces that were already gleaming. The manager, a woman in her fifties with dyed red hair, had her attention focused on something out of sight behind the till. He thought the whole place had an air of distraction, as though waiting for something to happen. The walls were covered in framed photographs of the narrow byways of the city, specifically mapping the local vicinity of Spui Square, with its awnings and tall, lean façades. In some of the photographs the square's wide cobbled space lay bare, and in others it was alive with the bustle of a market day. There was even a photograph of the Het Lieverdje, the statue of a ragamuffin unveiled last year. Metternich had taken an instant dislike to it, its arrival having drawn further tourists to *his* square and, if he could admit it, had somehow heralded Edith's deterioration. His eyes darted through the monochrome streets, from photograph to photograph, thinking for a moment that he might catch a glimpse of her there, some clue to her clandestine life. A waitress caught one of his stray glances and approached with a smile. Even this polite exchange became a confrontation, common niceties having become so unfamiliar to him. While ordering a coffee he anxiously sought a surreptitious angle into her confidence. He was no detective, however, and only achieved giving the girl the impression that she was dealing with an imbecile, a man who floundered even in the shallows of social etiquette. As she returned with his order he was still wracking his brain for something to say, and so forgot to thank her. Instead he just mutely watched her come and go. The redhead behind the till had thrown him a disparaging look, no doubt to emphasise his ineptitude. Yes, he had long since become socially incompetent. And what of it, he thought,

The Horned Tongue

growing indignant, taking out his wife's diary and opening its pages with undue force. And just as he was thinking that it was probably not the subtlest form of investigation, he was joined by the man who had only seconds before been hiding behind the pages of his newspaper.

I will take this opportunity to reveal that I was the man Metternich met that day and that it is down to me to tell his story, as no one else will. He has long since been forgotten as so many of my charitable causes are. I'm not popularly known for my compassion or modesty but then my enemies, those priggish guardians of history, have seen to that and think nothing of slandering me, so I must make an exception here at the risk of seeming boastful, after all it is left to me to rectify their lies. I can't leave it to those idiots who call themselves my followers either, to prove that even I have my moments of philanthropy, though I might be forced to take a circuitous route. So where was I? Yes, the old bookseller, Metternich was in a quiet corner of the café, considering how to hatch his plan, when a stranger approached him.

Metternich had made a move to hide the diary once more in his coat when the stranger gently tapped the back of his hand with his fingers and said, "Please, not on my account. I'll not interrupt your reading for long. I only wondered if I may join you for a moment, Pieter."

Metternich was taken aback and to further confound him, his name had been delivered in a seemingly feigned foreign accent. "You know me?" And then with a second thought, "Oh, you know my shop, my bookshop—Metternich's. I'm sorry. I don't . . . " It was only then, when the stranger had turned to focus his full attention on Metternich's face, that the old man noticed his eye: the right one unmoving and lightless, as though nailed into place and his left a deep emerald.

The Satyr and Other Tales

"Let me introduce myself," the stranger lowered his voice and, removing a black glove as he offered his hand, planted himself in the seat closest to the old man. "Professor Woland." The name seemed to ring a bell with Metternich, but his memory had been playing tricks of late. Still, he chanced a guess to avoid any awkwardness.

"Mr. Woland? You're a book collector?" Yet the professor seemed to sense his ruse with a smile.

"In a way, Pieter," he patted the bookseller's hand that still rested protectively on his wife's diary. Metternich slid the volume across the table into his coat and whispered:

"With respect, that volume is not for sale."

The professor held up his other still gloved hand to draw the waitress's attention. Metternich couldn't hide his envy at the stranger's charm, the waitress returned in seconds with an espresso, her face all coy admiration. With his little finger raised he took a sip, then smiled.

"Now, Pieter, where were we? Yes, you could say I'm fond of books, but rest assured your late wife's diary is quite safe. No, it is another book I have in mind, a particular book that was nevertheless close to Edith's heart." And of course the bookseller's face, upon hearing the stranger speak of *his* Edith in such familiar terms, flushed with rage. He let out a grunt he hadn't intended. Having turned a few of the other customers' heads, he smiled nervously and slid his fists from the table. The professor held up his gloved hand in appeasement as Metternich snapped under his breath, "How do you know? You knew Edith? Spit it out and be quick about it."

"Pieter, let's not misunderstand each other. I don't wish to make a scene. I'm sorry if I have you at a disadvantage. I became acquainted with your wife only to the extent of knowing she had fallen in with a bad lot, the wrong crowd so to speak. You must have known she was prone to such

The Horned Tongue

things." The professor seemed to struggle with sincerity and the bookseller sensed it.

"And of course you are acquainted with this 'wrong crowd', professor?" Metternich grimaced.

"Let's keep this friendly. We've both seen better days and the last thing we want is to make a spectacle of ourselves in front of these good patrons. Two old men brawling on a Sunday afternoon just wouldn't do. Now, how can I put this? I can only beg you to respect my confidence as I do yours. You must trust me when I tell you I have Edith's best interests at heart."

The bookseller refused to give an inch, returning his smile with a stare. The professor was undeterred and continued, "Very well, I can see that I must take other measures. I wanted to avoid this but now I can tell there is no other course. The little street urchin out there in the square, the statue you call Het Lieverdje. To most folk around here it's charming and the tourists seem to flock to it. But to you, Pieter Metternich, it is a mockery. Your wife never bore you a child, and by some cruel coincidence, when that statue was unveiled last year, in May 1959, you felt aggrieved, for that urchin's little face seemed to smile as your wife fell into sudden decline. Her heart, I believe."

The old man was about to protest, but sat silenced instead, staring over the professor's shoulder and out of the window onto Spui Square where the monument of the child stood.

"So now, Pieter, you are asking yourself—how could he know that? Now that I have your full attention I can return to the matter in hand. You see that woman behind the counter? That's Mrs. Lusher. She knew Edith very well indeed. And even though she refuses to show it, she also knows me. Don't be fooled, she is ashamed and really quite nervous that I have turned up here unannounced.

Pieter, she is a thief. She has stolen something that is very precious to me and I want it back; a book, my book, a private manuscript in fact."

Metternich listened to all of this as though from a great distance. Woland's voice seemed somehow isolated from the sounds of the café around him, the radio, the clink of cups on saucers, the grumble and hiss of boiling water . . . his voice moved slowly and smoothly ever-closer. When the bookseller turned his attention to the professor, he was caught in the glimmer of that one green eye. He lost all sense of how long he'd allowed his own eyes to linger there. He turned to look at Mrs. Lusher, who had clearly been staring at them both for some time, and with one glance Metternich seemed to compel her to quickly retreat through a strip-curtain in the doorway behind her.

"So you see, Pieter, if you're looking for a guilty party you need search no further than that woman and her cohorts, her little coven of charlatans. If you want answers then you must seek them there." At this Woland looked up at the ceiling and the bookseller's gaze followed, imagining the rooms that lay above his head.

"But you must be cautious. They have a few tricks up their sleeves. For one thing there are the scarecrows. They mark their territory with those things. You'll know them when you see them, a hotchpotch of household things strung together, horrifying phantoms they are . . . horrifying, intolerable, you see . . . well, suffice to say, it's not my place to approach this Mrs. Lusher and her sisters, and that's where you come in. There are rules, let's say there are certain strictures of conduct that I must abide by—but you, Pieter, you can disregard all of that, you have some leniency there, my friend, owing to being . . . well, owing to your marriage to Edith. And I can only ask, no, implore you to go there for me . . . and for yourself too, of

The Horned Tongue

course . . . to find out for yourself . . . and bring back my book if you would be so . . . "

Metternich sensed the shift in Woland's tone and saw in it an opportunity to take the upper hand. "This book of yours . . . this manuscript. How will I know it when I see it? It has a title?"

"It does: *The Horned Tongue*. You'll retrieve it for me? Although I'm sorry that I must insist that you don't read it."

"And what will I receive in return?" The bookseller surprised himself. He didn't want to seem like a soft touch. After all, this creature Woland had known Edith and all about his loss, and was quite prepared to toy with his grief just to get what he wanted. So Metternich planned his own game.

"When I come to your shop to collect my property, let's say on May the first, that's another day and night from now, you will already have your reward. I can say no more, only suggest the way. Strictures you see . . . "

"I'm not sure I do see and, to be clear, you seem to need help of another kind. Professional help I mean." Metternich noticed a thread of fire in the professor's green eye that told him he must tread cautiously. "I'm sorry. You see, I'm a simple bookseller and all this talk of scarecrows and secret bargains is beyond me. All I know is that I intend to pay Mrs. Lusher a visit because of this." The old man patted the diary in his pocket and allowed himself a breath of relief, having avoided provoking the lunatic, at least for a short time. He reasoned it would be more fruitful to show this poor soul some compassion and said calmly, "I'm sure that you can see my predicament. I can't simply break into this woman's home and steal something you claim is yours just on the strength of your word, the word of a stranger. I'd like to, believe me I would. But really it just can't be done." The bookseller felt a shiver of embarrassment.

Had he overstepped the mark? Woland seemed strangely deflated and the old bookseller didn't want to risk disappointing a man so evidently deranged. Yet he couldn't so easily explain away this stranger's knowledge of his wife, so he felt compelled to stay a while to learn more. If there was a hint of shame in the professor's eye, it was soon devoured by the wolfish light that suddenly animated his entire face. An idea had occurred to him and he expressed it with barely-concealed relish.

"Quite so, Pieter, you are right. How could I expect you to simply swallow my story? What *man* would? Men always require some demonstration. I wanted to avoid such excesses, to be fair, but now I see I have no choice. Come now, follow me if you will." Woland shot to his feet, immediately standing to attention and, briskly folding his huge newspaper under his arm, pulled on his right glove with surgical precision. The old man's heart dropped. The last thing he wanted was to leave with this madman, and just as he was mustering his refusal, Woland planted a hand on his shoulder and whispered in his ear, "You didn't know her. That's what the voice says, isn't it, Pieter? It gnaws in your ear at four in the morning. It's the first thing you hear when you open your eyes. Don't you recognise my voice, Pieter? It's me that you hear, and if you want me to stop . . . " The bookseller met the professor's gaze as he spoke, and for a second saw in the green bead of his eye a tear of pity. He would play along with him for the time being.

"Where are we going?" The old man muttered as he got to his feet, realising for the first time that Woland stood head and shoulders above him. He ignored the bookseller's question and was already opening the café door. Metternich reached into his pocket and placed a handful of guilders on his saucer. He walked out into the sharp air where stallholders in hats and scarves were busily arranging their

The Horned Tongue

books for the Sunday market. He thought he should be sheltered in his warm shop, in the hope of catching the trade of stray tourists, but instead he sadly joined the professor at the corner of Het Spui Street. Woland turned and sidled up close to the old man.

"Come along, Pieter, I need to show you something that will put a different complexion on all of this." In the frosted light of the square Woland had taken on a severe aspect. He seemed much taller, lithe in fact, and surely his eyebrows had thickened into wild, dark arches. A hungry confidence informed his slightest movement and facial expression. Pressing closer to the old man's shoulder he whipped the newspaper out from under his other arm. Opening it with a violent flourish he unfurled a huge map that like a wall obscured the bookseller's view of the street ahead. "Here!" Woland cried, and jabbed a place on the map with a leathery finger.

When Woland folded the map away, a new scene erupted, filling the bookseller's senses. They were standing in Zorgvlied cemetery. Metternich knew it immediately, it was where he'd put his Edith to rest. Still dazed by his arrival, the old man watched Woland stride off down a tree-lined avenue, tucking the newspaper under his arm again.

"I'm sure you know the way!" He called out behind him as Metternich spun this way and that, still convinced he'd find some trace of the vanished Spui Square. Only once he'd scurried after the professor did he sense the mild air, the warm scent of flowers, and birdsong in the trees. This wasn't just another place, it was another season.

"Spring last year to be precise, Pieter." The professor had stopped at an open graveside. The bookseller tried to catch his breath, deciding to keep some distance from the madman turned sorcerer. "Come closer, I want you to witness this." Woland pointed at the headstone.

The Satyr and Other Tales

Metternich knew what the name would be before he saw it. And then he felt nauseous at the evidence. A wreath of dry flowers crumpled underfoot. He said miserably, "So you want me to see my wife buried all over again, is that it? Is that my punishment? You wanted to bring me here before it all happened, before . . . " The old man was holding on to his rising anxiety with both fists.

"No, Pieter. Not before." Woland turned to him with pity in his one good eye. "No, see that wreath under your foot? You left that here the day you said goodbye. Remember, Pieter? You put her down there, in the ground, with all her secrets. This is a few days later. Edith was exhumed, but you wouldn't know that because you couldn't find the courage to return. You see, Mrs. Lusher has friends in high places, as they say. Your wife's body serves her purposes now. Need I give you any further encouragement to aid me?"

The old man lifted the wreath of dead flowers in his hands, shaking his head, not knowing if it was in answer to Woland's question or in disbelief.

"Listen." Woland reached a narrow, gloved hand to the bookseller's stooped shoulders. "Do you hear that sound?" The bookseller felt the pressure of the sorcerer's fingers compelling him to lean over the edge of the grave. He could hear nothing. Woland urged him. "Listen closer, Pieter, do you hear her sobbing?"

"I hear nothing, you devil!" Metternich pulled himself free of the professor's hold. "Let me go back. Take me back! Please." He cried as he stepped away from the edge.

"Very well." Woland unfolded the newspaper to ever more unexpected proportions, thrusting it out between them until he disappeared from Metternich's view. He heard the professor speak from behind the wall of paper. "Very well, Pieter, but you will hear your wife's voice before we meet again, I can promise you that. And I will come for my book." With a lunge, the old man was engulfed in the pages of the newspaper. Moments or perhaps hours later he awoke still enveloped in ink-scented pages. He struggled to tear them apart, the crumpled paper falling about him. He was home in his armchair, alone by the window. It was night outside and someone had left the radio on. It whispered in a language he couldn't place. As he stirred to switch it off he found that a wreath of dead flowers hung around his neck.

II.

Metternich returned that night, walking through the back streets that echoed with the sounds of late cafés. He cautiously entered Spui Square, taking a minute to survey its deserted space. The statue of the urchin and the sparse trees were its only occupants, casting warped shadows across the damp cobbles. He stared a while at the façade of Lusher's café. A dim light had been left on and the awning had not been raised yet; there was no sign of life in the little aquarium of its windows, nor in the three floors above. He thought he saw movement on an upper floor, but dismissed it as a reflection of lamplight. Pausing for a moment at the café door he gazed at the table he'd occupied that day, only hours before. The stranger's mismatched eyes came to mind, the dead black button of his right pupil frozen in its socket, while the left never rested; with minute jolts it had searched Metternich's own, flickering from one eye to the other, as though animated by suspicions he'd rather not consider. To shake the memory, he moved from the window to peer around the corner. A narrow alley ran down the full length of the café's flank, however, what he'd assumed would be a thoroughfare ended abruptly in the muted light of a porch door. He made his way towards this sepia pane, all the time hesitating at his actions, stopping to wring his hands and look back down the street's tunnel at the familiar square now barely visible at its end. As he turned again, the light in the door had vanished. Not a sound could be heard there and he trembled at the thought that he was no longer in the city he knew. The door opened effortlessly and without a noise, as if it had been especially oiled for the occasion. He crept inside, the weight in his breath slowing his progress. He squinted and guessed that he was in a passage. He removed a torch from his overcoat. Fumbling for the switch, he turned as the weak beam of light revealed a tall motionless figure. It stood before another door at the passage's end, barring the way with its frame of dishevelled rags. A spasm lurched through Metternich's stomach as he saw that instead of a face the stranger had . . . a mop? With relief and subdued amusement, he approached the junkyard effigy. There was still something sinister in its artifice, in the fact that anyone would go to so much trouble to create such a thing. It had clearly been crafted with skill and devotion. Woland had informed him the circle used these dummies to mark their territory, and for a moment he questioned their motives, whether it could be a decoy, a warning sign, a ritual totem, or perhaps a strange hybrid of all these things, he couldn't guess. Were they quite sane? Metternich squeezed past the effigy to the second door and had his fingers on its handle when he hesitated again. Had there been an edge of intimidation in Woland's voice when he spoke of these people? He found it hard to believe that someone like him should feel so threatened by these séance-peddlers. And yet it remained unclear how Woland had come to hear of his loss or of Edith's involvement. How could he have been so naïve to take the man at his word and respect *his confidence*? Respect his confi-

The Horned Tongue

dence—what had he meant by this strange turn of phrase? Unless there was unsettled business and he was to act as an unwitting agent of Woland's revenge. And as he was turning the handle the question of the book came to mind. What could a book have to do with his wife? It was absurd. Steal a book? All he wanted was to understand why she had known these people and had decided to keep their acquaintance from him. Woland was clearly thinking he could take him for a fool. If he wanted the book, there was nothing to stop him creeping in there and stealing it himself. Yet he had come that far, he thought, he must press on and perhaps find some trace of Edith that would put his mind at rest.

The door opened onto a steep flight of stairs and he ascended to a heavy black drape. He tentatively parted the curtain and peered inside; he heard whispers somewhere in the darkness of the room. Off to his right, in a far corner, a dimly lit door stood open lending the space meagre definition. He could make out the edges of stacked crates and boxes. Shelves lined the walls holding tins and jars. He was in a room that served as storage for the café below. He turned off his torch and slowly moved to the door, following the growing sound of voices speaking in a contorted tongue. He was still standing out of the flickering glow of the doorway when he heard a woman's voice silence the others' chatter.

"Come in, Pieter. We've been waiting," she said between his heartbeats.

The second room couldn't have contrasted more from the first. It was much larger than he'd anticipated and surely out of proportion with the café's exterior. Woland's impossible map sprang to mind as he entered. He took in as much as a few glances would allow before focusing on the source of the voice. Had there really been more than one pi-

The Satyr and Other Tales

ano by the carved mouth of a grand fireplace? Had he seen a large glass ball on a silver stand above it? Had there been tall, unpolished mirrors and embroidered drapes reaching up into darkness where the ceiling should have been? He could not be sure if he'd seen great paintings; their oily sheen catching the fire and candlelight, yet the impression of untamed forests remained. As he stood there, like a child awaiting a scolding, the warm voice purred again.

"Please come nearer, further in so we can see you. We've been waiting." It was as though the room no longer mattered; it receded into shadow as his attention became fixed on the small circular gathering of faces around a table. At its head sat Mrs. Lusher, her face the texture of warm wax under a nest of red ringlets. She gestured to an empty seat at the table. The six other faces around its edges were turned away from him but he guessed they were probably women. All of them remained focused on Mrs. Lusher as she placed a small leather-bound portfolio on the table and pushed it across the polished surface, down an avenue of lit candlesticks, towards the bookseller. Metternich didn't move. He only glanced at the leather folder, enough to discern that its skin was decorated with a silver title and illustration. The old man waited for the woman to speak again, but seeing that her lips were pursed he cleared his throat and began.

"I'm sorry . . . " was all that he could muster. He'd wanted to say more but got lost along the way.

"He's sorry, sisters . . . too polite for a burglar. Perhaps he's a spy." The redhead looked into the averted faces of the other women and the old man thought he heard amused croaks and sniffles. "Please be seated." Metternich accepted her invitation and joined them.

"You came looking for Edith." Lusher's eyes flickered to her left, at an empty place at the table, the back of a

The Horned Tongue

chair pushed against its edge. All the bookseller could manage was a compliant nod, as he swallowed the urge to shout at her. "And Mr. Woland has sent you on an errand." He nodded again, finding courage to meet her gaze now, down the avenue of candlesticks to the face hovering at its end. He had not expected to find such sympathy in her eyes. It encouraged him to find his voice again.

"He asked me to find . . . let's be honest . . . he asked me to take, that is, to steal back something that was stolen from him. I don't know anything about it. I just want answers about Edith and why . . . why you saw fit to take her body from her grave." He'd successfully stifled his anger. He cleared his throat again. The sound of his voice shaping those words had scared him, not simply because he had made a demand, but because in saying it he was consenting to and legitimising their madness as truth. Yet he wanted to snatch those words back from the air, to swallow them, to drown them out with other explanations but instead his eyes fell to the leather portfolio on the table and he remained silent.

"He told you that? And you believed him?" Lusher struggled to stymy the irritation in her voice. "What do you take us for?" She searched her attendants' faces, as though some look they'd shared was enough to calm her, and she whispered to them, "Quite right, sisters. Quite right. It's to be expected. He's not to know. How could he know? I'll just get on with telling our side of it, if he'll listen." And addressing Metternich she asked, "You will listen, won't you?"

Again the old man nodded and as he did so he saw the edges of the wide leather folder had been sealed with wax and sutures. He looked down the long row of candles again as she spoke.

"You see, Pieter ... I may call you Pieter . . . Edith did speak of you, although not often. You see, she came to us. She became one of us. And Woland is why we are here. Before him, before he came, we only read books." Lusher looked to the others and received nods of approval.

"We'd meet once a week to talk about books, that's all. That's how it was. That's how it began; and our numbers expanded, as did our tastes. At that time Woland was just one of us, it didn't seem to matter that he ended up being the only man. We'd assumed it was just a coincidence when the other men left one by one. Little did we know that he was working his charm, honing our appetites, grooming us, shepherding and coaxing us, bringing book after book for us all to read, no matter what the rarity of the book, or the language—he could get his hands on volumes we could all read in translation. It was as though he'd inadvertently become the master of ceremonies. His enthusiasm, you see, was irrepressible. And his charm, you can't understand—we'd underestimated such charisma." Lusher paused to collect her thoughts, she'd started to tremble, though the bookseller couldn't tell whether it was out of fear or excitement. She continued, "He adored books, a certain kind of book. He was an aficionado of the diabolical, the infernal, or so he liked to claim. And then he started to show us his own work. He read to us every night. And that is when we started to speak with the dead. It was Woland—he showed us his tricks, that's how he first introduced us to his craft, and he had us approach it all as a game. Some left the group, or the circle as he called it, but some remained. And he had a few of us, the more *conductive* of us, speaking in tongues, in a language he said that had been lost to man long ago, an ancient tongue that seemed to erupt from our throats spontaneously, like fire. And he showed us the book he'd been writing," Lusher

The Horned Tongue

pointed at the sealed leather wallet, "and that's when his spell was broken. It was Edith."

At the sound of her name, Metternich took the soft leather portfolio in his hands. It was heavier than he'd expected. The silver words on its cover glinted in the light but made no sense to him. Yet the illustration drained the blood from his face. It was an unmistakable likeness of Woland, rendered as a baroque mask, from his lips snaked a tongue that was bifurcated into twisting horn-like tendrils at each tip. Metternich ran his thumbs over the puckered stitching and waxen edges.

"Yes, it was Edith. She'd been trying to please the professor and found a book in your storeroom, in your archives, that she thought would be to his liking. I can picture her now, sitting where you are sitting, she produced her find to the circle, Woland included. At first it hadn't been her intention to denounce him, but the more she'd read the more she realised. She said it was a little known book, translated from Russian, not even a book really, but a samizdat version, a rough manuscript by an author called Mikhail Bulgakov, in which a certain Woland featured. He was even described as having the same eyes. For reasons we couldn't then understand Woland detonated in a wild rage, cursing Edith on the spot before tearing the book from her hands and storming off into the night. You can't believe the man's magnetism. Edith was terrified. He is a madman, of course. Edith stumbling across his deception in that way must have acted as a trigger, although that's hardly an adequate explanation. I mean anyone might be mortified when they are found out to be pretending to be something they're not . . . but to be masquerading as a fictional character from some unpublished Russian novel—being unhinged is one thing, but Woland had clearly done his homework. If he's mad he seems to demonstrate great perseverance and consistency in his delusion."

"Demonstrate. That's what he said before he took me to Edith's grave. That he must demonstrate . . . that I require a demonstration, and he said something about it being necessary because I was a man. He meant *only* a man, as though he needed to make the distinction, implying that he wasn't . . . " The bookseller watched the candlelight glimmer across the portfolio's silver illustration.

"We're not asking you to believe that Woland was true to his curse, and that Edith, well . . . no one would blame you in thinking that he and I are as deranged as one another. That would be a reasonable conclusion. Edith said you'd think as much. But you see, whether Woland is an invention or not, whether he is a man or not, he appears to possess at least some of the peculiarities of his fictional namesake, as I'm sure you've noticed." In the flickering light the walls of the room seemed closer.

Metternich, still transfixed by the silver mask etched into the portfolio answered, "Having not had the privilege of reading the Russian's novel, I'm not sure I do. Why? Is Woland a famous madman in that fiction too?"

"No, Pieter, Edith said that in Bulgakov's novel Woland is the Devil in disguise." She said it without a shred of humour.

The bookseller let a respectful silence pass between them before carefully choosing words that might placate her. "I could take this manuscript, his manuscript, if you don't mind, as I will, after all, need something with which to humour him, and I'm sure once he has it he'll leave you all in peace." It seemed reasonable to him, it would appease the madness of both parties surely, and then he could have done with it, shut up shop and retire to the country. As he reasoned this through, awaiting Lusher's response, the room seemed to visibly shrink, to lose its glamour. The embroidered drapes became sackcloth, the paintings were mere junkshop prints, and here and there he spied those strange effigies again, strung together from brooms and rags and mop-heads.

"That's not what we intended." One of the attendants, an elderly woman wearing heavy mascara, snatched the leather portfolio from his hands and clutched it to her breast. Lusher pleaded with him, "Pieter, you must destroy his book, you must lure him to a place with deep water, and with him as your witness you must throw it in. Not a page must survive and you mustn't read it. No one must read it again."

"And if I leave the book? If I walk away from all this . . . and I don't care whether magic, *his* magic is real or not . . . what could really happen? If I leave it here with you and refuse to answer his knock on my door when he visits? He would tire of it eventually. He'd just end up in a nuthouse like all the rest."

"I can see that you still don't get it. He doesn't tolerate those who can't keep their word. A deal's a deal. Believe what you will, but he won't take it lying down, and there's not an asylum in the world that would have him. Have you forgotten your visit to the cemetery?" Lusher was on her feet now, her sisters turning to face the bookseller. He was surprised to see a few of the café waitresses staring back at him.

"Then you've convinced me he should have his book, if only to keep him off my back. After that I'll be leaving it to the authorities to decide what to do with lunatics who rob from graves. They can cart you all off for all I care!" Snatching the portfolio back with surprising ease, Metternich hurried to the door as Lusher called out to him. "Think, Pieter! Remember Woland's eyes. What of those?

Even a lunatic can't just whisk you away to Edith's grave like that. Destroy his book, Pieter. You're the only one that can do it. Do it for her. Take it to deep water, to the Singel canal, and throw it in!"

The old bookseller scurried down the stairs. How had she known about the cemetery? Why hadn't they tried to stop him? What did he care about Woland's eyes—he was a lunatic after all and it might be self-inflicted. He pushed the effigy in the passage aside as he stumbled on. Even in the alley, as he was closing the door, he thought he could hear her calling out to him. Reaching the square without once looking back, he made his way across its wide cobbled space. With the portfolio clutched to his chest, and his head lowered in determination, he refused to look at the wild shadows that the trees cast or the lonely statue of the street urchin. And yet he couldn't help but consider, if he were to do so, how he would entice Woland to the Singel canal; it wouldn't be so difficult, as it was only a few streets from his bookshop. Was it lack of sleep that made him susceptible to Lusher's suggestion? Nothing could persuade him, surely. Then another woman's voice reached him across the night. Even if he'd imagined it, it was enough to turn his head and make him peer over his shoulder. The square was empty behind him. He was drunk with fatigue—that was it. Then the voice came again, so insistent this time that he turned to face it. It called again, resonating softly against the cobbles and the tall façades of the square. He heard the voice, but didn't want to know it. It came again, as though sobbing and sounding like rainfall, "Pieter," she said. This time the sound drew his gaze to the statue, the moon sheared in half above it. And again, "Pieter," she said as he returned towards the figure of the little urchin boy on his dais. He looked about the deserted square, at the dead windows that lined it; there was no

The Horned Tongue

sign of anyone watching. Another whisper came and this time he could see a thin light animating the urchin's face, making its features as fluid as mercury.

"Edith?" He heard himself murmur as he touched the statue's hand, looking up into the little waif's face. "Edith, is that you?" And perfume answered him; her perfume, the scent of jasmine from an unstoppered bottle dissolving into the air about her dressing table. The hard sculptured features had softened into the face he'd first loved. She was young again. Yet her brow furrowed and told him she was in pain. "I'm mad, Edith," he whispered, tucking the leather manuscript between the urchin's feet so he could reach both hands up to cup her face. He looked about once more, ensuring no one was making a fool of him.

This was no ventriloquism, be assured.

"I'm going mad, Edith, for you. Is that how I get you back? Didn't you always say I spent too much time alone with my books?" He felt like laughing. Was it rain or were her cheeks wet with tears? He held out a hand to the air and felt raindrops. "It's only raining. Edith. I'm sorry, Edith, I'm sorry."

Her voice was close to song, as if trying to calm a child. "Yes it's raining, Pieter, and tomorrow the canal will be full. Don't read his book, Pieter. Take it to the canal, Pieter, trick him there and throw it in." He could smell her perfume, wet on his hands. As the rain grew heavier, Edith's face lost its light and sank away to become a statue once more. The bookseller wandered off into the night, pushing the leather portfolio inside his overcoat while clutching his arms tightly around himself. He soldiered on, thinking of her, thinking of embracing Edith. Head bowed, he made his way back to the bookshop and their home above it. The wind and rain urging him on.

III.

The old bookseller slept uneasily. With my manuscript on his bedside table and his wife's diary open on his chest, he tossed his head this way and that, mumbling in his sleep, on the verge of waking but still dreaming. Yes, he dreamt as I watched him, I sat there at the foot of his bed and listened to him speak in his sleep. It would be the easiest thing in the world to have reached over and snatch what belonged to me. Or so you'd think. But no, that's forbidden. It would have spoiled everything we'd been working towards. So, he was dreaming and speaking, and in his right hand he still clutched a pen. He'd been reading Edith's diary and attempting to make sense of all the strange little notes she'd made when she was alive, all the near-illegible scribbles in her hand. And what was he dreaming of? He dreamt of me, Woland.

In the dream he'd adopted the role of a detective, plodding through an endless night, busily finding and searching through hidden rooms. He'd made the ingenious discovery that all of Amsterdam's upper floors and secluded attics were interconnected; one only had to find the corresponding concealed triggers to unlock sliding doors or hatches. And as he dreamt that he was looking for evidence of his wife's disappearance in these secret passages, events took a turn for the worse, as they often do in these cases; the pursuer became the pursued. It was his turn to be the game, to be the quarry, and he took to hiding in dusty lofts crammed full of papers, books, and photographs. And every time he faltered he thought he caught sight of a huge black cat closing on him, or the glint of an empty eye in a slash of moonlight. And finally, as he was waking, as he was clambering through an attic window from a room filled with lithographic machines and antique hand presses, shadows were closing in. Shadows dressed in uniforms, with red armbands and leather gloves. And just as he glimpsed the gleaming concentric rings of great canals stretching out to the horizon, someone caught his ankle and pulled him down into darkness.

The old man awoke at four in the morning with the impression that there'd been someone else in the room. He looked to the window where Edith's dressing table lay. The mirror was empty as was her chair. Yet he'd been writing; he found he still had a pen in his hand. He remembered he'd been writing, trying to decipher Edith's diary. Much of it had been scrawled in smeared hieroglyphics he had no hope of understanding. Yet there was a sentence that stood out as being immediately more legible, scrawled across two adjacent pages, it read:

> Witchcraft once started, as we all know, is virtually unstoppable.

It was cited—Mikhail Bulgakov.

The pages had a brittle texture. They'd become crinkled and creased with the pressure of her writing. Absent-mindedly he turned to the next page, even though he knew the remaining pages had been left untouched. Where there had once been blank pages only the night before, a passage of writing had now appeared. He was certain that it was new. The hand in which he'd found the pen upon waking ached, and the heel and knuckles were stained with traces of ink. Like a needle to his heart he realised the minute screed was written in Edith's handwriting. He trembled as he read:

> Woland told us that there are many secret games and that it is not always our choice to play them.

One day we might wake in the midst of play, only guessing at a game's existence after suffering the consequences of having broken its rules unknowingly. I remember he compared them to the games we find ourselves playing in dreams. They have no rhyme or reason to our waking minds, yet he said only a fool would say they vanish with the dawn. We play them without knowing. We're sleepwalkers, hypnotised and seduced. We ensnare each other and ourselves in their gambits, their intrigues. We dance to silent music. His book is one such game. Call it the lost tongue of the Devil if you will, he said. It will teach you how to speak its language until you can speak no other. Be warned, he said, for when you speak the language of dreams, others will distrust and shun you. But he told us not to fear— for we will have the satisfaction of his knowledge.

He looked at the pen in his hand and let it fall from his grip. The entry was entitled "This Walpurgis Night". Turning the page again, to ensure there was nothing else, he felt another sharp prick to his heart at finding a hand-drawn diagram, a map tracing a winding route from the bookshop to a place on the Singel canal a few streets away, the canal Lusher had mentioned. Metternich remembered his dream and sensed its resonance with the plan before his eyes.

He turned to his bedside table and took the leather-bound manuscript in his hand and, putting Edith's small diary on top of it, he got out of bed and shuffled from the bedroom down the landing to his study, still half-asleep and in his dressing gown. Sitting down at his desk, the night pressing against the window, he switched on a lamp. He dismissed the thought that, in that light, the high bookshelves that lined the walls resembled a tomb. Taking a letter knife he worked at the wax seal and stitched bindings of Woland's book, trying to ignore the silver illustration that glinted on its cover. The pages were unlike anything he'd encountered before; soft and malleable with the slightest trace of oil. As he turned each page an aroma caught his breath. It wasn't ink but the scent of jasmine. He was drunk on it.

He'd sat there until the room glowed with morning light. He could hardly recall how, upon first leafing through the manuscript, he had been confronted with page after page of incomprehensible sigils and letters. Nor could he remember how those snaking lines and strokes and loops had started to make sense. All he knew was that he understood, and there'd been a moment, a culminating moment, an epiphany, when dawn was slowly arriving, that he could recite passages out loud to himself. Some part of him, some trace of that old man, still faltered at the strange garbled tones of this new voice as he struggled to articulate the sounds that this new tongue demanded. His mouth and larynx ached. Yet with it came the intoxication of singing, of wanting to fill others' ears with his song, a song that was at times guttural, even bestial. The words seemed to dance from the page into his mouth. He and the words became one. Yet at that moment of ecstasy, a vestige of the old man he'd known sputtered a thought of doubt once more and made him hesitate. It was enough to silence him in a second.

Shaking, he shut the pages of the book and swept it from the desk onto the floor. Dismayed he put his hand to his throat, massaging it with thumb and fingers, swallowing in an attempt to find his own voice. The panic subsided as he opened Edith's diary to the map she'd used his hand to draw. Could he remember what he'd been singing? The verses faded but had left an impression. As he followed Edith's map with a trembling finger he recalled the song. Had it been a history? Yes, a folk tale or fable, but not only of some Golden Age of the city's past, when science and magic were secretly one, but a time ordained to come, a time heralded in song. It was Woland's song and he wouldn't sing it, he refused to be his chorister, his messenger. He remembered Edith and Lusher's appeals to him to destroy the book. Invigorated by that thought, he crossed the room to his bookshelves with the diary in his hand. With the other he traced along the vertical spines with a finger, looking for his book of local street maps. Trembling once more he saw that all of their titles had transformed; they'd come to resemble the script of *The Horned Tongue*. He pulled a random volume from the shelf and flicked through it to find that all of its pages were filled in the same snaking hand. He threw it to the floor and continued. He knew the collection well and could recognise the required book by its colour alone. He found it and marked the page he needed with a thumb. Woland would not stop him, no matter what he was. He was back at his desk comparing the hand-drawn map to the one printed in his book. He was sure of the route—he'd take the manuscript to the place marked "x"—a cluster of buildings on the water's edge, condemned warehouses that should have been demolished years ago. He remembered them from childhood. Even then it was forbidden to play there by the Singel canal, folk said there were hidden rooms inside, and their floors waited to collapse under unwary feet. Now all he had to do was follow Lusher's instructions and wait for Woland to come.

He spent the remainder of the day downstairs in the shop, preparing for the professor's visit that night. He sat at his desk gazing at row upon row of books. Some were

The Horned Tongue

still stacked in boxes in the aisles from days before and he knew he didn't have the strength to log, price, and order them. He tied Woland's manuscript up in string and sealed it in a large padded envelope. He put the package in an old school satchel and loaded it with glass paperweights from his study. He pictured it breaking the surface of the water and sinking through cloudy depths.

The bell on the shop's door tinkled and roused him from daydreams as customers came and went. It was getting late. He'd sold nothing that day, for none of the customers, even the regulars he'd recognised, greeted or approached him. All had simply browsed for a matter of minutes and left. Yet when the last customer, after picking up several different volumes and comparing them shook his head, Metternich's attention was drawn. Sensing this, the customer, a young English tourist, gave the bookseller a bemused frown and asked, with a book in either hand, "Don't you have anything else?"

Metternich pushed himself from his chair as the tourist approached. The young lad put the books on the desk between them and opened both in unison at random pages. He continued, "I mean, are they all like this? What is it anyway? I don't mean to be rude but . . . well, is it a joke?"

The old man saw the same script, the sigils of *The Horned Tongue* writhing across the pages. He slammed the books shut and said, "Sorry. It's late. We're closing." He ushered the young man, who smiled nervously, to the door and locked it behind him. He stood a while looking at the bookseller through the pane, then shook his head and walked off. Metternich watched him go; he turned his shop sign around on its string and pulled down the blind. He picked up the nearest book from a stack on the floor. By the paperback's cover (a depiction of Ebenezer Scrooge by a headstone, a cowled companion by his side) it should have been a copy of Dickens's *A Christmas Carol*. Instead he saw that the contagion had spread. His entire stock had been transformed overnight. He'd been wrong to assume that only he could see it. The clock above his desk told him it was past seven. Hadn't Woland said he'd visit him that day? Or would it be in the small hours of the next morning when he'd come knocking? Why should he wait? Surely he should go and be free of the book once and for all. He hurried to his desk, put the satchel over his shoulder, and turned out the lights. The bell on his shop door still jingled long after the old man had gone.

He followed the map torn from Edith's diary, down the main thoroughfare of Het Spui Street at first, but then into narrow byways, away from the square and into the evening. While pausing at intersections to get his bearings, he witnessed things that perturbed him. Firstly, he'd overheard the conversations of passers-by—they seemed to be whispering in the contorted tongue of the manuscript. And then there were the street signs—their lettering grew increasingly warped as he hurried on. And lastly there was the cat. At every corner he'd turn to look back at the way he'd come; out of panic at first, but it soon became obsession. He thought he'd glimpsed something slip out of sight. Then he was certain; at the corner he saw a large black cat's tail whip behind a newspaper stall. The streets were emptying, so he hurried on. In a narrow alley he came to a steep drop of steps. He turned and saw Woland's silhouette leaning against a streetlamp as it flickered into life. Guessing he'd be caught if he descended the steps, he took another alley on his right. He picked up his pace; the doors he passed in the cramped lane were mostly boarded-up or missing, the plaster of the walls was cracked and stained. The further he went, the more the streets seemed neglected. Occasionally, through the gaps where other stairs descended, he glimpsed the glint of the canal below. There was the definite aroma of damp and decay in the air. The weight of his satchel exhausted him, and seeing no sign of Woland behind him he stopped to catch his breath.

He moved on, and after taking the next turn, found himself unnerved again. The street ended in a cul-de-sac. The little square had been forgotten for some time. There was a forlorn tree in its centre, and a railing lined the edges of the terrace to its left where a park bench lay in disrepair. Metternich stood a while panting. The canal was visible again, shimmering through an alley formed between two tall, dark buildings. The closer of the two was an ancient warehouse, its slated roof shining just above the lip of the terrace. As Metternich approached the railing, he saw that the warehouse possessed a small balcony separated from him by a gap of only a few feet, however his stomach turned as he looked down into the deep lightless ravine of the street below. Yet some enterprising vagrant no doubt had bridged this gap with sloping planks torn from the bench. They were secured on the far side by a jumble of indiscernible detritus; ropes and crates and broom-shanks, or so it seemed. It looked anything but safe, yet he was desperate to give his pursuer the slip. He still had the crumpled page of Edith's diary in his hand, and when he opened it out he saw the map had been leading him there all along. Squinting, he made out a diminutive window behind the balcony's railings. It was the only means of escaping the terrace without retracing his route. At that instant something caught Metternich's watchful eye. A great feline shadow slid up the walls of the street behind him. It seemed to rear up onto its hind legs to walk like a man. He needed no further persuasion, and clambered under the railing, propelling himself across the gap, barely touching the makeshift gantry, before falling onto the boards of the balcony opposite. As he lay in pain, trying to account for this feat, the silhouette of debris that held the planks in place tottered. As it did so, it seemed to rise up and turn to expose its mop head of writhing string. A moment later the effigy collapsed into the alley below, the planks clattering as they fell with it. Alarmed, the old man prised himself through a tiny window, oblivious to the brittle shards of glass that snagged his clothes.

He tumbled onto bare floorboards in a cloud of dust. As he stood up, his head and elbows struck against crumbling plaster and he guessed he was in some kind of attic, although its diminutive size rendered it useless for any purpose he could imagine. Once his eyes had adjusted to the gloom, and his burning throat to the dust, he found a doorway to a steep set of stairs leading down into a pungent darkness. The rails felt damp and unstable in his hands. With each movement something creaked or cracked or crumbled around him. He cursed under his breath and the building groaned back at him, as though grumbling in its sleep. A fungal door gave way to a room that belonged inside a shipwreck. A few rays of meagre lamplight pushed through newspaper-encrusted windows. The sulking floor had cultivated mould so dense that it made walking across its slick surface treacherous. The old man crossed the moist floor on hands and knees, avoiding the room's centre where the boards sank into a pool of shadows. As he passed through another door and down a further flight of musty stairs, he had to resist the idea that he was being swallowed. Although he descended through floors that consisted of no more than a single empty room, he thought he saw other doors in those leprous walls that he was not prepared to consider. And he glimpsed things that he dismissed as a trick of memory; in corners he

The Horned Tongue

thought he'd seen some of Lusher's crude effigies, and in others Woland's calligraphy upon the walls.

As he opened the door to the room that must, he thought, finally lead onto the canal outside, he stumbled and fell under the weight of his burden, the satchel flying from his grasp. Exhaustion had stolen his purpose and he lay there with his eyes tightly closed.

There was a round of applause.

"My dear Pieter, well done! You made it at last."

It was Woland's voice, but when the bookseller looked up to see him, he saw Edith's smiling face instead. She was nude and sitting on the professor's lap. She was as young as the first day he'd met her. Woland was playing with her curls, twisting them in his fingers as she fluttered the pages of her diary in her hands. As the old man got to his feet, he saw Lusher standing by their side; she was naked too, her hand resting on the back of the armchair in which they sat. And all around the room Lusher's naked sisters were smiling, lit candles in their hands. One of the waitresses was already dropping his satchel to the floor and unpicking the string that bound *The Horned Tongue*. The walls were daubed with its writing, and in each corner stood makeshift totems. The bookseller's eyes darted to the door and the dirty window beside it. He watched the mirrored light playing on the water's surface until the oversized head of a cat reared up on the other side of the glass to obstruct his view. There was no escape. It had all been lies.

Rubbing his hands together, Woland received his manuscript from the waitress. He opened its pages and offered it to the old bookseller saying, "You will sing and we will listen."

People sometimes think they know Metternich's name when someone mentions it. They remember nursery rhymes and the warnings their mothers gave them when they misbehaved. Yet no one recalls that it was I, Woland, who reunited him with his beloved Edith. No, all they remember is the rumour of this man, as though in a dream. Some say they've seen him sing from a book by a statue of a little urchin boy in Spui Square, but then every city has its vagrant evangelists. No, when they remember him at all they do so as a game. For there are many secret games and it is not always our choice to play them. One day we might wake to their mystery, only guessing their rules. They are the games we play in dreams. Only fools think they vanish upon waking. We play them without knowing. We dance to their silent music.

Don't pity the old bookseller, my friend, for he got what he wanted in the end.

The Lost Reaches

I.

The house rose up from the snowbound clearing, faintly luminous against the high shagreen wall of trees. It seemed to have frozen at the point of collapsing. Its toy turrets, windows, balconies, and roofs all contorted into perplexing angles, its contours thickly encased in white, as icing on a cake.

While advancing across the snow, with the wounded man strung on their shoulders between them, Marek caught Jan's eye, and although they wanted to conceal any doubts they had from their vulnerable charges, they couldn't resist exchanging a look of disbelief. In all their time as scouts in that wild region they had never heard of such a place. The woman must have seen the astonishment in their faces and frantic with exhaustion, lost her footing, pitching headlong into the snow. A third man, with the sunless demeanour of a bureaucrat, went to her aid and thought to calm the woman by clasping her hands in his, which only served to panic her further, for the man's face was white with fear. Marek heard her demand, "Where've you brought us?" as they trudged into the shadows cast by the house. Before anyone could answer, her wounded husband retched, blood spattering the snow at his feet. She rushed to help the couriers support his slackening body as they pulled open the two stout oak doors and stooped across the threshold. Taking one last look at the stars, the bureaucrat pushed the doors shut behind them. Once inside the sound of his words seemed muffled as he stuttered to the other four: "Won't their dogs follow the blood? Won't it lead them here?" But no one was listening.

It was as though they'd been expected. Preparations had been made. Warmth greeted them in the hall and candlesticks arranged on polished tables and sills lent the space a clouded light. It had all the expected characteristics of a grand house, with candelabras, trophies, tapestries, carved banisters, and carpeted stairs, yet its shrunken proportions had them crouching, huddled together. The two couriers were the first to comprehend that they could all stand upright with ease once they'd entered the hall from the cramped passage. The silence of the house seemed to demand reciprocation, and although they struggled to carry the wounded husband to a couch in an adjoining room, they did so in hushed tones and cautious movements. The open fire they'd found there bathed them in its heat, and the husband had soon fallen unconscious while Marek attempted to staunch the gunshot wounds in his shoulder and chest with dust sheets heaved from the furniture nearby. Like the world outside, the room was layered in white, covered in thick starched linen. Its pale plaster ceiling hung less than an inch above their heads, giving the impression that the entire house had been compressed and would at any moment close around them.

II.

Within an hour the husband was dead. Waiting until the others were preoccupied, his wife vanished upstairs. Despairing, she'd hid somewhere in the far reaches of the house. The remaining three agreed that Jan and Marek would wrap her husband's body in sheets and carry him down into the cellar while the bureaucrat went in pursuit of the widow.

They'd found an abundance of wine and cheese in the cellar, rack upon rack stretching along low narrow tunnels, and while rooting around they'd discovered paintings wrapped in sackcloth and bound with string. They dragged several out and arranged them in the hall at the foot of the grand yet squat staircase, propped against crates they'd filled with dusty bottles. As they knew it would be unwise to move on now since their encounter with the NKVD patrol, they'd decided to lay low in the house until the following evening. Although it was a risk to stay there, the situation had instilled in them a strange confidence that encouraged them to disregard the world outside. For now, they'd drink and eat, appreciate their luck in stumbling upon this place just as they'd feared it had finally run out. This was not the first time their lives had suddenly turned to nightmare; they knew when death was close that life could take on a hallucinatory clarity that demanded unlikely strategies. Their nerves depended upon casually ignoring the threat. So Marek uncorked two bottles of red with a penknife and put one at Jan's feet as he busily cut at the strings around a covered canvas. Before pulling the cloth away from the large concealed rectangle Jan paused to lift the bottle in the air in a silent toast as Marek reciprocated. They both put the bottles to their lips, taking a glug of rich wine. They allowed themselves a laugh against the gloom of the hall as Jan returned to unveiling the canvas. Their discovery soon silenced them again. There against the banister in the candlelight an image glowed back at them; it depicted the very room in which they stood. A woman descended the staircase as a man awaited her with arms outstretched imploringly, prostrated in dishevelled clothes on the lower stairs. Their attention was drawn again to the woman, her face concealed by a mask and headdress that was a hybrid of peacock and owl. It merged into the shoulders of a heavy feathered cloak parted by a lithe buttery thigh and belly in the glister of the chandelier above her head. Particular emphasis had been given to her left foot, which was bare and slightly elevated, seemingly in the act of being proffered to the man to hold and perhaps kiss. A crimson slipper lay on a lower step.

"I know this," Jan whispered under a spell as Marek turned to him. He continued in a hushed voice, "Not this picture but the man . . . the artist."

Marek was on his knees peering at the lower edges of the picture, as he touched the canvas he murmured, "There's no signature." And he frowned back at his young comrade.

Looking down at Marek crouching in the half-light, a synchronicity momentarily occurred to Jan, of Marek's posture and the depiction of the prostrated man in the painting. He shook it from his thoughts and whispered again, "You remember the teacher from Drohobycz?" Marek looked up at him blankly and took another slug of wine. "Mr. Schulz—you must remember him. I know you'd long since left the academy by then, but he was known in the neighbourhood." The older man shook his head dumbly as the wine brought tears to his eyes. "He must be still there now, in town. But back then some of us broke into his classroom and found his private case, a leather portfolio. We graduated the year he came and there'd been rumours you see. None of us had really believed them, to look at him. A recluse or so they said." Marek had already put down his bottle and was cutting through the binding on a smaller canvas as he listened to the lad. Jan's bottle was half empty now and fuelled by the wine, his eyes glazed with recollection. "We'd all seen a mural by Mr. Schulz . . . that was one thing, it was all regalia . . . national pride—but these, these sketches we spied that night in the classroom left us all . . . well, I don't have the words . . . it was like a secret, like hearing something you shouldn't . . . then can't forget."

Marek's eyes wandered around the room and he murmured. "What is this place? What's it doing all the way out here in the middle of nowhere?"

III.

As the widow escaped down the passageway she tried every door in turn only to find a dark, uninviting space. In her flight she passed painting after lurid painting, each quickening her pace. Returning flashes of the recent past fuelled her panic and she thought of how she'd abandoned her possessions by the roadside as the border guards raised their alarm and pursued them back into the forest. She was thankful though that she'd decided to wear all of her favourite necklaces. The bracelet too, although she knew she would no longer admire its blood red rubies. She thought of the home she'd left behind in *Lwów*; how they'd stolen away at night so that the last glimpse she'd had of her little palace was in shadow, the grand hall so dismal and lifeless.

She moved on into another corridor without noticing the way she'd come or how she would return. She wanted to lose herself there, deep in the house. So she had no way of knowing how she'd come to be there, in that room. She stood awhile absorbed in its silence, its lines softened by shadow and lamplight. Her eyes drifted from the chaise longue that occupied the centre of the room and the empty costumes hanging behind it to the countless cabinets that formed the perimeter of the space. The cabinets sank away into shadow, row after receding row, their glass panels gleaming as she squinted to discern their contents. It was a museum of sorts, that much she guessed, although admittedly one where the humdrum artefacts were somehow at odds with the grand nature of their presentation. Depending upon how she focused her attention, the depths of the room seemed to shift, tempting her to advance. And before long she found herself walking down polished aisles, with her fingertips outstretched to trace the panes and frames of the cases. She followed the whims of one glance to another, allowing the things she glimpsed to coax her quietly into a labyrinth. In the subdued light, a pane might shine jet black or bright silver, throwing back her reflection as she passed; a drawn face with welling eyes. The artefacts she spied through the glass panels; dolls and stuffed animals, porcelain crockery and ornate cutlery, children's shoes and family portraits, span delicate webs of associations that soon dissolved just as she thought she'd grasped them. The artefacts seemed eager and restless as they stirred in the shadows, enticing her into making fresh correspondences; new memories from old, she thought. It occurred to her that she was following a pattern, from shoe to doll to glove to fork, as another kind of logic drew her onward to the dead end of an avenue. There behind the glass was an array of portraits, envelopes and letters, displayed in layers against lace-edged fans. The same face looked back at her again and again. The same name was scrawled across the end of each love letter: *Bruno*. She whispered his name under her breath. The man's many faces stared back at her through her reflection in glass, some sharing a knowing smile or downcast eye. A murmur lingered between them. And his prominent ears in some photographs seemed comically simian, she thought; his dark hair swept slick from his forehead. Yet that sly humour she sensed was part of a deeper charm played out in his sensuous mouth, his ink-drop pupils. She happily surrendered to them all, that brotherhood of shy faces in the cabinet.

IV.

The bureaucrat was lost. Although the interior was compact, its layout puzzled him. It seemed that whichever way he turned, an aspect had slipped or shifted or a new feature had suddenly appeared. Indeed he was unsure how long he'd been wandering as certain details (such as the mildewed pattern in the wallpaper or the gilt curlicue on the edge of a picture frame) had drawn his attention so acutely that he had to shake himself free from a lingering fascination. He'd not had the chance to notice the pictures when they'd first arrived, compelled to find a dying man sanctuary. He'd been devoured by fear and lost an hour in an instant. Later, as he escaped the two couriers, who couldn't even remember his name, he'd been surprised at his relief at the man's death. He was glad that the stranger had taken the bullets instead of him. Did that make him inhuman? He would no longer hinder their flight across the border into Hungary. And now he could console the stranger's pretty widow with the sympathy he was confident he could fake. Why should he lie to himself? No one remained that could make him abide by a world that had betrayed him, abandoned him, allowed him to stray into this region that within an hour had made a mockery of all the laws he'd known and made his own. He'd always suspected it and now he'd never be fooled again. If his fellow men came to view him as a coward, a liar, a monster, then so be it. Their world was ending. The paintings he'd hesitated to study in the passage seemed to echo his guile. He carried a candlestick to light his way and in its quivering flame he examined each painting in turn, hardly aware that he muttered to himself as he went. The events of the night had released something in him. He could sense it itching in the back of his skull, something had been worked loose and he felt elated, capable of anything. If he wished he could abandon the rules he'd formerly followed to the letter. All he had to do was let go, let go of all the pretences and obligations others had held him to. He could slide freely away in whichever direction he pleased. That night he'd been spattered with another man's blood. He'd felt that man's life suddenly torn from the scheme of things, a page ripped and discarded from a vital ledger. The relief he'd felt at leaving the occupied city for the wilds of the Carpathian forest had soon diminished: it seemed as though the trees and snow conspired to swallow them whole. Yet these paintings returned him to a mystery that Man, out there in the world beyond the house, in all his arrogance and violence, deemed unreal or insignificant. These paintings spoke of an understanding of experience that everyday life was too insensible and intolerant to consider. In contemplation of those paintings, he knew he could mourn the loss of the man he'd once been only the day before.

Each canvas depicted an interior reminiscent of the house, perhaps capturing the likenesses of rooms he'd yet to see or never find. And through those rooms strange figures roamed in pursuit of one another, locked in inexplicable games and allegiances. In a particular triptych great stag beetles of prodigious size with iridescent carapaces clashed and tore at each other or struggled upended on polished floors, while others danced with half-clad women under brilliant chandeliers loaded with exotic birds. In other pictures, boys with mawkish expressions on their outsized and creased faces grovelled in adoration of debutantes' naked legs. Sensuous almost luminous, those legs were stretched across fur-covered pedestals or draped like vines from garlanded swings. One particular countess in that scene captivated the bureaucrat. Her eyes smiled down at him with secret relish, a riding crop gripped in gloves across her lap.

The paintings and framed sketches were unsigned yet shared the same hand and consistency of symbolism. They seemed to depict the same event: a celebratory masked ball where the women were in costume while the men wore sober civilian clothes. The walls of the cramped passages were cluttered with these images and the bureaucrat found himself successively drifting to each in turn down the hall, reconstructing the events of that imaginary masque as he went. Some of the pictures were representations of the same room, shown through varying perspectives, some acutely skewed into disturbing angles, their inhabitants occasionally possessing hideous and comical proportions. Where windows were depicted in the walls of a chamber, the glass was left a blank white, as if to suggest that the house had been entirely encased in snow.

Along the passageway masked and feathered women stared back from delicate paintwork. The pictures coalesced with heavy shadows and their brushstrokes seemed to writhe at the bureaucrat's approach. Did his senses register the faint aroma of incense prickling his nostrils or its dense smoke clouding his eyes? Or was it a memory, the house's memory lying dormant in the filigreed wallpaper and in the worn carpets? And reaching the passage's end, he lingered in a corner by an oval window, letting intuition guide his movements until his cheek pressed against the cool polished panelling of a narrow doorway. There he relived the sensation of plunging his face into the deep scented hair of a boudoir. He was close to tears, cradling his face in his fingers. He would never see those feline girls and maternal widows again. Drohobyscz was as good as dead and so were they, lifeless in invaders' embraces. There was the sound of movement and voices on the other side of the polished door. It could only be the widow Josefina. He turned the glass handle and his pulse quickened at the thought of her.

V.

Spurred on by Marek, Jan was getting steadily drunk. Although the fire in the drawing room still blazed they'd not moved from the stairs, making a token gesture of vigilance. Had the border patrol found them in that moment they'd have been able to do little more than sing them a song. They'd guessed the border wasn't far and although Jan often followed Marek's example, the older man had failed to demonstrate his customary fortitude and discipline. Instead Marek's lips spilled stories as his eyes twinkled and roved around the rich furnishings of the hall. At the sight of the trophies mounted on the walls, he set off on reminiscences about childhood hunting trips in the Carpathians. The younger Jan was more cautious, half-listening to the seasoned trooper and yet attentive to the wind brushing snow against the windows. They'd brought further canvases from the cellar and uncovered them at the foot of the stairs where Marek had uncorked a bottle of Węgrzyn in preparation. The slick surfaces of the paintings slipped under Jan's gaze. His eyes slid down the half-dressed contours of masked courtesans and pooled in their supplicant lovers' lids, finding fear mingled with infatuation. Marek was oblivious to the young lad's bewitchment. He himself was mesmerised by the thought of his quarry on the edge of a crisp clearing in a great forest: a woman shivering on her haunches, naked apart from a feathered headdress, turning her gleaming eyes into the crosshair of his rifle's sight. Jan tried to shake him from his reverie, but his eyes were fixed on an autumnal tapestry that spanned the entire width of the wall above the staircase. Marek's delirious eyes unnerved the young lad and he backed slowly up the stairs, hesitating to look down at the drunkard in the hall, drawn by thoughts of finding their charges, the widow and the bureaucrat. As he reached the landing, still hearing Marek calling out to an imaginary presence, Jan felt the wine addling his own movements. Vestiges of animal forms writhed in the details of the balustrade he clung to for support. As the room's contours softened and warped, he was halted by thoughts of the past. He turned to climb the steps, Marek's voice mocking him as he went. From the gibberish Jan could pick out familiar names that sparked memories. The sound of the wind wailing circled the house and with it the room seemed to spin. The wine had made him proud and bitter. He began to despise the drunken old trooper for abandoning him to these events, to face this house alone. He'd depended upon Marek, ever since he'd been recruited, they all had, but in his present condition he was no good to anyone. He found it hard to resist berating the drunkard from his vantage point on the mezzanine. Something seemed to coax him to do so. Thoughts rushed through Jan's head, compelled by the leering bestiary in the ornaments and tapestries around him, and the wind outside, whipping at the walls. Yet he made out a softer note in the maelstrom, a feminine tone, murmuring from the passage behind him. To hell with Marek, he thought, he'd find the widow and they'd head for the border together. The walls of the passage that led from the landing were lined with numerous paintings and drawings, some of which were hanging askew, so he guessed that the bureaucrat had passed that way. He couldn't remember the man's name so called out "Josefina!" instead. As he advanced, he tried the glass handles of each door until he found one that opened and slid into the shadows.

VI.

The bureaucrat found Josefina slumped in furs across a chaise longue. In the muted lamplight glass cabinets loomed on every side. Numerous costumes adorned tailors' dummies. Empty plumed headdresses and avian or feline masks crowned vacant cloaks. They left the uncanny impression that their wearers had either vanished into thin air or suddenly abandoned their vigil to roam naked through that mock museum. One of the stands was completely bare. At its base lay Josefina's clothing in a crumpled pile, she'd exchanged them for the ritual garments that were wrapped around her otherwise naked body. The bureaucrat had to move so close that he was within inches of her face before he could discern that she was still breathing. He speculated to himself about the circumstances that might have led her to donning one of the feathered and sequined half-masks from the archived displays, however, he was soon distracted by the sight of Josefina's white thigh sliding from under the mother-of-pearl lined cape. He could sense her heat rising to meet his palms as they hovered above her skin. He wanted to inch the garment aside without rousing her from her slumber. Her lids flickered tantalisingly in a dream but didn't open. He imagined that she dreamed of him, even urging him to undress her. He risked brushing her cheekbone with a fingertip as she swallowed a murmur in response. She slept on as he teased a few black strands of her hair from the headdress on to her naked throat and shoulder. The thought occurred to him that she hadn't undressed herself. Perhaps some light-fingered assistant, not unlike himself, had crept in while she dreamed, and by sleight of hand transformed that refugee into a captive countess. As he slid the robe from her shoulder, she awoke but showed no sign of surprise or resistance. He instinctively backed away as she sat upright, a dazed look in her eyes. Indifferent to her exposed skin she lifted her feet up onto the chaise longue and pushed herself backwards to adopt a regal pose, her left hand drifting from the side of the chair to support her chin. She let out a languorous sigh.

"I have been dreaming." She absently gestured to a cabinet in the shadows of the chamber and demanded, "Bring my slippers, boy."

The sight of her lying prone across the furs had intoxicated him, and he obeyed without thinking. His fingertips trailed the shining glass of each compartment door as his eyes roamed the cabinets' contents. He swept along the first row in search of her slippers. Before his eyes could linger long enough to discern each artefact or curio, they flickered on to the next in line. There were photographs of the same man; again and again the same impish face smirked back at him, scattered throughout the relics displayed in the mirrored cases. There were locks of hair attributed to this man's lovers. Many of the objects, having peculiarly private and mundane aspects, made for unlikely exhibits: a pocket watch, a wallet, a comb, a pair of braces. Each had been tagged, and in one particular display, beside the slippers, there was a labelled phial of dark liquid with a name marked clearly on it: *Schulz*. The toes of the crimson velvet slippers rested upon the handle of a Luger pistol. A tiny key protruded from a copper lock set into the wooden frame of the cabinet. As he took the key between his thumb and forefinger he heard Josefina purr.

"This museum holds shadows of things that will be as well as shadows of things that once were."

Somewhere out in the trees many shadows were moving stealthily as one entity, boot and paw moving tirelessly over frozen ground and across crisp white fields following the trail and scent of blood. Beasts strained on leashes as moonlight glinted on cold lenses and gunmetal. The men and dogs exchanged abrupt grunts or snorts, enough to fuel and direct their pursuit of the fugitives.

VII.

Old Marek sat alone, slumped on the lower steps in the entrance hall. He had only just acknowledged that Jan had left him there, surrounded by uncovered canvasses and swigging from a bottle of vintage wine. He groaned something incoherent to the empty hall, the echo of his voice only served to chastise him further. He lashed out at one of the paintings with his foot, yet in the attempt slipped from the stairs on to his backside. The bottle rolled across the floorboards out of reach, spilling wine as it went. Enraged he struggled to his feet, which took him far more effort than he had expected, and grabbed the nearest picture in both hands. With one movement he cracked the frame and bent the painting in half. Not satisfied with this vandalism, he attempted to flex the frame this way and that in an effort to tear the canvas itself. He tore at the picture's edges, grunting until he was red in the face, spittle foaming at his lips. A loud cracking and splintering sound from behind him, echoing his own actions, stopped him from his destruction. He turned to see a doorway where there had been no doorway before. Marek stifled a whimper at the sight before him. The sudden breach in the wood-panelled wall opened onto a conservatory mottled with sepia light. The perspective seemed wrong to him as he stumbled to the newly emerged door, running his fingers over its edges to ensure its palpability. As he did so he was drawn to a small window set into the wall to his right. He recalled that the window had been there before, but seemed to have slid from its original place to accommodate the appearance of the breach. As he peered through the window he felt his jaw slacken: he had expected an annex corresponding to the conservatory, yet there was nothing to be seen but dark snow-speckled air. Marek backed away from the window, sending the wine bottle into a spin across the floor with his heel. Only then did he notice that the remains of the wrecked canvas depicted the same grand conservatory. As he returned his gaze to the gloom of the garden, the old trooper swore he'd seen sleek naked forms flicker through vegetation. Crossing the threshold he could make out several narrow broken parquet pathways winding through overgrown ornamental thickets. An occasional wooden crack or shudder sounded in the otherwise silent space, as though the new-born chamber were still settling into place. Three vast dilapidated glass-domed ceilings gave a dull luminescence to the artificial jungle below. A multitude of tropical plants rose up around him as he edged along a quiet path, running a trembling hand along buckled and rusted railings. Vines and creepers, ferns and tendrils surged across the haphazard path he attempted to follow. He was parched and wished he'd brought another bottle on his journey. He turned to see that the route behind him to the breach was no longer visible. In places the vegetation resembled aspects of misshapen human and bestial anatomies. Between glances great yellowing leaves became half-masks and vines lacing tree trunks were exposed ribs. The vegetal walls of the way ahead were fixed at the moment of decomposition. A pervading fungal sweetness scented and thickened the air. There was another flash of light or skin through a break in the undergrowth; Marek pushed on, wheezing as he tried to disregard the decay of the garden all around him.

VIII.

Josefina reclined in the snaking strands of incense the bureaucrat had lit in her honour. Having already kissed and slid the slippers on her feet, he returned to the cabinets again to examine their contents. He thought that they had expanded and multiplied in the murk of the room. He neared one of them until his breath misted the glass panel that he passed, trailing a hand across its surface as Josefina half-sang a drunken monologue.

"Listen, little boy, you will soon remember as I have remembered. Where are you wandering, little boy? Don't go far, you might get lost. And I have duties for you to perform tonight. Listen, boy, you must prepare for the arrival of their carriages. They will be cold and ravenous from their long spell away from us. We must prepare for their games. You have seen their amusements all around you in those paintings. It's time to wake them and remember the lost times. It's time for you to run your little hands through scented hair once more. It's time again for you to write on ladies' mirrors with your tongue. You'll find boots in those cabinets, my boy, and riding crops and furs. You'll find masks and feathers and pearls. Long ago in a forest, on the border between this world and that, the countess dreamed an artist . . . and so built this house . . . so that nothing of his might be lost. Whether the rumours of her intentions were true, no one can say, yet it seemed that the only thing the museum lacked was the artist himself; if only she could coax him there before it was too late. I suppose some might think this a fairy tale. So much the better if they do. Bring me those pictures, boy. Bring me those pictures!"

He drifted in and out of glistening aisles, from one row to another, not caring to note his route. All the while the bureaucrat could hear his countess's whispers. Occasionally he paused in his wandering to press his hands to the panes and staring between them, with the tip of his nose touching the glass, he could make out small model dioramas of devastated towns and cities. Crumpled maps and photographs lay heaped behind them. He muttered the place names he read in those shadows: "Kraków . . . Przemyśl . . . Góry Wysokie . . . Dwikozy . . . Sandomierz . . . Drohobycz." He refused to accept what was captured in those photographs: ranks of withered bodies and mounds of white limbs. Such events could never come to pass. No world could endure such a cost.

He heard his mistress calling to him and found his way out of the maze of cabinets, following her song. She was still reclining with her eyes closed, inhaling the heavy incense. With her lids still unopened, she gestured to the walls around her, demanding that he unhook some of the paintings and bring them to her. He did as she commanded, dutifully placing each canvas on the floor, in the order that she instructed. Turning in her seat she slid her feet onto the floor. Opening her eyes she pointed at her heel and commanded him to kneel. He did so and bowed his head in compliance.

"Now look, little man. Look at these pictures. What do they tell you? Are you clever enough to say? Don't answer. You're not important. We must let the house respond. They are all memories. It seems that you've forgotten our friends that brought us here: the two couriers, Marek and Jan. You must have heard of the Biali Kurierzy. No? Should I tell you their story? Although this is no fairy tale, I can see that I must speak to you as I would a child." Josefina's gaze was distant as she patted the bureaucrat's head. As he nodded beseechingly, she began her story and he smiled.

"Long, long ago . . . or was it only last year? How quickly things are lost. Poor Jan was just another boy scout then when the invaders came, and he and his comrades had to become soldiers, joining the Szare Szeregi . . . The Grey Ranks. It was Marek who recognised Jan's gifts; such knowledge of the terrain of the borderlands and the forests in one so young was rare. So Jan was handpicked to join Marek's division. Marek, at the age of forty-seven, was one of the respected and elder men of the White Couriers, the Biali Kurierzy, and had served in the Polish Army. It was his task to take fresh-faced youths, the oldest only in their mid-twenties, some promising athletes from the Junak Drohobycz academy, and turn them into fighters. But more than that, the Biali Kurierzy were tasked to smuggle fugitives, enemies of the new state, to Carpathian Ruthenia, and further to Budapest. All of those mere boys were subsumed into an underground resistance. So much had happened since the inception of the Biali Kurierzy, last year, in '39. Jan saw his comrades slowly vanish one by one. Some executed by the Gestapo while others would simply never return from smuggling their human cargo across the border. So they were presumed lost, while rumours circulated that they'd fallen into the hands of the Soviet NKVD and were tortured. Are you trying not to yawn?"

"Countess, it's just that your voice is so lilting . . . so close to dreaming."

"Very well, insect; I'll continue. You were once one of those fugitives, only hours ago, one of those condemned by the Terror to be deported to Siberia. What crime did you commit then? None, of course."

"I am only a Polish national, my mistress, and a civil servant of Drohobycz."

"Well, then you are twice damned by their laws. And what was I before I came to this house? The wife of a writer, that is all. True, we were society people back in *Lwów* . . . and left to depend upon boy scouts for our safety! Lost in a forest. Where was I?"

"You were showing me these paintings mistress."

"Yes, so rumours circulated that our salvation lay in the hands of these boys, and arrangements were soon made for the aristocrats to be trafficked through the Eastern Carpathians. Perhaps it was their intention to bring us here all along . . . to this house. They say the Biali Kurierzy are not quite human. That they have gifts that we mortals, we city dwellers, could never understand . . . they have been appointed by a greater authority. We have been so fortunate, do you see? We have been blessed . . . chosen. We have been elected to reside here in this . . . house . . . this museum. We are all that is left of a vanishing world. We will make this house our own. It speaks to me. It tells me that I must serve it and you in turn must serve me. I will be the custodian and you will be my curator."

"It would be my honour, countess, but what of these paintings? They have stories to tell also, stories of carriage rides through forests at night to a grand celebration in this house, stories of fugitives in the snow stumbling upon a refuge, stories . . . no . . . the history of a lost artist of Drohobycz. Or an artist not yet lost."

"Yes, quite so, my little curator; these paintings conspire to tell us something . . . to remember something . . . while the enemy burns books in Berlin. If this house is a vessel, then I will be the figurehead on its prow."

"You have such a turn of phrase, my countess; so eloquent."

"And you are becoming quite the expert at grovelling at my feet. We should put your talents to greater use however. We should make a start on your duties. These paintings will be the first objects worthy of our attentions. We must wake them from their sleep, unleash their events."

"How will we do that, mistress?" The bureaucrat clasped his hands together in anticipation.

"I will hum a rousing tune and you will dance a Hajduk, of course."

He hadn't danced a Hajduk since he was a boy. The very word called to mind raucous moments in childhood, surrounded by the beaming faces of his family. Josefina started to clap her hands and the bureaucrat, unsure of himself, rose to his feet and began jumping self-consciously up and down on the spot. She spurred him on, caterwauling and yelping as he started to spin on the spot. When one of his steps crushed the edge of a canvas underfoot he began to slow in his movements, but she called for him to continue, indeed goading him on, challenging him to make his dance more furious, and in doing so crush the paintings beneath his stomping feet. As he span around and around, hearing the frames crack under his heels, glimpses of something caught the tail of his eye. He couldn't stop to confirm these suspicions, for his mistress insisted he kept spinning until he was ready to drop from exhaustion and the pictures were no more than shreds and splinters. As he spun madly on, aware that he was making a fool of himself, the tip of his shoe caught the edge of a frame and sent him crashing to the floor. Josefina was laughing behind him, and as he turned while picking himself up, he noticed the room about him had changed. Aspects depicted in the paintings had suddenly bloomed in the alcoves and contours behind his mistress. New crimson drapes hung heavily from the rafters. Marble pillars and statues of mythical beasts flanked painted recesses. Yet that was not all, the dimensions of the chamber had changed, and human figures could be seen milling about in the shadows, as though awaiting commands. Some were young women, and they were laughing at him as he dusted himself down.

"Our guests have arrived." Josefina rose to her feet and gestured to the half-seen figures on the outskirts of his sight. Timidly, they emerged from the gloom. The first were the men in dishevelled clothing. Some were fully dressed, only their ties hanging askew, while others resembled survivors from a desert island, except the bureaucrat could already discern, due to the wheals on their exposed skin and the leashes some wore about their throats, that their hardships and injuries had been inflicted by their keepers, who followed in their wake. Their youthful mistresses stepped gracefully forward, as though their movements had been choreographed, with their heads held high. It occurred to the bureaucrat that not a single one of them was entirely convincing in the part that they played. They resembled young, local women, lacking in the etiquette of aristocratic appearance and conduct he had come to expect. It was as though they'd worn fancy dress for the occasion. Furthermore, all seemed to carry their grace with difficulty, as if it was a burden, another performance that they had neither the experience nor the energy to maintain for long. All were sallow-faced, perhaps malnourished. As they neared the dizzy bureaucrat, he could see that their eyes looked weary and spent by the things they'd seen. They seemed to wear their jewels, fine gowns and fur stoles on sufferance, like dolls dressed by a spoilt child. One of the young women immediately broke away from the row her sisters had formed, and strode up to the gawping servant. Without a moment's hesitation, and with all the force she could muster, she struck him across the face.

"Now you will remember me." The girl was a foot shorter than him, yet her raised face was fierce and determined. The bureaucrat thought he recognised her, a baker's daughter from Drohobycz, yet he dismissed the idea as he was certain her family had been amongst the first to be taken. He had, after all, seen the documents with his own eyes. She struck him again, yet this time with less vigour.

"You will learn soon enough. After all, you are here to yearn for the past. It is never how you imagine it. If you have come here expecting idylls . . . childhood is not a retreat. Stand up straight when I am talking to you." She half-turned away and looking back over her shoulder measured him from head to foot with a glance.

"What would you say if I told you that you had already crossed the border? Don't answer; just think." The bureaucrat looked to Josefina who was now parading along the row of other debutantes.

"She has no answers." The girl pointed to the frames and torn canvases at his feet. "You have started to break the seals I see, so now this house has started to remember. It has started to wake. You will join us in our procession and we will guide you to a place that the couriers could not. There can be no turning back now, once you have planted your feet in this direction. Come now boy, take my hand and we'll begin. Josefina will wait for Jan, for he too will soon join us." The bureaucrat felt the girl's gloved hand slide into his and pull him away towards a door that he had not seen before. The other debutantes quietly followed in single file.

The Lost Reaches

IX.

Marek couldn't understand what he was seeing; somehow the clearing that the path had led him to opened out onto a street bathed in flickering sepia light. It was palpable enough to convince him he was there, in broad daylight, however the attendance of an audience transfixed before the spectacle suggested that he was merely witnessing a cinematographic illusion. Yet there was no discernible division between the vegetation and the street. Roots, vines, and branches continued undeterred into the fabric of the cobbled lane and buildings that constituted the vignette. The audience was composed of partly clothed youthful women and men in dishevelled formal attire. They lounged around a loose arrangement of armchairs and chaise longues, with the air of spent passion, as though he had just arrived after the conclusion of an erotic liaison. The old trooper shook his head, attempting to rid himself of the dream. The great screen remained flickering before him. He waited awhile, expecting the silhouetted audience to move, but all remained still. Feeling the weight of alcohol on his senses, he moved from the edge of the vegetation and made his way across the clearing. As he did so he was half-aware that a scene was being played out on the screen, yet his attention was focused largely on the dark reclining figures before it. As he neared them he could make out the illuminated features of one of the women, her face almost concealed by a plumed, wide-brimmed hat. He decided against calling out her name yet he was sure he recognised the woman as the one they'd been charged to escort across the border, the widow Josefina. Her eyes were closed and her breast rose and fell as though in sleep. At her feet there was a tangle of bodies, hands jutting from sleeves, and men's faces staring up into the soft light, almost adoringly. Having seen no evidence of a projector, the thought crossed his mind that the audience was the true source of the illusion, an idea he wanted to forget. A movement on the screen drew his attention away. In the film the slight figure of a man in an overcoat, left the doorway of a baker's shop and hurried along a lane with high featureless walls to the mouth of another street. Marek thought that the man's gait suggested that he wanted to make himself as small as possible, to perhaps shrink and vanish from sight. He carried an indiscernible bundle close to his chest. At the corner, where the sunlight almost entirely bleached all of the other features of the streets beyond, a man stepped into the other's path. Without any hesitation this second man, a uniformed officer in peaked cap and jackboots, levelled a pistol. The officer's arm recoiled slightly, followed by a wisp of smoke from the barrel of his gun. Marek had expected to hear the shot. The victim instantly dropped to the pavement where he stayed, splayed out across the ground, not quite motionless at first but finally coming to rest, as his right arm fell lifeless by his side, allowing the bundle to tumble into the gutter. Some way back up the lane, a girl in an apron at the baker's door retreated into the shadows, both hands pressed over her mouth. The silent execution played out again and again, returning to the moment that the man left the baker's doorway with what Marek guessed was a loaf of bread wrapped in paper, and ended with the girl vanishing from view. The impression that the audience had fallen asleep while watching this scene repulsed him yet he felt himself succumbing to the relentless and hypnotic loop of the film. Then a distant noise reached him and broke the film's hold over him; from beyond the glass walls of the conservatory, he heard a dog barking, and then another and another.

The Lost Reaches

He pulled himself away across the clearing and into the undergrowth once more. As Marek retreated through the ornamental garden, the cinematic memories returned to him in flashes; the street captured in the film seemed so familiar to him and yet he'd never heard of any such event occurring in Drohobycz. The remnants of the alcohol still lingered, whispering unfounded ideas to him as he fled through the overgrown avenues, hoping for the exit to rear into view. Could those events be happening in Drohobycz, in his absence, or were they events yet to come? As he staggered on, the leaves of the overhanging vegetation seemed to blacken yet the breach was now in sight. He turned as he crossed the threshold and witnessed the entire garden behind him flicker and vanish before his eyes, leaving a dull black pocket where that world had once been. The hallway had changed. Its proportions had somehow diminished. Even the banisters, tapestries, and carpets had lost some of their former detail. He was still trembling as he climbed the stairs of the hall calling out his young comrade's name. He was silenced by the ferocious bark of a dog as the main doors to the hall were battered open.

X.

Having found no light switch Jan edged forward as features of the room slowly emerged from the near-total darkness. The room seemed insubstantial, its features flickering into life, as if only waiting to succumb to formlessness once again. Sliding planes of silvery light occasionally glimmered for a moment then vanished. With arms outstretched he continued, waiting for contact as he paced on. His fingers found the hard edge of what he now guessed was the first of many glass cabinets, and slid along its wooden frame to a corner. Their contents were no more than perplexing shapes heaped together in shadows. His hands searched every pocket until they found the familiar rattle of matches in a box. Even when the match flared upon ignition and settled to a steady glow, he still struggled to make out the walls of the room. Row upon row of glass cases receded into the all-engulfing darkness as the wind outside whipped across the eaves and whispered something almost coherent to him. Lost somewhere in that sound he thought he heard the distant baying of a dog. Just as the first match burnt his fingertips, he began to make out familiar shapes. The spacious case was filled with toy sailing ships displayed on a painted papier-mâché sea. He broke the glass with a jab of his pistol butt and lifted out a large schooner. Holstering his revolver again, he held another lit match to the ship's main sail and waited for it to catch alight. He held this makeshift torch above his head as he turned on the spot, trying to find his bearings. He placed the burning boat on the parquet floor and took another armful of ships from the case. He lit and placed another on the floor; he walked on, leaving a trail of burning toy ships in his wake, until half an aisle had been illuminated. Stuffed birds looked on from the rows of cases to his right. Other avenues of curios glinted all about him, yet the end of the room was still not in sight. This one chamber defied his understanding of the house's dimensions. Looking back at the row of burning toy ships it seemed to him that his very actions were taking him further and further out of reach of the world he had known. He thought of Marek and wondered if he'd drunk himself into unconsciousness yet. Then he thought of Josefina. She meant little to him and yet if his time there in the house was to have any purpose or sense he must follow the commands of the mission. Marek should have known that, god knows he'd impressed that rule upon Jan many times before. It was essential for the integrity of their union, the couriers working in no more than pairs, had to be determined, it was crucial that they remained focussed on their knowledge of the borderland in order to remain a step ahead of the NKVD. Again a dog was baying through the wind outside.

Anxious that the flaming ships might start a larger fire, he returned to extinguish them underfoot. He cast about for something to use in their stead. The glint of a mounted candelabra caught his eye. He pulled it from its fixture on the wall and lit some of the dusty and broken candles as best he could. With the last of the ships' flames snuffed out, he returned to his search. He walked to the wall where he'd found the candelabra and paced its wood-panelled length until he came to a heavy green drape. Moving the material to one side, he found a doorway that opened onto another room similarly filled with rows of glass-fronted cabinets. He drifted from pane to pane, holding the candelabra to each surface and cupping his hand to his temple, peered inside. In the murk he made out the oiled carapaces of large antlered beetles, some the size of his fist, all impaled by hatpins to the pages of opened books. In another case he found an assortment of eggs arranged in a descending and snaking scale from the back to the front of the display on a bed of feathers. Some showed signs of hairline fractures. In yet another he was mesmerised by the exhibits: propped on a miniature easel was the pencil sketch of a face he knew. It was proof that he'd been right in recognising the paintings he'd unearthed from the cellar. Here was the artist himself, Bruno Schulz, his timid yet saturnine face staring back at him. The delicate crosshatched shading under his left eye, in his black hair and deep in the furrows under his cheekbones held him breathless for a moment. A pattern emerged from the scored pencil-markings to slowly approximate the wooden panelling of the house. Indeed, the artist's face slowly folded in on itself, shaping shadow-cornered chambers and stacked concertina stairwells. Jan felt himself swaying back and forth. His gaze was drawn away from the self-portrait to find crumpled pages amongst boxes of nibs and pencils. Paintbrushes lay in bundles across half-concealed drawings of hobbyhorses and diminutive men. Jars of ink glistened like rubies, emeralds, amethysts, and sapphires. In one corner sat a buckled homunculus of tubes and tins of paint fused together. It seemed to him that the cases' contents alternated or resettled themselves in new arrangements whenever his eyes darted from one to another. Yet there was incense in the air to coax him away and he followed the scent to its source. In the room's centre, amongst costume displays and grotesque statuary, he found an unoccupied chaise longue. Immediately before it, the broken remains of several paintings were strewn across the floor. One of the cabinet doors stood open, inside there was a Luger pistol resting against an ancient loaf of bread. All around it were phials of dark viscous liquid, each labelled and bearing an illegible scrawl.

XI.

The old trooper barely had enough time to register that the shape that darted across the entrance hall and up the stairs toward him was a dog and not a shadow. All he could see was the blur of its snarling teeth and its fixed merciless pupils as its weight bore down on him. For a second he could have believed that the dog had sprouted further heads yet, somehow in the panic, time had become impossibly slow. He understood at a glance that another two of its kind had joined the fray as Marek fought to reach the pistol in his holster. He was suddenly on his back, wrestling for his life on the stairs. Their teeth had soon raked his exposed flesh while tearing at his clothes, putting their weight into each bite as they shook their heads. He knew in another second it would be too late to act. Then, like sliding on his wedding ring, his finger found the trigger. He was suddenly deafened and disorientated. He lost count of how many rounds he'd fired, only that he didn't dare stop. Cordite stung his eyes as the dogs' black bulks whimpered and slumped and slid away from him. Their blood left a sharp metallic scent in his nostrils. And then at the main doorway there was a crack in the air. The balustrade near his head exploded into splinters. The sound had come from a gathering of snow-encrusted shadows, uniformed men, their faces hidden under goggles and scarves and peaked caps. There was an unbelievable pause of hesitancy, of indecision. Then, when one of the shadows barked muffled orders to the others, Marek returned to firing his pistol randomly in their direction as he struggled to his feet. He'd half-seen some of the border guards fall, yet others levelled firearms in retaliation, some pistols, others rifles, as he made it to the doorway above him, shaking with adrenaline. A hail of gunfire erupted as Marek threw himself forward, the panelling of the passage exploding in a cloud of sawdust as he did so.

Halfway down the passage he understood that he could no longer use his left arm. His hand was red and almost numb. He tried to form a fist but it refused. The crack of another gunshot filled the corridor. The darkness was on his side. The bullet shattered the oval window at his shoulder as he manoeuvred to return fire. Seeing that his target, a silhouette at the passage's end, had already sidestepped into cover, he instead turned his pistol on the lock of a door to his right and disappeared inside. In the pitch darkness he stumbled up steps. Up he climbed, half-crawling and spluttering on dust, gritting his teeth against a bone-deep agony. He'd lost all sense of direction, that in somehow crawling he no longer knew which way he turned or whether he was ascending or descending. He dismissed the idea that he had been swallowed and slowly digested by the house. He could hear vermin scurrying away at his approach then the air became suddenly clearer and as fresh as spring water. Perhaps his pursuers had taken another route knowing that they would be able to wait for him in hiding somewhere ahead. Yet the raftered space he fell into was silent and still. As he found his footing, pulling himself upright by grasping a nearby crate stuffed with straw, he looked about, wheezing on the dusty air. The only source of light came from below, glowing from an opening in the floor almost ten feet square. His heart throbbed with a loud and irregular rhythm in his head. Although he glimpsed the dark blood soaking his left shoulder and arm, he dared not examine it closely. Instead he dragged himself onward to the banister that edged the opening in the floor. From there he could see down into a grand mirrored ballroom, half-obscured by an enormous chandelier that was suspended from a beam in the attic roof by means of a chain and pulley. He stared at the glittering cut crystals and candlelight as he felt his head growing heavier, noticing something on the branches of the chandelier. Were large birds perched there, huddled together? If so, he had not seen their like before. He thought that he could hear faint piano music from below, and the stir of distant voices. Was it that bureaucrat and the widow that he could hear? Perhaps Jan would be there with them too. He should warn them. Yet the attic space became stifling and now he clung to the railing to stay upright, his head loose on his shoulders. He thought of crying out for Jan, but he couldn't muster enough breath. As he attempted to do so again, something crossed the corner of his eye. In the clutter of the attic space he could make out great avian heads on slender necks stirring in the half-light. Nests had been built in the gaps where a few of the balustrades that edged the opening in the floor had been broken through, presumably by formidable beaks. Huge eggs lay nestled there in lustrous plumage and shredded pages. Something that could only be a hybrid of pelican and archaeopteryx reared up from the shadows and tried to spread its great wings in the cramped space. Yet as Marek slid cowering and exhausted to the floor, the tyrant bird rearranged itself in its nest and continued quietly roosting. Lying on the boards, with distant piano music playing in the ballroom far below, the old trooper remained transfixed by that bird's huge eye, glimmering amber in the dim light. As death took him into sleep, he held up his good hand to see its fingers elongate and sprout feathers. The last dream he had as a man was of being a bird perched upon the branch of a chandelier above a grand hall while boys and women danced far below.

XII.

The bureaucrat looked behind him to see the procession of debutantes and their chastised servants traipsing through the dim passageway. He had just learned that the young woman who led him by the hand called herself Adela. She wore a loose silk robe that shimmered in the lamplight. The robe's grapevine pattern drew him onwards, leaving him mesmerised and almost oblivious to his surroundings. In time he understood that they had descended a stairwell into a chamber devoid of furniture and lined with tall draped windows. The sound of soft laughter and excited words stirred from the others as they gathered behind him. Large covered canvases stood stacked at angles against the walls. Adela made a sweeping gesture with her hands and the women dispersed to the edges of the room. They began pulling the dustsheets from the paintings, turning the pictures so that they faced the room. Before the bureaucrat could absorb what they depicted, Adela had pointed to several of the paintings and the women did as instructed, stamping the frames underfoot. A few tore them apart with their bare hands, and some were so enthused by the prospect they even buried their teeth into the canvas as they did so. As each picture was destroyed in turn, a corner or stretch of room came to life. Copper candlelight spread across the walls as a great chandelier slowly emerged from an opening in the shadowy ceiling. It appeared as if from thin air, first one icicle then another grew to form an inverted shining glass citadel. Strange birds fluttered down to perch on its branches. The bureaucrat backed away and as he did so turned to view the whole spectacle taking shape around him. The entrance, which had formerly been a single oak door, had doubled in size and split into two. Bright baroque mirrors pooled in the once drabs walls. Vegetal murals unfurled across every surface. Candelabra sprouted like stray tree roots from the plaster. As the chamber's fresh wonders settled into place, the debutantes and their servants took their places in two opposing lines facing each other in the centre of the floor, with the anxious bureaucrat standing between them. Adela took a step forward and addressed him.

XIII.

Jan thought he had heard the baying of a dog somewhere, this time within the walls of the house. Then from behind the chaise longue the widow stepped out of a shadow. She softly smiled at him, a feathered cloak hanging loose around her bare shoulders and slender neck.

The widow led the young courier to the first aisle of cases. In the corner of each cabinet, Jan found a peeling label glued to the pane. It depicted by means of a web-like diagram how the contents of the individual cabinet might be interrelated, although understanding that each must possess such a label he could only guess at the magnitude of the schema that was at play all around him. Josefina pointed to another case in which old maps and charts had been heaped or pinned to boards. Each displayed similar schemas, yet caught in their webs were tiny portraits the size of postage stamps. He found her likeness amongst them, as well as his own, each face was linked by faint pencil lines and arrows and threads. Dogs barked as feet thundered in a nearby passage.

"Come, we must go now." The widow took Jan's hand, suddenly animated as a puppet by its strings. After passing through numerous doorways they were soon sweeping down stairs through looming shadows, the walls turning. They descended the stairwell as great bestial statues in alcoves swept by them, the sound of barking following close on their heels.

"Come now join us in our dance. Let us celebrate this last night. Tomorrow all this will be gone." Adela held out her hands to the bureaucrat. Yet he wanted to tell her that she was wrong, that Josefina had promised him a place by her side, as the great curator of a lost world.

As she took his hands into hers the others followed suit, falling into a trance. Executing movements instinctively, they enacted a ritual to the slow tempo of piano music. As they began to turn in each other's arms, their feet following a pattern of soundless steps across the polished floor, the bureaucrat heard the house shift, groaning around them through its stone and wood and glass, as though stirring from sleep.

"The house is remembering for the last time. It will soon die. These are its final moments. We are honoured." Adela whispered in his ear as they danced on, the silver depths of candlelit mirrors gleaming as they swept past, barely aware of their fellow dancers spinning about them.

Josefina and Jan stood watching the dancers glide across the great ballroom floor, observing Adela and the bureaucrat at the centre, the others spinning in measured orbits around them as the piano played a hypnotic minuet. The widow led the young courier by the hand and they weaved their way through the dancers to join Adela and her partner, the great chandelier glittering overhead, strange birds looking down from its branches.

The high doors to the ballroom were flung violently open. Two black mastiffs straining on leashes emerged snarling from the shadows of the threshold. They were followed by a mass of men garbed in long heavy coats, their faces half-hidden by scarves, their eyes shaded by the peaks of their caps. The dogs were unleashed as the men advanced into the ballroom, raising their firearms. To Jan's astonishment the piano continued playing as the guests retreated across the dance floor. Several debutantes and servants dropped to the ground as rifle shots cracked the air. Jan returned fire and their captain fell clutching his shoulder. As soon as the dogs gained the centre ground, shards of light cast by the great chandelier overhead danced across their backs. At their touch the beasts were instantly struck down, as if by lightning, writhing where they fell. As the patrol gathered in dismay, dropping their guard and gesturing to one another in confusion, each in turn suffered the same fate as the dogs, grasping at their

The Lost Reaches

own throats or chests as if in great agony, black ink bubbling from their mouths.

Adela and Josefina emerged from the gaggle that had cowered at the far side of the ballroom. Smiling, they crossed the dance floor to witness dense shadows coagulate around the prone forms of the dogs and their masters twisting in convulsions upon the floor. Out of the dark, viscous masses new forms took shape.

The music played on as Jan stepped forward. Beyond Adela and Josefina the black glistening carapaces and antlers of huge beetles reared up where their enemies had lain only moments before. The bureaucrat stood dumbstruck by Jan's side, gripping onto his sleeve with both hands. Jan tried to shake him off as he advanced to join the two women, his pistol still in his hand. The crowd behind them started to mutter to each other, debutantes reasserting themselves over their servants once again.

Then the great stag beetles began to dance, and as though to mirror their crablike movements, the music took on a staccato rhythm. With every fourth strike of the piano keys, the beetles performed a mindless turn in precise unison, the components of a greater machine. The debutantes all rushed like laughing children to gather in the light of the chandelier and enjoy the spectacle. None of them were the least concerned by the fact that the high wooden panels of the hall around them groaned as it contracted and splintered in time with the music. Indeed, Adela and Josefina had begun to mimic the insects' movements spurring the others to follow suit. Even their servants were instructed to ape their steps.

Jan paced the length of the wall, keeping his distance and his eye on the doorway at the far side of the room. The bureaucrat was still pestering him, clinging to his sleeve and making whining appeals for Jan to protect him.

By then the debutantes, servants, and beetles were dancing as one, performing the ritual one last time as the house shrank around them. They danced on and on, turning, retreating, and advancing in time with the music as Jan and the bureaucrat reached the open doors. For a moment the bureaucrat hesitated and Jan could see in his eyes that he wanted to plead with him to take Josefina with them. Without a word Jan turned away and plunged into the darkness of the shuddering passage. He was angered to hear the bureaucrat calling out to him as he climbed the stairwell. The music faded behind them and statues crashed across the steps as they ascended. They passed through distorted rooms that aged in an instant; the drapes and furniture decaying before their eyes, the brittle glass of the cabinets splintering, their frames collapsing sending their contents tumbling to the floor to disintegrate into dust. All the while the house shuddered and groaned as it contracted. By the time they reached the entrance hall, they were bent double, walking with their backs against the ceiling, as the house slowly shrank around them.

Lying exhausted in the snow, Jan watched the house collapse as though it were folding in on itself; the bureaucrat whimpered nonsense by his side. Jan thought of Marek somehow still alive and lost within the shrinking house. The stars were sharp in the pool of sky above the clearing. All was silent in the wall of encircling trees. They stayed there until the house had almost vanished, its walls as thin as paper, and just as it seemed to be slipping quietly into the earth, the bureaucrat clambered across the clearing and snatched it up in both hands, laughing.

The Lost Reaches

XIV.

By morning the house had disappeared, although the bureaucrat said otherwise. Jan hoped he was lying when he claimed he'd swallowed the house when his back was turned. Without shelter, they had to press on through the forest. What other choice did Jan have than to complete what he'd been instructed to do? And besides, even though he was now mad and repeatedly refused to tell him his name, he knew the bureaucrat still trusted and depended upon him. He still had to be delivered to safety, Jan felt he owed him that much. For a mile as they walked they discussed viable routes through the borderland, more as a way of distracting his charge from his mania than anything else. Yet even when Jan managed to wrestle the conversation back onto concrete subjects, such as the names and courses of rivers, the bureaucrat's tone would suddenly change. So they marched on through the green depths of the pines and firs, the bureaucrat lagging behind, staring up at the sunlight breaking through the branches and talking more to himself than to his guide.

"Yes, the river San . . . the Tysa, the river Prut, Prut, Prut . . . the Seret." Yet soon enough, as Jan knew only too well, the subject would slowly return to the house.

"It's a shrunken head and we're its dreams. Of course the house has a museum. Why wouldn't a head like that . . . like this . . . have a museum? And I see now that it has plans. It wants me to be its curator, its emissary. We have to play out its games, this little house, fit for dolls, filled with conniving schemes . . . and she is part of it all, Josefina, the lovely Josefina. See how easily she's made herself at home. I see myself in all of those tapestries and paintings, in all of those glass-eyed boys pawing at delicate feet. I remember now, that was me and will be me again.

The life in here is all that there is: nothing before and nothing after. Together we remember everything. What I forget, you remember and vice versa. I see it now . . . that all along I knew everything. We . . . together . . . know everything. All I needed to do was wait, to listen. I remember all that is to come. The snow is pressing in, it's gathering, smothering everything . . . all time and space . . . even the stars are falling snowflakes. Here I'll leave my mark. I'll hold court to honour those who were carried off by the night. Their light stamped out under the heels of another history. Their names have all but been forgotten now. In this house, in this head I'll remember them. That's all that's left."

The Feast of the Sphinx

I. The Dangerous Hour

10th September 1939, Prague

Nemec lacked the resilience to be a saboteur. He didn't have the nerve; in fact I appeared to be the only one who sensed the extent of his instability. I wanted to wash my hands of him as fast as I could. Their report identified the prisoner as a known "degenerate" and something he'd said when arrested had made them suspicious or, worse still, curious. The Gestapo foisted this case on us just to see how we'd squirm.

The day they brought the prisoner in they descended like birds of ill omen, their long leather coats sweeping through the corridors of Police Headquarters. Mercifully they considered anyone lower than the Superintendent a waste of time, so someone of my rank seldom had to speak with the Gestapo directly. No one wanted to come under their scrutiny as those who had often ended up in Pankrác Prison or worse.

Almost as quickly as they commandeered buildings the Nazis started to confiscate valuables, and it had been this factor that had put Nemec under their spotlight. He'd spoken of lost treasure belonging to some aristocrat or other. In my book, claiming to possess a great secret or the answer to a mystery tended to indicate madness. Yet it wasn't the prisoner's insanity that had warranted the label "degenerate", but his meagre reputation as an artist deemed abhorrent to the Reich's constitution. By all accounts, he existed on a list of undesirables designated for immediate arrest. While my colleagues know me as a stickler, it never ceased to surprise me how much energy the Gestapo expended in the pursuit of absurd misdemeanours.

I knew it wouldn't take long before my most trusted colleagues were relieved of duty; some demoted and others sent off to God knows where. Most of my superiors vanished. They were old-timers, and Czechs at that, deemed too lenient and institutionalised for the new regime. Replacements were brought in from Germany after a month of tuition; a mere four weeks of familiarisation in local bureaucracy and customs and "the Czech character". A core of my peers remained, those the Reich deemed dependable. Steadfast was the word they'd used. They demanded all meetings should be conducted in German. So they favoured their fellow countrymen and hardliners. I'm both, the first by birth, the latter out of necessity. I quickly lost my taste for it when they took the city. Discipline is one thing, that's something to believe in; there's structure in punishment just as there's dignity in work. If you discipline someone, you take the shapeless matter of who they were and work them into something better. Yet these bastards have no rules. They claim to abide by some ancient law lost to everyone but themselves; it's just an excuse. It's not order that their law promises but cruelty. They take pleasure in it. It's a secret game to them; they play with power like a child stumbling on an ant's nest. They accused my men of turning a blind eye when German shops were vandalised and looted and burned. And when commands came that in the event of further demonstrations or student protests we were to shoot into the crowds no one believed it. No one wanted to believe that day would

The Feast of the Sphinx

come, but that day came and went like so many other days until one morning you found yourself having breakfast with the Devil. So it was in the shadow of such times that I received the prisoner Nemec into my custody.

From the early days of the occupation unspeakable stories circulated about the Gestapo, so the prisoner's fear was such that there was no need to deprive him of sleep. We only had to hold him for a single night before he became compliant enough to interview. At first I thought they'd sent me a bewildered boy to question. I could tell immediately there was something not quite right about him; he wasn't all there. I gestured for the prisoner to approach and he did so, slowly and obediently, slipping into the chair without a noise. He seemed dazed. His clothes were dishevelled and dirty, his skin and hair powdered with dust. He cut a ridiculous figure: a shell-shocked dandy.

He'd been caught tearing Nazi flags from statues in Wenceslas Square. He'd told the soldiers who'd apprehended him, that he was trying to find someone hidden underneath; surely a sign he had lost his reason. They'd interpreted his actions as a threat. Before the occupation, someone like him would be deemed a waste of time but now everything was viewed with suspicion.

"I'm Ritter, Inspector Ritter. You're being held on suspicion of resistance activity, you understand? They've agreed to let me question you in advance. I try to intervene where I can, but you must realise that I'm largely powerless where they're concerned . . . anything less than full cooperation will mean immediate transfer to Pankrác . . . to the wing under their command. You can expect no mercy there. If you give me what they want, there's a chance they won't interrogate you. Understand?"

The prisoner nodded, his eyes lowered. I opened the paper file before me and took up my pencil.

"To confirm: you are Jan Nemec, born May 14th, 1908? And what did you do before . . . before all of this?"

"I'm a painter . . . at least I was."

"Speak up. A painter? Of what exactly?" There was something about this Nemec I didn't like: his thin hands, his nervous eyes . . . his mouth a sickly almond shape. I instantly detested the weakness I sensed in him and resented the discomfort he made me feel.

"Portraits."

"Portraits?" I put down my pencil expecting to see Nemec smirking at my expense.

"Yes, portraits." He continued in a deadpan tone.

Nemec had an unfortunate air about him; a pull of some kind. Not that he was aware; it wasn't charm, more an odd sort of innocence that provoked distrust. Madmen make most people suspicious; it's as if they have something precious to hide, something unobtainable.

"You'll have to give us names . . . addresses: of your friends . . . your family. We'll make a list then whittle it down." It was difficult to gauge my approach; I found myself pitying him, as if comforting someone infirm.

"Friends?" the ghost finally mumbled. "They're all gone. Some fled the city. Others ended it. Cyanide."

"You'll need to do better than that. You need to divert them. You need to put other names between you and the Gestapo. If you don't, they'll come straight to you. They'll take you to Pankrác and that'll be that. Understand?" The prisoner's eyes went from searching the shadows to fixing his gaze on me. It wasn't a look of defiance or fear. He seemed oblivious to the threat of his predicament, as is often the case with the demented, yet there was still something else I couldn't work out. It was as though he were on the outside looking in, observing, trying to figure out what made me tick.

The Feast of the Sphinx

"Are you a Jew? If you are there's only so much I can do to keep the wolves at bay. You'll need proof or they'll assign you to a transport. Do you have papers?"

"No sir, I'm not a Jew. I have papers at home proving that I'm Czech. If you let me go there I promise I'll call back in a few days. It's her, you see. She's out there somewhere . . . in the city. I have to get back to her, if she'll let me."

"Who? Your wife? What's her name?" I took up my pencil again adopting a smile.

"No, not my wife. She doesn't really have a name, not a name that would help you find her."

Slamming my hand down on the table didn't rouse him from his daydream. "You're not helping." I told him, "The next time they call I could let them come for you . . . I don't want to do that, but if you force my hand . . . this is your neck on the line not mine . . . so what is this woman's name and who is she to you?"

"I was told to call her the Countess."

"The Countess? That won't do," I told him. The Gestapo demanded answers to impossible questions. They demanded to know who the prisoner knew; they wanted names, addresses, photographs. They wanted to know what his roots were, how and where he'd lived, what places he frequented, what friends or lovers he had. They expected no less than his soul on a plate. Yes, I could speak Czech. Did they think I could read minds too; me, a mere inspector? And always the same threat came through my superior: that they'd send one of their own to oversee the case if I lacked the stomach. I knew what that meant; if I failed, my fate would be no better than the prisoner's.

What could the Gestapo want with someone like him? That word they'd used in the cable—"degenerate". He wasn't a Jew. He was no more than a painter. If he was part of the intelligentsia, then he seemed incapable of agitation. He was delirious when he was first brought in, yet this soon gave way to a strange calmness. There was no edge to him, as you'd expect to find with someone in the resistance. He didn't have the hands for it, for one thing; too delicate. I couldn't see the point in putting him through an interrogation. There'd be no practicable outcome, but I had my orders.

The way I saw it the sooner I got rid of him the better. So I asked the questions and reviewed the transcriptions. If I doctored anything it wasn't because I wanted to conceal or deceive but survive. What would be the point of documenting what no-one would believe? Yet what was expected of me? How much should I let through unadulterated? Is that what they wanted? Did they want me to document the prisoner's ravings in detail or sift for truth through Nemec's madness? Did they believe there was a hidden code in what he said?

As was always the case with the Gestapo, I delivered my reports and received no replies. I worked in a vacuum, fearing that a lengthy deliberation was under way in a distant room somewhere, and sooner or later I would be summoned to take their test.

Normally in cases such as this, making the prisoner afraid could have results. Yet I knew with someone like Nemec, instilling fear would only make him forget the finer details; he'd cut corners with the truth and confess to things I wanted to hear. I couldn't risk that. With suspects like Nemec, it's important not to get drawn in. It was difficult to strike the right balance. In a way I had to gain his trust; I had to become like a doctor or confidante to him. Yet his trembling hands sickened me. He was an innocent. It was as if there was something missing, like he didn't have a solid hold on this world, and for some reason it was that vulnerability that held my attention. If nothing more, I was curious where the prisoner would lead me.

"So, tell me, Mr. Nemec, how did you come to be here?"

"Well, soldiers arrested me in the Old Town Square, of course. I admit that I tore down their banners from the Jan Hus monument. What of it! You think me a saboteur or spy. I can't deny that I am an agent of another power, if you will; unknown to me almost as much as it is to you. I'm only a messenger. She speaks through me. I'm her vessel, you see. But if you listen, be warned, you will not sleep easy tonight. You will become a part of this just as much as I have. I know your secret. You want me to lead you to my mistress, and that is why you have kept me alive. It's inevitable; you are only a man after all. To follow, you must be silent and listen. Yes, sit in that chair and be quiet. How should I begin? We walk through a dream when we remember."

The prisoner was agitated. I told him to begin simply as I didn't have time for riddles. I told him to be calm or he would lose his only chance to tell his story. I told him to remember where he was before all of this had begun: before the city was occupied.

"I didn't want to know. No one did. No one wanted to admit that it was the end of an era. No one wanted to speak of the sour taste in the air. Yet everywhere you could hear talk of people leaving Prague. The headlines were everywhere you turned. The Sudetenland had been taken. President Beneš ordered mobilisation. It only made those within our circle want to drink more. It made us scurry to our old haunts, to find sanctuary in the familiar, knowing it was our last chance. Soon the life we'd known would be swept away.

"So by night we returned to the Montmartre Café, our sanctuary in the Staré Město. For once my infirmity was an asset and I knew I would fail the call up. Yet my friends, a small circle of poets and painters, were not so lucky, and it seemed that with each meeting they became steadily ill at ease at the prospect of their military duty. Escape plans were constantly dreamt up but dissolved by morning. Every evening became another excuse to drink until we dropped or were thrown out. The proprietor tolerated us because he knew it wouldn't last much longer. Everyone knew that these were the final days."

The prisoner was rambling. I told him he needed to focus. I told him I knew the café. He smiled softly, as if humouring me. I couldn't believe the conceit of that little worm, but I bit my tongue and let it pass.

"Then as a policeman I'm sure you'll know that the rooms *above* the café have quite a reputation. The proprietor, who had once aspired to opulence, became a victim of his own success. The place wasn't so much decorated as disgorged; all peeling paint and faded brocade. Yet this atmosphere of decline only served to cement the loyalty of his faithful clientele and deter those with orthodox tastes. It was in that cavern of mottled mirrors and shabby drapes that I first encountered Otakar, the Countess's servant.

"It was still early evening. I was discussing the finer details of a liaison with one of the girls there when something caught my eye in a mirror. Regardless of all the revelry, I remained transfixed. Some way off in the crowd of the mirror there was a face, and it was as if the face glowed. I experienced what I thought was recognition, yet I didn't know this man. He was a stranger to me. Yet there was something remarkable about him, like a bearded figurehead rising above the spume of bodies. I watched this Neptune advance, emerging from the sea fret of incense and tobacco smoke. Unmoved by the lewd displays all around him, he proceeded to the corner where I waited, just as my female companion for the night retreated.

The Feast of the Sphinx

Friends reclining nearby were roused from their inebriation. With his long shabby coat and mane he loomed over us. I could have easily believed that he was a beggar.

"He must have said my name several times to rouse me from my stupor. He asked naïvely if I was Mr. Nemec, the great artist. My friends nearby laughed, and although it was obvious this man had not come to collect a debt, my instinct was to shake my head.

" 'I am Otakar. I come with a message and a request,' he said. The man's weathered face, wild hair and beard gave him a leonine appearance. As he approached, he held out his hands in a conciliatory gesture. My companions awaited an exchange with some amusement. So when the man nervously murmured his unusual name again they couldn't conceal their mirth. This time I felt only pity, and in seeing that I refused to share their joke my friends started to chide me. As I stood up to leave I realised it was decisive. I hadn't expected to burn my bridges so soon, if at all, and although I had no idea why I had done such a thing on the spur of the moment, I still tried to apologise for my former friends' behaviour as I walked with the stranger from the room. The old man held up his hands emphatically as he shrugged; he was an old Slovak after all, he said, and had long since become accustomed to such things in Prague. Before I could reassure him further he began reciting a speech that had clearly been rehearsed.

"On the landing of the stairwell his amber eyes met mine, and perhaps it was my drunkenness, I don't know, yet as he spoke I felt myself soothed as if by a song. He delivered a formal invitation from his mistress, who he didn't name, but said that she knew of my reputation as a portraitist. I tried to tell him that he was mistaken. He said that my attendance would be expected immediately and although the nature of the position prevented him

The Satyr and Other Tales

from stating how long my services would be required, he assured me that his mistress's reward would be substantial and that she'd provide for all my needs. He emphasised this last point with a knowing smile. Had there been a prospect of seduction in the remark?

"I thanked him, but tried in apologetic tones to decline; I'd found his offer difficult to follow and perhaps it wasn't the best time to discuss business as I'd been drinking. He wasn't listening to my excuses.

" 'You expect me to go with you tonight?' I said. Otakar's eyes smiled as he nodded.

"By way of diversion I suggested that we escape downstairs to the café instead. Once we'd found a corner suitably quiet to conduct our business I asked a passing waitress for coffee and *slivovice*, gesturing to the old lion. He nodded more in obedience than agreement. I waited for him to begin. I didn't think it was unreasonable to expect an explanation, yet he remained sitting there in silence, smiling. It crossed my mind that I might be in the company of a simpleton.

"As the drinks arrived he asked me if I had any plans. I told him that I'd been on the verge of leaving Prague, after all according to the latest reports the city would be occupied within weeks. I turned the question on him and I pressed him on whether his mistress meant to stay when so many were already fleeing. Then my sarcasm got the better of me when I remarked, ' . . . . or is she expecting friends?'

"Otakar downed his *slivovice* with a reproachful look. What did he expect? Prague was about to be overrun and he'd come to me with that proposal.

" 'You could return to your old friends of course, Mr. Nemec.' Otakar gestured to the empty space around us, 'Or you could always drink yourself to sleep so when the jackboots come hammering through the Staré Město

The Feast of the Sphinx

you'll not hear them. Failing that you could run, if you have somewhere to hide. Do you have somewhere to hide, Mr. Nemec?'

"I admitted that I had nowhere to go. The rooms that I rented would be seized, the owners being Jews. Yet still I demanded to know why his mistress needed me of all people. I wanted to tell him that he was mistaken, that I wasn't a painter of any repute, but refrained at the last minute.

"He said that he didn't know why. He only knew that if his mistress had charged him with finding me then I must be worth the trouble.

" 'Now you must come,' he said and only then did I really notice the size of the man. The span of his hands and the expanse of his face were unnatural.

" 'You could at least tell me her name,' I said. Perhaps I had heard of her. He became evasive then, saying that she wasn't well known, not anymore.

"What did he mean? Had she been famous once? I must have demanded her name repeatedly, far more than I recall, for the rest of the small room turned its attention towards me.

" 'The Countess . . . you must call her the Countess and that is all you need to know.' He whispered, cupping his mouth with his hand.

"That was not a real name, I told him. He'd have to give me more than that. I was stalling him, of course. I wanted to learn more about the old beast's mistress, yet I needed to defer the decision he expected me to make. I raised my hand to order more drinks, but Otakar shook his head and this time it was my turn to comply.

"He said that I would not know her name for her golden age had long since passed. That was the phrase he used: 'her golden age'. His manner seemed so grandiose that I suspected that it was a ruse, a joke at my expense, and said as much. And then I recall he said something I found curious. He apologised, saying that he had been away from the life of the city so long that he had forgotten how to live. He said that common etiquette and behaviour was now a puzzle to him.

"I didn't quite follow, but nodded all the same. 'You must have travelled far then?' I asked.

" 'No, the Countess lives nearby, in Prague itself.'

" 'But you said you were no longer accustomed to the ways of the city? I assumed that you meant that you lived with the Countess quite far from here.'

" 'Yes. You will see.' The old lion replied.

" 'I haven't said I would come.' I downed the *slivovice*. He must have sensed the lack of conviction in my words.

"He was as disarming as he was awkward, yet his manner encouraged candidness. Even though I suspected he was taking advantage of my drunkenness, I still admitted to him that there was nothing left for me in the city.

"He said that I'd returned to darkness only so that I could begin again. He said that was always the way, if I could only see it. His eyes met mine with such compassion that I had to look away. I recall retrieving my hand from his, surprised to find that he'd probably been holding it for some time. He said that my resistance was to be expected, but that I must prepare for what lies ahead. Yes, you think he was mad. I admit I thought the same at first. No doubt he is just another degenerate to you, someone that must be expunged. Perhaps for that reason I surrendered, in defiance of your kind. I would not expect you to understand."

The prisoner had fallen silent so I tried another approach.

"Mr. Nemec, like you I have lived all my life here in Prague. And although I'm German by birth, I am not the same as them. I am not the same as the men who brought you here. If I can keep you from them I will, but under-

The Feast of the Sphinx

stand this: I will not be made a fool of. I don't know what they want from you but I'm not going to make it easy for them." It was like humouring a child.

The prisoner sulked a while, but then made a strange twirling gesture under his chin as he picked up the thread of his story.

"So as Otakar absently twisted a finger through his beard, awaiting my answer, I finally agreed to go with him.

" 'We'll go then. It's not far,' the beast said, reaching across the table and grasping my shoulder. I could have sworn tears were welling in his eyes. Despite the old lion's reassurances, I soon found myself drifting for some time through unfamiliar lanes. It was as though he had taken us on a circuitous route with the intention of confusing me. I attempted to identify recognisable landmarks, a rooftop or spire, yet I'd underestimated how drunk I still was and the night's chill rather than sobering me up only numbed my thinking. Otakar moved on, occasionally pausing at a corner of lamplight, waiting for me to catch up with him. And as I did so, he'd grasp my shoulder again as a gesture of good will, as he had in the café.

"As I followed I became aware that the street narrowed as it descended. I wished I'd paid attention to the street signs as we walked down that secluded lane. I became increasingly aware that the buildings that lined the road were untenanted and in a state of disrepair. True, I am not unaccustomed to seeing neglect in some quarters of Prague, yet as there were no signs of occupancy, no lights in windows or noises at all, I felt that I was being led into a trap. As Otakar's thickset shadow shuffled on before me, his hands stuffed deep into his pockets, it seemed possible that he was intentionally keeping his face turned away from mine. I looked back to see the desolate lane. Only a few lamps remained lit. I turned again to see the old man waiting at a corner. Without looking at me, he raised a hand to gesture that we neared our destination.

"From the uniformity of the surrounding street the Countess's house rose up, an edifice from a bygone time. Misaligned rows of blank windows stared back from its mouldering face. It seemed rooted there, even older than the steep streets that snaked down to the Vltava. Fog obliterated any view of the city on the opposite riverbank. It was as though I'd strayed off the edge of the world.

"The house had a grandeur that was out of place amongst the other abandoned properties. From its imposing architecture, it struck me that it may have once fulfilled a long-since lost civic function, although I had no idea what that could have been. It was set apart at the end of that dejected street by the high rusted railings of what may have once been an ornamental garden. Various pieces of toppled or leaning statuary lay in the sparse undergrowth. I recognised in a specific pairing of weathered idols certain astrological characteristics; nudes with the countenances of Sol and Luna. With dawn only a few hours away, I followed Otakar up stone steps rising through a jungle of dying vegetation to a pale blistered door. Along the building's cornices I could make out the crumbling remains of heraldic beasts. As we crossed the threshold I wondered what kind of countess left her door unlocked."

II. The Furrow in the Mirror

13th September 1939

Without warning Nemec had blacked out, and after many attempts at reviving him the prisoner finally came round. When he did so it was late at night and the physician demanded that he should at least stay in bed in his cell if I insisted upon questioning him while he remained so unstable. Time was already running out for him in other ways; my superiors would soon demand progress.

Nothing could have prepared me for what I experienced that night. I admit I only have my own account to rely upon, for what that's worth, given the state of my nerves. I had demanded to be alone with the prisoner and ordered my assistant from the cell as his presence caused Nemec obvious distress. Yet my mistake was in making my transcription without a witness. In the absence of corroboration, I'd left myself open to criticism. It was as if I had set a trap for myself, inviting the scepticism that inevitably surrounded the events of this case.

That night Nemec changed. Of course he had never been the healthiest of specimens, the pale wretch that he was, but that is not what I mean. True, his decline did seem in some way unnaturally rapid, as if he were spiting me, his captor. And while his gaze became unbearable to meet, at times awe-stricken by something unseen to everyone else, that wasn't the worst of it: it was his voice. This voice was not simply a version of the prisoner's own. This was no performance or imitation. The shock upon hearing it was so palpable that I wondered whether I was still speaking to the same man. Indeed that night, as I sat at the foot of his bed, I doubted at times that I was in the presence of a man at all. He had become something else in that cell, his face floating there in the shadows, the blanket drawn up to his chin. In soft distracted tones he introduced himself as the Countess.

It was my duty to remind the prisoner that his time was running out and that he could not afford to play stupid games. It was duty too that told me to persist in using his real name, as much to support my own reasoning as it was a method to tether Nemec to the here and now.

"Nemec? Do I know that name?" The prisoner's head moved as if his neck was unaccustomed to its weight, his eyes rolling slowly under half-closed lids. Then a light singing laughter trilled from the prisoner's lips in tones that no man could mimic.

The voice continued to whisper, "You must return Mr. Nemec to me. He is the only one who can truly listen to me, after all this time in the dark alone with only my lion Otakar for company. My time has passed. My master is dead. No one remembers my face. Am I to be forgotten? Yet my dear Mr. Nemec knows me. Who else could paint my portrait?"

I had seen a woman put into a trance in the theatre once, and Nemec had that exact expression and manner; his head swaying to and fro, his breathing shallow. Then a terrible sound emitted from the prisoner's lips like that of an animal in pain, an unearthly whine that pierced the air. The walls of the cell rang with the sound. One of my men came knocking on the cell door, his troubled face appearing at the hatch; I told him that I needed no assistance and that I would shortly draw the questioning to a close for the night. The guard looked relieved. The small viewing hatch slid shut leaving me alone with the prisoner once more. Yet that was not the end of my audience with the Countess. Indeed it was she who dictated the pace and duration of our dialogue that evening.

"You are mine now," she said. "I would rather die than speak in another's presence. You belong to me, just as Nemec does. You too will be my confidante, an ally here in my secret court. This will be your only duty, you will serve me." The prisoner caressed his own face and mouth and there was strange grace in his movements.

Something in me wanted to silence that terrible, feminine voice. I've been known to apply other methods to bring prisoners to their senses, and indeed my hands were

The Feast of the Sphinx

gripping the prisoner's bedclothes at his throat when he spoke again in that singing tone, so I released him.

"I still think of my maker, the Emperor. At times I still await his arrival. Once he found solace here with me in this retreat. He would come to contemplate his collection if only to remove his worldly mantle for a while. And he would love me. Of all the artefacts he adored, even more than agates, none were more precious to him than my eyes. He said that through me he could gaze upon the world's secret faces." The prisoner fixed me with his eyes.

Did I scream at Nemec to wake him up? Yes, I shook him, demanding that he remembered who he was. Yet that unearthly voice returned as if from a great distance.

"I have no name, or at least lost it somehow along the way. He called me Countess, yet it may have been part of the game he liked to play. He sometimes teased me, saying that I was his muse."

I thought of calling the physician in to assist me, yet I had to minimise the risk of rumours spreading that I was indulging this madman. So in his place I tried my best to adopt the role of analyst, to play along with Nemec's game, to see if some scrap of evidence could be retrieved from his lunacy. The prisoner looked about the cell from his bed, ecstasy surfacing in his expression. His face thrust upwards towards the ceiling, sighing in awe, he waved a thin arm through the air, his thumb and forefinger pressed together as if sketching an imagined and majestic interior. As he did so the Countess continued speaking.

"My master built this palace for me alone. He did not tell me who or what I was or why I must never leave its confines. He seldom spoke in my company. All that I know is that he was a great man. The books he brought me were my only mentors. From their pages I learned that I was not born as man is born. I was made."

Nemec fell silent. A further change seemed to have come over him, his face softening in the lamplight became a low moon lighting the barren field of his bed. Fatigue was getting to me. Before I could stop myself I found that I'd addressed him as Countess, and without correcting my slip of the tongue encouraged the prisoner to speak on.

"The Great Work, that was what my master called me. I have been known by so many names. In the pages he left here in my sanctuary I have read of others' failed operations. I have found my likeness in the diagrams of many rare books, yet know I will never meet another of my kind. I have been alone too long to believe that's possible. Had he hoped that this house and its galleries might serve as my education, indeed as my life, and that this secluded world would be enough. I have seen those illustrations of clay infants curled up asleep in vessels. I am nothing but the vital component of a greater process. I am not an individual. I am this place, this house . . . this event as it unfolds."

Nemec was sitting upright, naked to the waist, his skin the colour of chalk, his long throat craning upward. In the sinews of his scrawny frame I glimpsed another quality I struggled to identify: was it a kind of elegance? Had his skin become smoother, finer, or even lustrous? I asked the prisoner where the Countess was hidden, but it was as if he hadn't heard me. Nemec dwindled into the background now, as the flame of the Countess glowed into the cell.

"My master decreed that I should become a rumour so that his enemies would never find me, and that the world could never contaminate what I might become. He desired for me to no longer believe that we had ever known each other. He said it would be better if even I no longer believed what I was, so that if captured I might be mistaken for a common lunatic or fool. Though there is no denying the evidence of my anatomy." Nemec stretched out his thin, naked arms as if in supplication.

The prisoner defeated me that night. I could do nothing but listen and transcribe what the Countess proclaimed to the room, as if delivering a sermon to an invisible audience. I asked her who this master was, yet the voice was oblivious to anything outside its dream.

"Who am I to doubt my master's wisdom? He had his reasons for hiding me here, so far from man, so long ago that I have forgotten. And yet he would come here to consult me for he believed me to be blessed, he believed that I was an oracle. It saddens me still to think that such a man could so easily fall victim to charlatans. His desire to believe in the poetry of this world was all too much for him to bear alone. Indeed his physician, the celebrated Paracelsist Maier, was consulted. That is why I was made, to be his secret companion. Yet emperors are only mortal men, and so I am alone again."

I watched as Nemec pretended to draw upon the thin air between us with his fingertip. It took me a moment before I realised he was tracing the contours of my face from his perspective. I was too tired to protest. I felt my fists loosen as I watched his lips.

"How he tired of the intrigues of court, retreating into the secret theatre he'd made within these walls. He neglected his crown to trace the lines in my palm, to find the great in the small. He called me his precious stone. He said I was the gold of time. My body was his bestiary. The languages of birds and flowers and beasts commune beneath my skin." The prisoner reached out, his fingers finding mine as the aromas and songs of a garden fell into the darkness between us.

The guard awoke me in the early hours of the morning. He said he had found me asleep in my chair at the foot of the prisoner's bed, slumped forward, my notebook open on the floor. The prisoner was still awake, yet silently stared up at the ceiling. I ordered the guard to tell no one of this.

III. Hide Yourself War

14th September 1939

I asked my deputy to wake me after a few hours' rest in my office. I would resume questioning Nemec later that day. Let him sleep, I thought, then drag him from bed and see how he acts, see if this Countess shows her face then! So once awake I gave my orders to the deputy to rouse Nemec and have him brought immediately to my office.

The creature that my deputy manhandled into the chair squinted back at me like a mole. His shirt was still unbuttoned. If his skin had possessed its own inner light last night it showed no sign of doing so again. I told him to pull himself together. Nemec composed himself without acknowledging the mistreatment he had just suffered.

The prisoner claimed to have no recollection of our previous dialogue. I asked him straight if he was protecting someone who was in hiding. If so, I said, he was putting himself at unnecessary risk. I stated that anything that he confided in me need not be disclosed to the Protectorate's command. We could strike up a bargain. If the fugitive's whereabouts were made known to us we could at least deflect Gestapo enquiries. I suggested to the prisoner that with his cooperation we might find this Countess together and thereby eliminate her from the investigation. Kindness always caught them off guard. Sometimes it paid to humour such suspects as from time to time an indirect approach unearthed something useful. There must be some semblance of truth to what he was saying, I thought. If we could only lure Nemec into playing along, with his assistance we could perhaps make preliminary searches and find something that may at least defer my superiors' demands. I suggested that he could show us the general area in person; by returning there he might better recall the events prior to his arrest.

"No, I won't take you there; it is out of the question. And besides I'd struggle to retrace my steps without Otakar as my guide." I could see my deputy's anger rising at the insolence of this waif. I dismissed him from the room to be alone with the prisoner again, pouring him a cup of water.

"So, Mr. Nemec, if you recall, you were recounting how this manservant, this Otakar, took you to a house somewhere that night, the night you met him above the café? Let's return to that point now." I wondered again if the Countess's voice that I had heard only the night before might return if provoked with the correct line of questioning. From my office window one could see the Vltava snaking beyond the rooftops wet with rain. As the prisoner stared into the distant streets outside I have no doubt that he was imagining the secret route to her hiding place. When he spoke his voice sounded resigned to defeat.

"I remember thinking how lost I was as I crossed the Countess's door that night. Was it a trap of some sort, I thought? Whether it was the alcohol I do not know, yet a part of me didn't care. I had nothing to lose. In fact I welcomed whatever disaster might come. I followed as Otakar slipped into the shadows of the passage ahead. As we reached a pool of lamplight he gestured down a tilting passage and patted my shoulder when we reached a doorway to the left.

"The room was much taller than it was broad. He offered me a seat by an open fire, the only source of light in the confined space. Shadows wavered about the peeling walls. There were no visible windows, only high heavy drapes drawn across the far side of the room. He sat before me in a wing-backed chair surrounded by towers of books and clutter. Etchings depicting naked forms flickered in the gloom. A low table occupied the space between us. The old lion poured me a drink from a decanter I hadn't noticed and leaning forward in his chair slid the glass towards me across its polished surface. We raised our glasses in a silent toast and I downed the drink in one. My heart dropped as I saw my host empty his glass upon the fire, causing the flames to erupt at once. The concoction went straight to my head. Relaxing into his chair with a sigh of satisfaction, Otakar began to speak. Casting his eyes toward the high ceiling, it struck me that he was recalling a rehearsed speech, something he had been told to recite.

" 'Trust me and surrender,' he said. 'Few know these paths and fewer still are prepared to risk them. My mistress only appears to those who do.'

"I tried to speak, but he silenced me with a wave of his hand, untying then slipping a black kerchief from his throat which had previously been concealed by his beard. Whatever it was that I'd been so foolish to drink was quick to take effect. My eyes began to burn and blur.

"Otakar's amber eyes gleamed hypnotically. As I attempted to speak again, finding my tongue numb in my mouth, he shook a finger at me, and running the length of black cloth through his hands, rose to his feet and walked to the rear of my chair.

"He whispered, 'It is customary that guests of the Countess undertake a test, a trial.'

"He brought the cloth down over my eyes and plunged me into darkness. As I swallowed my panic I felt him tying the blindfold at the nape of my neck. I tried to lift my hands, but found the effort laborious. It was then that I

The Feast of the Sphinx

realised I was weak, as though my limbs were perpetually waking from sleep. I'd been poisoned, and expected at any moment to choke. While the concoction may have impaired my body, my thoughts raced, multiplying in response to the least sound or movement. With a hand under my elbow he encouraged me to stand. He brought another glass to my lips; I struggled against downing its contents and managed to splutter some down my chin. He tugged at my arm and instructed me to follow. Only then did I understand that, by some sleight of hand, he had bound my wrists behind my back. Due to the drug, my movements became leaden, my progress slow. He led me from the room into the hall, I am certain of that much; where I was taken after that I don't know. He simply said that my compliance in the ritual would be necessary if I wanted to meet with the Countess. With the sound of doors opening and shutting, we moved through rooms pungent with damp and dust. A hand on my shoulder suddenly pushed me forward and I stumbled onto wooden stairs. Otakar began to speak again as I slowly found my feet, the concoction already addling my balance, I kicked each step as I slowly and unsteadily ascended in darkness, stumbling and striking my head again and again. His voice resounded around me in the enclosed space of the stairwell. Perhaps he repeated these words like an incantation for they stay with me now.

" 'Something must be lost. That is the way with pacts. We roam the threadbare seams between day and dream. Here maps lose their form, borders warp and the moment devours the watchful and the unwary alike. No one can meet my mistress without walking these paths.'

"As I climbed the stairs I became aware of faint hypnotic music playing somewhere above me. The steps seemed to loosen under my feet as the tight stairway forced me to contort my body. As the ascent suddenly grew much steeper, I pressed my knees against the steps to keep my balance. My heart was pounding in my chest. I heard wings beating about my ears. All the while Otakar's voice rang out around me.

" 'Something must be lost. That is the way with pacts. Something must be given. Something must be sacrificed,' he chanted.

"Another door opened into a room filled with sickly incense. The faint music I'd heard earlier suddenly became much louder. I entered to the sound of warped violins. As I stepped forward I was met by many hands that spun me on the spot until I staggered this way and that, my disorientation heightened. Those same hands tore at my clothes and slapped and pinched my flesh. A muffled cacophony of animal calls broke out in distant rooms. Other limbs contorted around my body, interlocking with my own arms and legs in an unseen dance. Lithe bodies pressed against me as long locks of hair whipped against my face and were stuffed into my mouth. Other laughing female mouths found mine only to slip away to bite playfully at my throat and fingers.

"I was guided again through another door to another staircase, even steeper than the last, where the wooden steps creaked beneath my weight. I reached what I imagined was a confined attic room, its floorboards shuddered underfoot. I couldn't help myself. I admit it, I laughed. I was delirious. In that same instant I expected to have my throat cut. Again someone took hold of me and propelled me across the room. Other hands caught me and within a second I found myself sitting upright in a chair. My hands had been freed of their bindings. I reached up to pull away the blindfold yet many people grasped my hands and pushed their naked bodies against my palms, guiding my fingers across contours and into furrows. I thought of the Countess and called out her name.

"All the while Otakar was speaking another incantation.

" 'At each turn a new mask blossoms in the night. You must forget how to be human. You must become monstrous.' He said these words again and again as he untied the blindfold. My hands still trembled, yet my seducers were nowhere to be seen. The effect of the drug was levelling out, as if reaching a plateau in the reverie it induced.

"I spluttered at the centre of a circle of light. I could make out a wall, and fixed to its crumbling surface was a large oval picture frame. Both Otakar and the source of illumination lay somewhere unseen behind the chair. From out of the darkness, a pair of hands thrust a wide wooden board into my lap. There was a blank white page pinned in place.

"I was still shaking as a panel slid open within the empty oval frame. A face slowly appeared through the black aperture.

" 'The Countess,' Otakar announced from the shadows, as a hand gripped mine, pushing a pencil between my fingers.

" 'Be quick now, begin your study, your portrait,' the lion whispered. 'Be quick, try to catch her before she vanishes again. If she lingers then you'll know that she favours you.'

"It was as though my hand moved of its own accord under her gaze. Trembling, I tried to draw the face within the large oval frame. I do not know how long I was there or how many attempts I made to retrace the pencil across the page only to see it dance in unintended directions. Yet a picture took form all the same, a spectral portrait of a face surfacing through clouded water. Each time I looked upon the face I wanted to tear myself away, and yet I was compelled to return my gaze again. A light shimmered beneath that face's new-born skin. There was a promise behind those half-closed lids. The tip of a scarlet tongue traced the line of her lips. Was there something fearful in the beauty of that face, or something in my own fear that I found alluring? The Countess's mouth quivered as if unaccustomed to speaking. Instead she gave out a cry, yet I could not say whether it was anguish or satisfaction.

" 'Come closer.' Her tone fell somewhere between a purr and a sigh. As I took a few steps from the chair my eyes followed a line from her chin down her long slender throat. Her breasts were partially veiled in the shadows by a fan of lustrous feathers. Her thick black hair was pinned high upon her head and was adorned in some way with clusters of precious stones. The darkness of her chamber on the other side of the oval frame swam about her; heraldic murals on the dim walls stirred into life, great baroque limbs and wings unfurling. I wanted to reach through that aperture and touch her porcelain skin. A smile played at her lips as I tried to do so, yet she slipped further back into the recesses, her face glimmering in green shadows as if its flame may at any moment be extinguished. As she plunged into the gloom, I caught sight of the supple arch of her spine and the restless tail of a great cat.

" 'Come back to me,' she said before finally vanishing into the night.

"The drawing was snatched from my grasp. I tried to complain, but Otakar tied the blindfold around my head once more and, taking my arm, led me back the way we'd come. We walked on through passages, and I heard many doors open then close behind me. When he removed the blindfold again I was standing at the entrance to the house, the ruined garden before me and the quiet street beyond.

The Feast of the Sphinx

"Otakar walked some distance with me, how far I can't be sure; his hand on my shoulder guided me along unfamiliar lanes. When we parted he said that I should find him at the café the following evening and to tell no one. His words lingered as I walked on alone through the early morning. My hands were still trembling, traces of pencil lead on my fingertips. As I returned home exhausted the statues that I passed readily joined with my memories of the Countess's house. With a building momentum, and with the gravity of sleep, each statue seemed to greet me along the way. They became characters in the same drama, and it was inevitable that I would take my place amongst them. As I crossed the threshold of that greater story, I hoped that all memory of my own life would be lost in its many passages. I longed to be no more than a rumour in the streets of Prague. I hungered to see her face again. I wanted only to please her. That morning I fell into bed and dreamt that the Countess spoke to me. She predicted the coming of the enemy."

Nemec was revived by his recollection. I asked him what the Countess had told him in his dream and when he spoke, it was in her voice again, yet this time the prisoner didn't flinch. The transition had occurred within the blinking of an eye.

"Nemec, do you hear me, Nemec? I speak to you from the other side of the mirror as you sleep. Do not try to resist and I will tell you of things yet to come, things that I have seen on this side of the glass.

"From the darkness I see crowds emerge, herds silently fill the streets. They wander quietly without aim, nervously eyeing an army of strangers arriving in the city. These strangers all look the same. These men in uniforms swarm around the monuments. They are everywhere, marching in rank and file. Each bridgehead is guarded and at every corner sentries watch for those who have too much to say.

"And then the suicides begin. People throw themselves from windows and bodies fill the Vltava. People cry out in the streets, begging to leave. It is too late. The Josefov shrinks behind walls of shadow. Dreamers are imprisoned. Only the devout are allowed into the castle on the hill to pay tribute to a man on a high balcony. He returns their salutes as banners glisten with blood."

With that the prisoner fell into a deep sleep.

IV. Night After Night

16th September 1939

The prisoner slept for most of the previous day. I thought it was wise to let him recuperate before I pushed him further. I had to be his guide and judge how best to pace our approach. The last time I spoke with him he'd become exhausted by recounting a dream. When he speaks with that other voice it burns him out, as if consuming him from the inside. My colleagues could never appreciate what I might have found in this prisoner. His presence in the station had put them on edge, as if they feared that a wild animal or disease was in their midst. I barely understand what it could mean, yet I see something in Nemec, some kind of promise. It would be madness to admit such things to others. They know nothing about the suspect's obsession. Did I dream of the Countess last night? Yes, I followed Nemec to her hiding place. Paintings of strange beasts on walls stirred into life. The prisoner was there too, yet unharmed and full of vitality. The Countess instructed him to draw my portrait; he did so wearing a blindfold. I expected that he would at any moment be executed. Did she speak to me with the pris-

The Feast of the Sphinx

oner's voice? Her house must be found. If need be I will search for it myself.

The Superintendent called me to a meeting. An official representative of the Protectorate had telegrammed directives. A timescale for the resolution of the case had been agreed without my consultation. Irrespective of any findings, it would seem the outcome had already been decided.

I had Nemec brought to my office again; the view over the city served as a tool, a stimulus that perhaps offered him hope of reuniting with his mistress.

"Tell me, Mr. Nemec, what happened then? This Countess, was she . . . is she a beautiful woman . . . an artist like you perhaps? Did you serve her in some way? You must recall her name, surely?"

"You ask many questions. One thing at a time, please." The prisoner smiled back at me vacantly, a dummy without a ventriloquist, baring yellow teeth. It took every effort to refrain from striking him across his insolent face. Perhaps sensing this he quickly resumed his story.

"I have dreamed of my journey home from the Countess's house many times, Otakar walking some distance behind me, prowling in the shadows. I recall as I walked I lost the thread that might lead me back. Try as I might, I could not imagine a route back to the Countess's house. I can think of no way back there now. Those streets have vanished into thin air.

"Despite my hunger I didn't stray from my apartment for days. I was under her spell. In her absence I made drawings, trying desperately to recall some semblance of how she had appeared to me. Night after night I filled pages, countless delicate drawings of hands and lips and eyes depicted from many perspectives. As I ran out of materials, I returned to the same pages and covered the surfaces with further layers and textures. In the knotted fabric of these drawings, I chased a single golden thread that would lead me back to her, back into the web of her flesh.

"An uncommon quiet in the street one morning roused me from bed, and at my window I looked down to find the pavements almost deserted. The few people I saw pass by seemed fretful. From time to time I could not resist returning to the window to peer down into the street again. That same subdued air deterred me from venturing outside until evening had come. The common life of the city had been disturbed; it seemed people had retreated from one another. The few I passed on my return to the Café Montmartre looked about pensively as they went on their way. I found that I did the same, wary of shadows in back lanes, walking with the impression that I was being observed. Fear had arrived through anticipation alone. It was as though unseen enemies already occupied the city. I thought only of reaching the café, to meet my guide Otakar, believing I would find solace there. At first he did not come.

"So for days and nights on end I waited. I came and went, always returning to my own room, yet yearning to join her in hiding, to become her servant. I saw her face everywhere; in the folds of my bed clothes, or the cracked surfaces of walls; that face with the texture of butter and of chalk, with drowsy opalescent eyes and lids half closed. I was mesmerised by her long slender throat, her delicate hands that at times were claws, her black hair falling loose from a jewelled circlet to snake around her naked collarbones. Her mouth of moist petals whispered something I couldn't discern. The fine blue lace under the surface of her skin occupied my thoughts in the small hours. It was the same in the depths of every night; I watched her in the darkness emerging from the fabric hanging at my window. Her body as curtains on a theatrical stage, a deep blue silently opening onto a rich red that bled like ink blossoming in water; as I entered I knew I was lost. I knew I would drown in her. Every night to the soft drumming of a great heart I welcomed the coming of that ritual where she beckoned me back into her lair. That was the secret discipline in her game. It was as if with every attempt I was picking at the seams of the world with my pencil and letting something through, something uncontrollable. And with each attempt I felt an increasing compulsion, a pleasure in abandoning myself to whatever I was unleashing through my actions. It felt as though I was taking revenge upon the world.

"Each morning I'd awake in a city more afraid. As rumours of the encroaching enemy increased, so did my desire to escape to the house. And each evening I'd make my way to the café to meet with the ancient lion Otakar in the hope he would be there to take me to her again.

"I recall how the old lion had said that I should never try to call at the door without him and should never bring friends. That request was easily granted; I hadn't seen my friends since meeting Otakar and thought it likely they'd fled the city for good. I admitted to him that I'd panicked and tried to find the place alone, yet the route always eluded me. He said that was to be expected, only in longing to return would I will him to answer me.

"After days of waiting I found my guide again, seated in the corner where we'd first made our pact. Through the many nights that followed we performed our final rituals, coming and going along the course of a spiralling path that orbited her secret heart. Every night was the same. All our words, all our gestures were scripted. I knew Otakar would again escort me back to where I would be blindfolded and led to an ever-deeper chamber of the house.

"There, as before, I would see her face emerging at an aperture in the wall. Each time her face appeared to differ, sometimes the bone structure had changed, or the colouration or elasticity of her flesh had altered. On some nights she was little more than an adolescent and on others a wise beldam, her history evident in the lines of her skin. At first I suspected a ploy, that the Countess was a part played by many actors or a small cast expert at disguise. Yet it seemed that Otakar hinted each time we met that my perseverance would be rewarded, that in time I could become a trusted witness to her transformation. On one such night as I was leaving I remarked that my initiation appeared to be nearing completion, yet my enthusiasm proved premature. Otakar only spoke to say that he would meet me again the following evening. As I descended the steps to the street he called out to me that tomorrow would be different, tomorrow we would prepare for a great feast.

"In my dream that night the Countess escorted me to the muddy shores of the Vltava at dusk. I glanced behind me and saw her there, stooped with one hand covering her face while the other waved me on towards the water. Behind her the black branches of the trees seemed singed, as though curling at the edge of an unseen fire. The mud pushed up through my toes as the sky sparkled like water. I stood there a while watching strange forms I knew did not exist in waking life cross a bridge. In those silhouetted bestial shapes I found an echo of those I had seen painted on the walls of the Countess's palace. Within the dream it occurred to me that I was witnessing the demonstration of a principle or process that I must fathom.

"The monstrous procession embraced every animal form and every imaginable stage of metamorphosis. While it seemed these hybrid beasts were locked in mating, it slowly became clear that within the contortions of that host something else was taking place: maws opened to bite at flesh and claws tore at sinew. Just then I felt the

The Feast of the Sphinx

Countess's hands on my shoulders. She was pushing me to my knees and although fearing her motives I silently acquiesced. She smeared my face with handfuls of mud from the Vltava, forming a mask. We lay together at the water's edge. When I awoke I could still feel her mouth pressed to mine."

While transcribing the prisoner's story, I imagined her mouth too. I poured Nemec a cup of water and surprised us both when I carried the drink over to him while he remained seated in his chair. He looked up at me and, hardly daring to believe what he'd just experienced, thanked me. I was quick to redress the balance.

"So why should she choose you of all people? I mean, look at you, you're little more than a vagrant."

"So you believe me then? You have started to believe she exists? The others, your men, laugh and deride me when I speak of her." The prisoner shrank in his chair.

"What? You mustn't speak of her to them, understand? This is only between us. You must see that you can trust me. You must have guessed that I'm holding the wolves at bay single-handedly. Any day now a call might come from the Gestapo, you understand? And it lands on me to answer them. What would you say if I could arrange for you to look for her? You'd still be in my custody of course and under supervision. Yet it might take us closer to where . . . "

"No, I can't take you there. Even if I knew, I would not show you the way. I can tell by your face that you've started to hear her voice too. Do you see her in dreams? That is as close as you will ever get, I'm afraid," Nemec said quite matter-of-factly, without satisfaction.

Still standing before him I struck the cup of water from his grasp, and before I knew it I had Nemec's throat between my hands. I could have effortlessly throttled the little wretch, yet I took one look into his eyes and my grip slackened. He fell unconscious to the floor. At the sound of the scuffle a guard entered. Instead of ordering him to take the suspect away, I had him help me prop Nemec back up in the chair. I dismissed the guard for the evening and told my colleagues I would be staying late. They knew better than to question my methods. Despite their superstitions, I told them, Nemec posed no real threat and besides the night-watch would soon be on duty.

V. The Phantom Object

17th September 1939

It was becoming difficult to shield Nemec from my superiors. They were growing impatient. If only a diversion was possible, or a reprieve, or a deal that could be brokered. And if that wasn't enough reports of the prisoner calling out from his cell at night had become common knowledge. A rumour had started to circulate amongst the night-watch that the prisoner conversed with an imaginary companion, a woman. Some had taken to provoking him in the hope that they might hear him speak in tongues. Since the occupation began things became increasingly bitter, as though there was a contagion on the air. Its symptoms seemed particularly acute in those who held positions of authority. I sensed that certain officers of lower rank had become insolent enough to openly express their suspicions about my motives towards the prisoner. If I disciplined them for insubordination I ran the risk of drawing further attention to the case. Is this an indication that my methods, my preoccupation with this case, had come under scrutiny elsewhere, higher up the chain of command? It doesn't take long before rumour becomes reputation and you're tainted by association.

The Feast of the Sphinx

The prisoner's confiscated possessions arrived today from his apartment. They were delivered to my office in a crate that showed distinct signs of having been tampered with. I had no doubt they'd passed through Gestapo hands first as some of the artwork had been crumpled and torn. I had greatly underestimated the significance of Nemec's belongings as evidence. Besides the reams of obsessively executed drawings, there were pages of long scrawled passages, some clearly attempts to recollect his supposed encounters with the Countess, while other strange texts had seemingly been written under the influence of this alter ego. I'd consulted our resident physician and he'd given me some ideas, guidance if you will, in matters of interpreting such behaviour.

There she was, the seductive face of the Countess, in hundreds of obsessive and overlaid renditions. In some her mouth had been depicted in such tantalisingly sensuous detail that it was as if one's fingertip might be moistened at its touch. There were nude studies where great sinuous lines brought numerous limbs together in interlocking patterns. Anatomical sketches embraced cornucopias of strange fruit and baroque vegetation. Yet through it all the ghost of the Countess could be traced, her countless graceful hands dancing from the page, her eyes rolling up into lids half-closed in ecstasy.

I considered how I might confront the prisoner with these visions, to see if they might act as a trigger. I pored through the pages of his haphazard journal, searching for useful clues:

> *Finally I was allowed to follow the Countess deeper and deeper into the house. Each room was a cabinet, great glass panels clouded with dust half-concealed countless curios and treasures. Every time she turned*

to peer over her shoulder her face had changed in some almost indiscernible way. With deft fingers she slipped her gown from her shoulder to show a breast glowing in the lamplight, as if illumined from within. With a flick of her wrist, a fan of brushes or quills appeared which she used to deftly execute a spontaneous image upon the nearest wall. I tried to follow her every movement, to grasp her method and technique.

There were rooms hung with ancient unfinished canvases, layer upon layer, collapsed and torn in the half-light. Her hands danced across the surfaces leaving impressions of leaf and feather in ink. In those spaces she would elude me, my hands slipping from her skin. She would vanish only to emerge a moment later in another corner of the chamber, on all fours on her bed, somehow a fusion of cat and swan. Opening great wings she revealed a further dance; the soft clay of her flesh became malleable to her touch. Her skin's surface gave way like milk to her fingertips. Her vulva was an imaginary fruit, a succulent and soft hybrid of pomegranate and pear. She allowed my gaze to linger a while, yet as she turned away shadows soon concealed the wonder again. I lived in and for that secret gaze.

There were more accounts, if that's what they were, recollections perhaps of a woman who had once tried to shelter him. Who had she been? An idealised lover or one of the women from the brothel? So far none of the passages mentioned her by name. Such a name might act as a key. The city's history glimmered from his journal, references that were oddly familiar to me from classes at school. Certainly every Czech and Slovak child learned of Rudolf II and knew him as the mad Emperor obsessed with alchemy and magic.

The Feast of the Sphinx

In the shadows of these chambers I could make out many large etchings by the artist Spranger on the walls, and although they mouldered in their frames, enough of the compositions survived for me to discern their subjects. These had not been pictures exclusively designed to arouse the Emperor. Certainly many of them depicted scenes of nude men and women caressing and coupling, yet the other characteristics of these scenes implied an ethos or code of some kind. If the illustrations were made to instruct, then these allegories of sensuality and love promised no easy satisfactions. No, these were encounters played out in secluded interiors, by secret pools and strange vessels, places hidden in desperation from the world's corrupting influence. Desire had made these lovers exiles. The dreaming temples in which these acts occurred took on a poignant air as the lovers' unions culminated in fierce transformations: phoenixes burning in an endless night.

While the cabinets were in a state of dissolution, I found a form of splendour there, as if the decay that invaded every corner possessed a tender appreciation of what it had come to destroy. Indeed a subtle mimicry of the etchings was taking place; from the decomposing furnishings and walls, the shapes of entwined beasts and lovers could be seen emerging and coalescing. From mirrors maps seeped and black fungal shadows flourished where they pooled. The passages and rooms showed signs of having been immersed in water for many years, as if the river that had once ran through it had inexplicably changed course leaving the place haunted in its wake. It was as if the interior had been formed by natural conditions rather than built by human hand, the cavernous impression emphasised by the indiscernible flotsam amassed along walls and the rotted rafters that had collapsed to form worm-eaten stalactites.

"Listen and dream, Mr. Nemec," she said. Remember Arcimboldo, the great painter who created the Wunderkammer, the Emperor's cabinets of curiosities? Who else could devise a palace concealed in the very heart of Prague, hidden behind secret doors that only my master could find and enter? The walls of that sealed world were decorated with the anatomies of impossible animals, of vegetation and fruit only glimpsed in dreams, with murals of great lost gardens depicted on the edge of decline; a celebration of decay, melancholy and formless night. He knew that I could have no other home, my beloved Vertumnus.

It was as though the voices of Nemec and the Countess became less and less distinguishable as the obsessive dialogue blossomed.

Arcimboldo promised me many halls of mirrors, iridescent mirrors in which I might see myself distorted again and again, a multitude emerging from the depths of the palace, roots and blossoms erupting from my many limbs and faces. After my master's death the palace and I were left to its shadows, abandoned to brood and gestate. In decay and neglect new forms proliferated, hybrids of dream and rumour yearned for release, for communion. This will be my feast day. Who will paint my portrait? Who will help me return?

The Feast of the Sphinx

VI. At the Golden Tree

18th September 1939

Again, the prisoner claimed to have no recollection of our recent dialogue. I showed him a sample of his belongings that we'd retrieved from his rooms. I informed him that he had been evicted as the property of his former landlords had been seized by the occupying forces. He didn't seem to care about the fate of his home, yet reached out to take the drawings from my hands, fastidiously smoothing the crumples and creases in the paper with his fingertips.

"Do these things of yours help you to remember? Who was she? You must tell me if you know where she is." Some part of me doubted the worth of making such an appeal to the prisoner's emotions when he so often seemed scarcely human.

"What is she to you? Your kind will never find her. She is not for you. She won't let you harm me. I belong to her." The prisoner's shoulders shook as if trying not to sob.

He reminded me of a wounded and cornered animal. Although I had received no further demands from above, the chain of command having become suspiciously quiet, I still wanted to give the prisoner the impression that a sword was hanging over his head. As if deflecting my questions, Nemec began to pick up the thread of his story, seemingly recounting the tale irrespective of whether anyone was there to listen.

"Each time I returned home the streets were quieter still, and those that passed by did so as apparitions. Even when gathered in greater numbers, in the nearby square for instance, others appeared to me as somehow insubstantial, as though a vital part of them was missing. I lived only for that hidden world now, anticipating the event that the Countess had called the Feast.

"Although it was still early evening when I arrived, Otakar was waiting in the café. He immediately got to his feet as I neared our usual corner. Without a word he looked to the door and touched my shoulder as he passed. I'd wanted to drink and eat but followed him out into the street all the same.

"As I trailed behind the old beast, I guessed that he was taking me to the Countess's house by yet another route. None of the streets were familiar to me from previous nights until we reached the lane leading to the house itself. The impossible thought occurred to me that there were many entrances to the house scattered throughout the city, so that no matter where I was, it was simply a case of knowing how to enter using a secret key. That key, which could only be found in trusting Otakar, allowed me access to the Countess's house, but at the cost of distancing me from the life I'd known. Each time I returned to the city's streets with a greater conviction that I was losing my home, my past, and my memory. That sense of unease stayed with me throughout our journey, as though the city I'd known only several days before had been replaced by an inferior simulacrum. I saw her likeness everywhere: in crumbling walls and in heaps of refugees' belongings abandoned along roadsides and in doorways. In the compulsion to return to her, I was losing track of time. This was the sacrifice that Otakar had spoken of. This was the pact I had to make.

"Immediately upon entering the house, Otakar led me to the room where he'd given me the drugged elixir. That seemed so long ago. If that was the same room then it had been emptied. The fireplace was dead and the space only dimly illuminated. Heavy drapes still concealed the far side of the room. I awaited his instructions.

"He blindfolded me once more and led me from the room through numerous passages and doors. This time my hands were left unbound and I was able to steady myself as I climbed the steep stairs. Finally he loosened the kerchief from my eyes.

"Otakar turned to me and said, 'We call this wing of the palace The Bestiary. Your arrival could not have come at a more auspicious time. The Feast . . . we are preparing for the Feast.' He was almost breathless. We proceeded through galleries now that were hung with portraits of women. At first I supposed that the faces shared a familial resemblance, but as I walked on I saw that they were not only attempts at rendering a likeness of the same sitter, that of the Countess, but all had been abandoned at various stages of composition and reworked only to be abandoned again. Some had been mutilated. Many of the faces were malformed and some bore the aspects of an owl, for instance, or a peacock or ibis. Some framed works on paper were badly creased, ripped, or indeed burnt in places, as though retrieved from a fire. Other canvases had been gashed and punctured.

"The old lion looked deep into my eyes and said, 'You will continue with your drawings. In return she will protect you, hide you. She will give you sanctuary now. The trial is at an end. You have waited long enough. Now the celebrations can begin.'

"I told him that no one would be safe in the city once the soldiers came. He simply replied that the Feast could not happen without me. So I was an honoured guest. That was why I'd been put through these trials. I was to join her court, to serve her and perhaps more than that. It was possible that these rituals and tests I'd undergone were to prove my mettle, to earn her hand.

"Otakar walked to the door, opened it and gestured for me to follow. At last I was able to join him without the blindfold. Yet no matter how much I questioned him about his mistress's expectations, he evaded me by speaking of the ceremonies of the household. With a lamp held high he advanced, casting a shadow that engulfed me.

"We walked through tight passages that seemed to have no reasoning or purpose to their plan. At times we passed dead ends filled with all manner of hoarded debris, and in others one could discern what seemed to be shrines: extinguished votive candles cluttered makeshift tabernacles from which dusty portraits peered. Some were familiar to me, but it took time before recognition fully dawned that they were varying renditions of the same subject: the Habsburg Emperor Rudolf II. For all the deserved awe surrounding that sovereign, the peculiar bearded crescent of his face and doleful eyes had always provoked an amused pity in me. Perhaps that was the only fitting response to a man who did not quite belong to this world, a man so steeped in tragedy and magic. We pushed on deeper into the house, only pausing for Otakar to tap the wall in such a way as to release the mechanism of a hidden panel that slid aside to allow us access to another passage. He turned and asked, 'Now do you really think you could find your own way out of here without me? You still need me to guide you, to bring you here every evening and return you to the world each morning.'

"In the light of Otakar's lamp my gaze followed the sinuous murals of feathered serpents along the walls. Under foot the threadbare carpet gave way to boards covered in either ancient seaweed or once-lustrous plumage. The scent of the place was intoxicating; incense mingled with the aromas of musty wood and plaster, evoking thoughts of secluded gardens rather than a house falling into dereliction. Had the old lion used the word sanctuary in some earlier conversation? If so, it seemed so appropriate that he should, although the house was much more than that: it was an institute of some kind, a place whose features had been built to influence its inhabitants. At times I heard movement through ceilings, floors, and walls. Occasional knocking passed from one wall to another seemingly in a chain of coded requests and responses. Somewhere deliberate or cantering footsteps could be heard approaching or diminishing. I heard the calls of beasts and birds, yet suspected their source was a gramophone.

" 'We're nearly there at her bed chamber, you must prepare.' We reached the end of the last gallery where Otakar genuflected before a door. He gestured that I should go first, and as he did so he placed a hand on my shoulder. Untying the kerchief from his neck, he secured the blindfold over my eyes again.

"I heard the door opening and was greeted by scents of moist earth and undergrowth. I was helped into a chair. I guessed that Otakar remained close by. As before, I heard the distinctive hiss of a panel sliding open and then a faint voice. It trembled through the darkness. There was something familiar in its cadence. The sense of recognition her voice provoked in me was fleeting, mischievously playing with my memories of voices I had once known throughout my life. She teased me, tempting me to think I knew to whom the voice belonged when it suddenly changed to become the voice of another. And just as I thought I'd grasped a memory, I felt its hair dance through my fingers.

"Like a child reciting a riddle, she addressed me:

" 'To gaze upon me is to find the great in the small, to find the mutable in the stable and secrets in the surfaces of things. I am the absent double, the mirror of the world, a jewel turning in the night. My body is the host for a great feast and you must sacrifice yourself at my banquet. Yet it is never the feast that is prepared for us, that is served to us at an assigned table. Nor is it the meat especially anointed for us by priests of whatever persuasion. It is not the satiation of a hunger for what is laid before us by way of a conjuring act. It cannot be found in contentment with the meagre scraps left for us by our masters each morning. The world is not a carcass waiting for our impatient hands to descend upon it. You cannot partake in the feast until you have foraged and hunted and been wounded by your quarry.'

"How I can recall that word for word I don't know, but that is what the Countess said to me that night. I will never forget. I would take you there if I could. I would tell you where to find her, if only to stop the pain. I will never know now. I cannot return. Tell me why you need to find her. I cannot confess things I do not know. I have no secrets to keep. I will tell you everything if you can only show me how. Believe if you will that it was only trickery to lead weak minds astray. If so, then I am weak. I was glad to surrender. Yes, I am certain there is gold there for those who know how to look for it, but I cannot take you there.

"Perhaps she expected me to solve her riddle. As I turned her words over in my mind, I felt Otakar's hands untying the knot of my blindfold. As the blindfold fell away, my eyes were dazzled by a constellation of candles scattered about the walls and floor. The room that took shape before me was a grotto filled with cracked and blistered mirrors, crumbling fonts and shell-encrusted effigies. I wondered what part these relics played in the rituals of that closed world. I had expected to see her bed, yet instead across the room, directly opposite the chair in which I sat, four sinuous pillars sprouted from the corners of an altar cluttered with paper, pencils, pots, and brushes. Between the pillars, set into the wall, there was an oval cavity serving as some kind of tabernacle. At first this aperture appeared empty but then, as I trained my eyes more intently on the opening, I could make out a spectral form shivering there. Flickering in the darkness there was the mouth and slender throat of a woman barely illuminated by the candlelight. It was as though a portrait had sprung to life in its frame. The mouth smiled widely but said nothing as Otakar walked towards the aperture in the wall. From the altar he took paper and pencils.

"As if in imitation of the incense burning within the recess, the Countess's face seemed to perceptibly shift and warp like tendrils of smoke. Her pale powdered complexion resembled that of a living bust, the head of a sphinx swathed in mist. Her black hair was drawn back from her forehead, fixed in place with a jewelled diadem and pins. Her eyes met mine, her pupils two bottomless ink-drops, growing ever wider.

" 'Begin, Mr. Nemec, put pencil to paper. Summon me from nothing. Find me in the darkness. Give me form. Feast your eyes. Feast your eyes on me.' That was how the final lesson began.

" 'Begin, Mr. Nemec,' she insisted. 'Your hold here is still weaker than you think, and soon you must return to the world out there.' So I began to draw. Every time I took my eyes from her face to commit a line to the page, they returned to find her face had minutely shifted, wavering in the candlelight. Her form and my hand were caught in a dance, where the lines that I committed to the page, far from delineating her features, only unmade the solidity of her flesh. Was that a further game within this initiation? Was it all part of her seduction?

"Otakar stood in silent contemplation of my work as I continued to draw. Just as I neared the completion of her portrait, the Countess would nod or clap her hands, and I witnessed my hand and the drawing retrace itself, the line devouring its own path, returning, circling ever-inward and backwards towards the first mark, the first scoring of the page, until there was nothing and I was left to begin again. As Otakar brought down the blindfold once more I understood that the game had no end.

"As we returned to the city outside, I imagined that we were somehow walking backwards. Without the ritual I would not remember, and yet somehow that same ritual was a game that made me forget. The passages we retraced were unknown to me. It was possible that through sliding panels, or the assembly of false screens, one might entirely alter the appearance of the interior. If the palace was a theatre, it remained uncertain on which side of the curtain its illusions lay.

"All I could think about was her voice, and her face suspended in the darkness of the aperture. I imagined her breath on my lips. I imagined trailing my fingers down her throat, her skin sprouting feathers at my touch. I thought of pushing my hands into the oval space as one would into the mercury of a mirror. Otakar stood before me in silence, no doubt satisfied to see me so intoxicated at the thought of his mistress, perhaps as he had been upon initiation.

"I will not take you there. I cannot. I do not know how to return. She will not admit your kind. She will not sing for you. Her mouth will never be yours. She multiplies in the darkness, beyond your reach. Even if you were right, that it was her intention to drive me from my senses then I would embrace it. She is everywhere, restless within the skin of the world, right under your fingers if you could only see it. And yet it pleases me to know with certainty that you will never see her, you who have chosen the path that consigns all other paths to darkness. It is you and your kind that do not belong to the world. It is restless. It cannot be tamed.

"Lost in the house I thought of how far away the streets of the city seemed. I wondered what was happening out in the city and whether time passed differently there. It occurred to me that a month might pass and I wouldn't know or care. No matter how much pain you inflict, I can only repeat what she has said to me. When I speak again it will be with her voice, her breath."

With Nemec locked in his cell I retired to my office. The others went off duty, and I heard the night-watch arrive to begin their rounds. Somewhere in the distant rooms below I heard a single voice wailing. The guards must have tired of trying to silence Nemec, and concluded the only choice was to wait until the prisoner exhausted himself. I could hear the tones of the Countess within Nemec's cries, yet resisted going downstairs. It was as if she was calling out to me alone. That night I refused to answer. I drank the *slivovice* I had in my office and unfolded the bed.

In the dream Nemec sat with me on a bench on the riverbank. Great golden branches creaked overhead. I listened as the prisoner calmly explained, "But Inspector, have you not realised yet? Of course I'm mad, how else could I make sense of all this . . . how else could I have got this far?"

"Don't mock me, Nemec, or I'll have you strung up on this tree here!" I said to him, pointing behind me as I stood up. There was laughter at our backs. Turning around I saw that Nemec was already hanging from the tree, bound by one ankle, swaying upside down.

VII. The Voice of the Forest

18th September 1939

The prisoner has become constantly agitated so I had to find some way of isolating him from the scrutiny of fellow officers. It was wise to conduct all of the remaining interviews in my office rather than the interrogation cell.

He finds solace in that other voice, the voice of the Countess. Now she speaks of retribution through him. When he speaks with her voice he becomes defiant. I was prepared to sit and transcribe everything that she said, still sifting for some sign that would take me to her.

"When they come for me they will find nothing they can understand. They will find nothing that they can possess. I am the embodiment of their punishment. My blood will be a mirror for their fears. I am the stone that is also water. I have destroyed myself a thousand times over and risen up each time anew from the alembic of this house. This labyrinth of answers lives in others' voices, in the breath that whistles through their bones. My body is the Bestiary.

"Mesmerised, you will see my face in the deepest reaches of a forest. Slowly you will discern the slightest movements and staring harder into the darkness, almost unbelieving, you will see my face as a jewel turning, each facet glimmering with another likeness. No sooner will you grasp the features of a face as it catches the light than another comes to replace it as the jewel turns on and on, eventually diminishing no matter how eagerly you follow it into the night.

"Mr. Nemec, soon we will feast together. You will come for me. You will hunt me out, deeper and deeper into the forest."

I waited until the prisoner was exhausted once more. He was failing fast. I knew he didn't have much time left. I ordered one of my men to assist me. We dressed Nemec in my long coat and hat and between us carried him down to my car awaiting us in the street. When he saw me strap on my pistol and holster, the officer became reluctant, even going as far as to ask me whether he should accompany me for the drive. I refused and threatened him with insubordination if he reported this incident to anyone else

The Feast of the Sphinx

in the station. After bundling Nemec into the back seat and taking the wheel, I caught the officer's eye and could tell from his expression that he'd disregarded my warning. He realised that I had crossed the line; soon I would be relieved of duty, questioned, and thrown to the wolves. None of them could see that the impossible demands such measures. As I pulled away into the night, I knew that I was alone.

I could see in the rear view mirror as the station diminished into the night behind us that the hat had slipped from Nemec's head. I called his name several times before he stirred. I reassured him he was safe, that we could speak openly as equals and that he had nothing to fear. Tears streamed down his face, yet his eyes seemed wide with a terrible joy as if the sensation was too much to bear. He looked through the window into the street sliding by. I kept my speed steady without accelerating to avoid drawing the attention of patrols and sentries. After a while I pulled into a secluded embankment overlooking the river and left the motor running. In the mirror I could see lights sparkling in Nemec's eyes as he stared across the water.

"I mean to find this Countess of yours tonight if it kills me. Can you give directions from here? I can't go back. Not now." The prisoner held my gaze with a demented smile on his lips. He seemed to believe me. Indeed he was reinvigorated by this turn of events, his small ghostly face beaming back at me from the capacious folds of my overcoat.

"I will take you to her. Let me show you the way. Yet you've not passed the trial quite yet. There remains much to accomplish. And I still must relate the rest of my story, Inspector Ritter." In the mirror Nemec was shivering and growing ever paler.

I joined him on the back seat, wrapping his lower half in a thick blanket. He looked strangely cocooned in that great woollen coat. His wiry hands, like talons, eagerly clutched the lapels to his throat. He noticed me remove the pistol from my holster. I assured him it was for our protection, in case we were approached by a patrol. I told him to return to the house of the Countess, to return to telling his tale.

VIII. The Wreckage of Dreams

19th September 1939

"As Otakar opened the door to allow me to leave that morning, as he always did according to our ritual, I found the door that once opened to the city only led me back into the house. The old lion instructed me to follow. He blindfolded me again and said I was finally ready. The Feast had begun. I was to go deeper and deeper into the house stopping only to draw the Countess wherever I found her. That was the game I'd come to play, he said. I was to hunt her out. He took my arm and led me on. Again I heard many doors opening and closing, although now it occurred to me that these sounds and my movement through the house could be achieved through theatrical trickery. As ever there were occasional sounds of knocking through the walls and footsteps tapping away overhead. Animals stirred in distant rooms. I imagined too that the other unseen tenants of the house busied themselves with hidden trapdoors and sliding panels. It even seemed possible that Otakar might be a man simply playing a part; that his beard was false and the wrinkles merely painted around his eyes. Without warning he stopped me with a hand on my chest. He removed the blindfold to reveal that we were at a junction of passages.

" 'You're on your own now,' the old lion said to me as he turned back the way we'd come. I watched Otakar disappear down the passageway, the swaying lamp in his hand casting wild shadows across the walls as he left. That was the last I saw of him. No grand speeches for a change, no goodbyes. No doubt he and the other servants would be turning wheels behind the scenes, manning the pulleys, lifting curtains, and lowering backdrops into place. I could picture them all preparing rooms for me to enter and pulling them apart once I'd left them behind.

"Was it any surprise then that of all the doors I tried from that junction only one allowed me to cross its threshold? The others were either locked or barricaded from the other side, allowing me only a glimpse of what might lie behind them in the semi-darkness. No doubt it was intended that I should spy through those cracks and see indistinct forms, like beasts moving through a forest. Although I guessed that they must be accomplished imitations, the animal calls unnerved me. I passed through an unlocked door, the only way left to me.

"The walls of that great narrow room were cracked from the pressure of roots snaking through the plaster in countless places. They writhed across the bare boards underfoot and formed a canopy across the ceiling. A table and chair lay in the centre of the room, their legs fused to the floor with lichen. A frail green electric light trembled in the ceiling above, showing the clutter of paper and pencils across the table's surface. I noticed an oval opening in the wall directly in front of the table. As I reached the chair, the Countess's face slowly came into view from the shadows of the aperture. I took my place at the table and eagerly took up a pencil, smoothing out a sheet of paper before me.

"She told me that Otakar was the name of her master's lion. She said the lion died only days before her master, as he lay dreaming of the beast on his deathbed. She told me that it was Pliny the Elder, in his *Naturalis Historia*, who said that lions were the only beasts capable of prayer.

"I gazed into the aperture to see her flesh become a translucent film beneath which a garden was budding into life. Fruit glistened like jewels under her skin. Turning to vanish into the treeline, she beckoned for me to follow her, saying that I must find her secret faces. Still clutching pencil and paper, I climbed through the oval frame and into the orchard of shadows. As she fled her face transformed, petals of skin fluttering around threads of bone. I pursued her through the trees, stone figures rearing up from the darkness. I'd seen those statues before, throughout the city. She paused at each in turn to reach up and caress their faces. She said that I must draw them all, that I must map the ancient faces of the city so that I would never forget. She put her lips to my ear and whispered her name. The sound fluttered as a moth vanished into the night air. She danced through the forest before me, her flesh as flame against the thickening shadows, turning this way and that, eluding my attempts to catch her. Then, after one last glance back at me, her body dispersed as embers up through the branches. She was gone. The house that had in turn become a forest was now only a memory too. Fading trees gave way to streets and soon I found myself walking through the city at the arrival of dawn.

"Keeping to the back lanes, I glimpsed soldiers sentried on the main thoroughfares. I passed unseen. How long had I been away? How long had the city been occupied? I thought and hoped that I was invisible, but it was not to be. With pencil and paper in my hands I made my way to the monument nearest my home, the Jan Hus memorial in the Old Town Square. From afar I could see the saint shrouded beneath red and black banners. As I crossed the square, voices called out to me demanding that I halt. I was tearing banners from the statue when the soldiers circled me."

"So you remember her name? Do you think you could tell me? It is a small thing, it hardly matters now." I saw him glance down at the pistol that was resting in my lap near my folded hands. I smiled to assure him there was nothing to fear.

"You're wrong. Her name is a key . . . a key to lock you in."

"Then what is it, this key?" I asked, allowing the prisoner to lean forward and whisper in my ear.

"Toyen," he said with my pistol at his head, and pulling the trigger he disappeared.

Acknowledgements

The author would like to thank Brian J. Showers,
Jim Rockhill, Meggan Kehrli and Ken Mackenzie.

The Satyr was first published
by Ex Occidente Press
in August 2010.

The Bestiary of Communion was
first published by Ex Occidente Press
in March 2011.

The Satyr was newly illustrated and the texts
of both books have been expanded
and revised for this omnibus edition.

The story from *The Bestiary of Communion* originally
entitled "My Mistress, the Multitude" has been renamed
"The Feast of the Sphinx".

About the Author

Stephen J. Clark was born in County Durham. His work has appeared in numerous journals and anthologies, having been published by Egaeus Press, Side Real Press, and Fulgur Press, among others. Regular collaborations with Tartarus Press have notably featured his cover illustrations for a complete series of Robert Aickman's strange tales. His debut novel *In Delirium's Circle* was released by Egaeus Press in 2012, followed in 2018 by *The Feathered Bough*, a fully illustrated second novel published by Zagava.

Swan River Press

Founded in 2003, Swan River Press is an independent publishing company, based in Dublin, Ireland, dedicated to gothic, supernatural, and fantastic literature. We specialise in limited edition hardbacks, publishing fiction from around the world with an emphasis on Ireland's contributions to the genre.

www.swanriverpress.ie

"Handsome, beautifully made volumes . . . altogether irresistible."

– Michael Dirda, *Washington Post*

"It [is] often down to small, independent, specialist presses to keep the candle of horror fiction flickering . . . "

– Darryl Jones, *Irish Times*

"Swan River Press has emerged as one of the most inspiring new presses over the past decade. Not only are the books beautifully presented and professionally produced, but they aspire consistently to high literary quality and originality, ranging from current writers of supernatural/weird fiction to rare or forgotten works by departed authors."

– Peter Bell, *Ghosts & Scholars*

THE PALE BROWN THING

Fritz Leiber

*"The ancient Egyptians only buried people
in their pyramids. We are living in ours."*

– Thibaut de Castries

Serialised in 1977, *The Pale Brown Thing* is a shorter version of Fritz Leiber's World Fantasy Award-winning novel of the supernatural, *Our Lady of Darkness*. Leiber maintained that the two texts "should be regarded as the same story told at different times"; thus this volume reprints *The Pale Brown Thing* for the first time in nearly forty years, with an introduction by the author's friend, Californian poet Donald Sidney-Fryer. The novella stands as Leiber's vision of 1970s San Francisco: a city imbued with an eccentric vibe and nefarious entities, in which pulp writer Franz Westen uncovers an alternate portrait of the city's *fin de siècle* literary set—Ambrose Bierce, Jack London, Clark Ashton Smith—as well as the darker invocations of occultist Thibaut de Castries and a pale brown inhabitant of Corona Heights.

*"Leiber has constructed a plot in which every single detail
adds to the whole, with suggestion and implication
used to stunning effect, so that our sense of dread mounts."*

– *Black Static*

Seventeen Stories

Mark Valentine

Mark Valentine's stories have been described by critic Rick Kleffel as "consistently amazing and inexplicably beautiful". He has been called "A superb writer, among the leading practitioners of classic supernatural fiction" by Michael Dirda of the *Washington Post*, and his work is regularly chosen for year's best and other anthologies.

This selection offers previously uncollected or hard to find tales in the finest traditions of the strange and fantastic. As well as tributes to the masters of the field, Valentine provides his own original and otherworldly visions, with what Supernatural Tales has called "the author's trademark erudition" in "unusual byways of history, folklore and general scholarship". Opening a book will never seem quite the same again after encountering this curious volume of *Seventeen Stories* . . .

> "*Valentine is a writer in love with the great tradition of the weird tale.*"
>
> – *Supernatural Tales*

> "*[Valentine's] is attentive to place and to the power of obsession, but one of his true gifts is an ability to suggest modes of artistic expression.*"
>
> – The Endless Bookshelf

THE DARK RETURN OF TIME

R. B. Russell

"I was searching for The Dark Return of Time on the 'net. It's odd, but there isn't a copy for sale anywhere, and it doesn't turn up on the British Library catalogue, the Library of Congress website, or the Biblioteque Nationale."

The past doesn't always stay where it should. It is as though somebody, or something, is forever trying to bring it painfully into the present.

Flavian Bennett is trying to leave his past behind when he goes to work in his father's bookshop in Paris. But a curious customer, Reginald Hopper, is desperate to resurrect his own murky origins. Hopper believes that a rare and mysterious book, The Dark Return of Time, may be the key to what happened before he arrived in Paris. In this quiet thriller by R. B. Russell, the futures—and pasts—of these two men will soon cross.

"A beautifully written and very clever work of art."

– Black Static

"R. B. Russell's The Dark Return of Time . . . *is a short thriller that opens in a shop selling second-hand books in Paris. What could be better?"*

– Michael Dirda, *Washington Post*

Lightning Source UK Ltd.
Milton Keynes UK
UKHW011243200622
404687UK00003B/869

9 781783 807413